First published in Great Britain in 2013 by Comma Press
www.commapress.co.uk

'Seeing Double' was first published in *The New Uncanny*, edited by Ra Page and
Sarah Eyre (Comma Press, 2008). 'Moss Witch' and its afterword were first
published in *When It Changed*, edited by Geoff Ryman (Comma Press, 2009).
'Lighting the Standard Candles' was first published as 'The Woman Who Measured
the Heavens with a Span', together with its afterword, in *Litmus: Short Stories from
Modern Science*, edited by Ra Page (Comma Press, 2011). 'Anaka's Factors' and its
afterword were first published in *Bio-Punk: Stories From the Far Side of Research*,
edited by Ra Page (Comma Press, 2012). 'Instant Light' was commissioned by
Stockton-on-Tees Borough Council and first published as a booklet by the same
name in August 2013.

A CIP catalogue record of this book is available from the British Library.

ISBN 1905583427
ISBN-13 978 1905583423

Supported by
**ARTS COUNCIL
ENGLAND**

The publisher gratefully acknowledges assistance from Arts Council England. It
also acknowledges assistance from the Wellcome Trust for its support in the
commissioning of 'Anaka's Factors' as part of Comma's *Bio-Punk* project in 2012.
The publisher also gratefully acknowledges the support of the Institute of Physics
for its support in the commissioning of 'Lighting the Standard Candles' in 2011, and
the commissioning of 'The Beautiful Equation' and 'Dark Humour' in 2013.

IOP Institute of Physics

Set in Bembo 11/13 by David Eckersall
Printed and bound in England by Berforts Information Press Ltd.

Moss Witch

AND OTHER STORIES

by
Sara Maitland

For Ford Hickson,

with love and thanks for his capacity for lateral thinking and flamboyant connection-making which has been an inspiration for quarter of a century.

And with thanks to Ra Page, the sort of proactive editor every writer longs for, and to all the scientists who nobly bore with my stupidities, answered my questions, taught me lots of new stuff and were patient and helpful as well as clever. I wish I believed they had as much fun as I did.

Contents

Her Bonxie Boy

AFTER CHRISTMAS SHE went south to spend the cold months in Portugal, with her friend Alice, as usual.

In late March she flew home. She stared out of the plane window through a gap in the clouds and imagined she could see him, beating his lonely way up the Bay of Biscay towards the Channel. But there was no urgency or even anxiety in the fantasy. She did not let herself open her laptop, but concentrated on how good it felt to know where he actually was.

One evening in the middle of February, Alice had looked at her shrewdly. The fifteen years between their ages did not often bother them, but it did occasionally give Alice permission to be a little maternal.

'Has something changed?'

Helen never knew how much Alice knew, or how much she understood, if there was a difference. One reason why Alice was her friend was precisely because she was never nosy, never intruded.

'What do you mean?' she asked.

'Well usually about now you start getting edgy, start talking about leaving, going north, back to your crazy island. You dither about rather fretfully. This year you seem so calm, so settled.' After a pause she added, 'I'm not trying to get rid of you, you know.' She smiled.

'Do you know something? That had not occurred to me. Isn't that nice?' They laughed and, if Alice noticed that Helen had completely ducked the question, she never gave the least sign of it.

But something had changed. And she *had* felt calm and settled.

It was cold and drizzling with a misty dampness when she landed, the spring seemed to be making its way north very slowly. She spent the night in her room on campus, but woke in the small hours, before the first faded light of dawn, sweating and clammy from a nightmare of big brown sea birds caught up in spinning turbines, sliced through, tossed across white-capped waves, headless, dead. She leapt out of bed and switched on her computer; the small white blip moved smoothly across the screen and she went back to sleep, exhausted but reassured.

Something had changed.

In the morning she went into the department. Walking across the campus she saw two Chinese plums were in delicate pale blossom, tossing on the rough breeze, fragile but determined. There were daffodils in clumps in the grass. It all looked tidy and pretty, out of tune with her own nervous restlessness. She had a meeting with her HOD and discussed her summary of the report she had prepared while in Portugal. It was a consultation paper for the EIA of a proposed offshore wind farm. She was an internationally recognised authority on Northern European sea birds; her research centre off Lewis was well known to the small number of people who knew or cared about Northern European sea birds. This was the sort of work she undertook most winters in one form or another.

When she had been sent the original brief for this wind farm she had had a fierce moment of panic that the northern end of the proposed site would be visible from the cliffs of Allt na Croite, but she quickly realised it would not; no turbines would disrupt her long views of nothing. She then felt obliged to work particularly conscientiously to punish her inner NIMBY. But in reality she did not really know – and no one knew. It seemed realistic to suppose that periodically some birds would fly into the turbine fins and die, but it was hard to guess how many. It seemed likely that the disturbance to the sea bed would shift the patterns of fish and that introducing 108 massive structures into an environment which had been entirely open for millions of years might even have an effect on winds and currents, but it was difficult to calculate just what those effects might be and impossible to guess how that might impact on the birds. Differently on different species was probably the best answer.

Both she and her boss knew that there was nothing startlingly original about her meticulous report. She was using other people's research, and there was not that much. She had picked deftly at the best study, from a pair of Danish offshore wind farms in the Baltic; it was pretty solidly evidence based. They had used both visual and radar observations and, on the whole, both travelling and feeding sea birds avoided the wind farm altogether, or flew rather elegantly between the turbines. The researchers could not and sensibly did not rule out the possibility that some birds might strike the blades which whizzed round at up to eighty miles an hour and recorded that there was a particular worry about eider duck: they 'were concerned that these large' – *she jolted in fear* – 'rather clumsy' – *her serenity returned* – 'birds might not be able to manoeuvre around the turbines.' The eider was not a significant species in her immediate context; but she conscientiously repeated the Danish conclusions on spacing.

She noted that lights, especially red lights, on the turbines for the sake of fishing vessels and aeroplanes, might disrupt birds' electromagnetic orientation in migration and appended the current standard advice: avoid all lighting where possible, but if absolutely necessary use low density white lights.

In the end, although she was being paid a lot of money for her thoughts, she could not really add much of significance to the RSPB's general observation:

Given the general lack of information about the specific impacts that offshore wind farms may have on birds, caution is clearly required...The available evidence suggests that appropriately positioned wind farms do not pose a significant hazard for birds... Climate change poses a much more significant threat to wildlife, and the RSPB therefore supports *wind farms* and other forms of *renewable energy.*

Her university would be pleased with her: research and impact, well-paid and pleasing to the Energy Company. Honest too.

'You know, Bob,' she said, 'eventually someone is going to have to get out there in a little boat and count the birds. We could do it from Allt na Croite; it might make a nice little fourth year project, or for one of the graduates.'

'Quite tough,' he commented. 'Can you do a risk assessment?'

'Oh blast,' she said and they both laughed. 'Perhaps we could get the Energy Company to pay for it – then we could send a local out with them.'

'Good thinking. When are you off then?' He knew her well.

'Tomorrow, I hope. Bill and Anis are supposed to come up in about four weeks and Chen Lee sometime in May. Do you need me down before that?'

'Don't think so. European Fisheries seem very happy and the grant's reconfirmed. Well done.'

In the evening she went to visit her mother. Nothing had changed. Nothing would ever change until she died. The old lady who had once been her mother smiled at her very sweetly and said that her daughter would come and visit her soon. She knew that they took extremely good care of her mother, at considerable expense which was mostly met by her brother. She knew too that the staff adored her mother and despised her for not coming more often. She no longer even tried to apologise or explain.

Later she rang her brother to tell him she was back and that she had visited their mother and found her 'well'.

'Oh,' he said, 'I should have realised you'd be back about now. I was planning on coming up this weekend myself. Why don't you hang on; it would be good to see you.'

It would be good to see him. 'Oh, I'm sorry,' she said, 'I can't. I have to get back to Allt na Croite. I'll be off in the morning.'

'I see. Your bit of rough is home from the sea, is he?' He was teasing her as he had done since she was about four years old. She did not mind.

'No,' she said, 'he's not back yet; but I'm expecting him over the weekend.'

'What exactly is it that he does? That keeps him away more than half the year?'

'I've told you. He's a sort of policeman for the Fishery people. He monitors boat catches. He's been off West Africa in the Atlantic, this winter.'

'I still don't understand why you always have to be there first. Surely he could wait a few days.'

Even to her brother it was more or less impossible to explain; to say, 'Well, you know, he's site faithful not mate faithful. If I'm not there when he lands he'll be down the hotel with that Mhairi McLeod and I'll not see him all summer.' Instead she says, 'It's a Hebridean tradition: a woman has to be there when her man comes in from the sea. His folk would find it very strange if I wasn't. They have a hard enough time with me as it is.'

'Well, give my love to the puffins.'

'Not puffins,' she said, but laughing because he knew perfectly well it was not puffins. 'I know, I know. Everyone except research ornithologists adores puffins, so sweet and pretty – cute indeed – but actually they're a nightmare. They get in a state and then you can never know whether their behaviour is a response to your intervention or if it's real "puffin stuff". And before you get onto it, not terns either, they're too flighty.'

'I know,' he says, 'when the going gets tough the terns get going. I do pay attention, you see.'

'OK, clever clogs, which sea bird am I the international expert in?'

He laughed appreciatively. 'Now you're name-dropping. But I do know: it's those big thuggish ones – with the heavy beaks and barrel-chests. They are not very bright and moderately bad tempered. But that aside, they're good to research because they are quite stable.'

'Oh God, have I become that boring? You should add that skuas have commitment; they're hard working and persistent and calm, and they live a nice long time too.'

'I've just realised,' he said, 'that that has all become exactly how I imagine your boyfriend. No, little Sis, whatever you are it is never boring.'

She asked about Kate and the children.

Later he said, 'I thought I might bring your nephews up; will you still be there at half-term?'

'You've never been,' she said.

'They've been too small. I think they'd like it now. Do you remember, years ago, when we went to Muckle Flugga, and you pointed out that skua harrying the gannet; all those aerial acrobatics, that skilful ferocity. It was rather magnificent – horrible but impressive. Unfortunately, I think the boys would love it.'

'Skuas drown kittiwakes too,' she said, 'just the thing for two pre-teen boys. Do come, it would be fun. It's a bit of a schlep though.'

'And I can ask your young man if his intentions are honourable.'

'They aren't,' she said. They laughed. She enjoyed him.

The next morning she left it all behind.

She stopped at the supermarket south of the Erskine Bridge for enormous quantities of coffee and then headed north up the A82, the most beautiful road in the world; the road to Allt na Croite. She drove, as always, with that strange mixture of recognition, sign posts and deep desire. Loch Lomondside. Crianlarich. Tyndrum. The long haunted pass through Glen Coe. Ballachulish. Fort William. Invergary.

She turns west. Her heart sings. The lovely lonely road through Kintail. Kyle of Lochalsh. The bridge, now free at last. Across An t-Eilean Sgitheanach, the winged island, with the Cuillin towering above the road, monstrous in their ferocity. Portree. Uig, where the road ends at the bottom of the steep curling hill. She is going beyond. Outwith the harbour wall there is nothing but sea and work and love and joy.

She is tired now. She has to wait for the ferry. It is cold and beyond the harbour wall the Minch is quite rough. She buys a beer in the bar and drinks it on her own. The ferry is not very full.

From Tarbert she sets off in a caterpillar of cars along the narrow road, but gradually the drivers peel off; she is alone, her headlights picking out the lochans as sheets of dark metal along the road sides. The sea is close. She can feel it even when she cannot see it or hear it above the car engine. In the village she parks the car and goes into the hotel.

She is welcome. Although she has not told anyone she is coming, she knows they are pleased. Even Mhairi McLeod, who goes behind the reception desk and finds a bedroom key.

'Come down when you're ready,' she says, 'Iain's in the bar tonight.'

She sits on the bed and opens her laptop. All day she has not looked and now she does. He is above the top of Ireland, though farther west, standing well out to sea and moving northwards steadily. He might arrive tomorrow. She smiles.

In the bar the men greet her with pleasure. 'Helen! Do bheatha dhan dùthaich! Ciamar a tha?'

She fumbles the response. She can just about say, 'Shin sibh. 'S math bhith air ais' and they laugh at her accent. Someone orders her a drink.

'Bha sinn an dùil nach b' fhada gus am biodh tu air ais,' one of the old men says and then says it again in English, 'We were saying so. Your birds are coming in now. Saw a first one four days back.'

They exchange news from the winter. It is her eleventh year... They know who she is; without belonging, which she knows she never will, she is accepted. They may even be proud of her; certainly there are pictures from the Colour Supplement article about her research centre on the wall of the bar. They speak in English for her.

'So, Iain,' she says later, 'any winter damage?'

'No, Dougie and I went over ten days ago to have a look. Everything's fine.'

'Can you take me out tomorrow?'

Suddenly, the bar is silent. Iain lowers his eyes to inspect his glass. The old men tut audibly; two of the younger men catch each other's eye, grinning perhaps nervously.

'Helen.' Iain sounds reproving. She is startled. There is a pause.

'Helen, what day is it today?'

'Saturday.' She is confused, almost interrogative.

'So, what day is it tomorrow?'

'Sund... Oh Iain, I'm sorry, I forgot.'

'Well, don't.' Then he smiles, laughing at her, momentarily like her brother. 'It's lucky you've come back from the godless lands. We can put you right.'

The Sabbatarianism still seems weird to her. But she should not have forgotten. She hears a small echo of the anxious fret that has driven her thousands of miles north in just three days. So near and yet so far; she needs to get out there. He is clear of Ireland now, out there somewhere in the dark. But she will not argue this one. She accepts her guest status. She likes it in fact.

Later, she prepares to go upstairs.

'First thing Monday,' Iain says, I'll come and help you load up – we'll want to be away before nine. For the tide. I'll see you in the harbour.'

'I'll be at kirk tomorrow,' she says.

'Guilt? You don't have to.'

'No, for the singing.'

'Tell you a funny thing,' Iain says. 'Last autumn we had an invasion. It was three Baptist ministers, and two of their wives, from Alabama. You can imagine. Half the children have never seen a non-white person... Well apparently, down in the Southern states, they sing like we do – they call it "lining" but it's just the same as Gaelic psalms. The precentor gives the line and the congregation pick it up. Different tunes, but the same thing, unaccompanied – but we're meant to say *a cappella* we learned. Theirs is a bit more cheerful and, for me, a bit less haunting, but it is the same. And – well, they'd come because some American professor of music has been saying that the Southern Baptists got their singing, their "lining", from here, from the Islands. Well, they did not want that to be true, because they've always thought it came from Africa and was their heritage from before slavery, and we didn't want it to be true because you know us – we don't really care for the idea that folk went from here and got rich and kept slaves – not our self-image, not Free Kirk. So, here's both lots not wanting it. But one of them has the real God-craic so the minister is all keen on him, and we end up singing for each other in the kirk like a Céilídh. Then it turns out one of their women gives the line and the minister doesn't like that so much. But, I think we all knew the professor chap, who is neither black nor Scottish, was right... The music migrating all that way, it made me think of you and your birds.'

9

It is a long speech for him. They smile at each other. And on Sunday in the morning she goes to the kirk and hears that beautiful, tragic singing and in the afternoon walks round the Calanais standing stones in the magical peace of the island Sabbath and feels soothed, briefly at rest.

It does not last. She wakes too early on Monday morning, before it is light and she cannot get a broadband connection and is fretful. The coffee is nasty and she does not want porridge; she wants to be going. He might have come last night.

She reverses her car down onto the quay, and starts unloading the boxes from the back. There are very few boats riding on the still water inside the grey rampart at this time of year, but there are two female eider ducks bobbing close in among the seaweed patches. The light increases; the wind, even in the harbour, is fresh; the grey of the sky breaks into elegant long bands of cloud. Although she feels impatient, Iain arrives in good time. They start to load his sturdy boat; they have done this before, often enough to work together smoothly, almost silently. Once she pauses and says 'Kerosene?' But he says that he and Dougie took sixty litres out the week before.

Finally, he starts the engine in neutral, climbs up onto the quay and unties the bow warp. He tells her to put the wheel down hard and she does; the nose of the little boat swings out towards the harbour mouth; he unloops the stern rope, drops it into the boat, jumps gracefully down after it himself and is at the wheel in a single practiced flowing movement. They run out, over the bar and into the open sea.

Depending on the weather and the tides, it is about a 45 minute run from the harbour to the island. The little boat smacks into the waves, but it feels more bouncy and cheerful than rough. She goes forward into the well at the bows and stands holding on to the rail, watching for the moment that they clear the headland north of the harbour, and she will get her first sight of the island lifting its cliffs like a beak towards the west. The business of loading had distracted and soothed her but now her urgency returns. She barely looks at the coast or the passing birds, only forward.

After a while, Iain calls her and she forces herself to turn, smile and make her way aft to join him in the little wheel house.

Things are not always what they seem. Iain looks like the local boatman; indeed he is the local boatman, but he also has a PhD in psychology from a Russell League university down in England. He had told them about it one drunken evening at the Research Centre about four years ago. It had been Chen's first year and he had hated it. He was good at the work, and probably now was confident enough to get on with it to the point of enjoying it, but that first summer had been appalling for him: he was scared of the northern light, cold too much of the time and darkly baffled by everyone's enthusiasm. His beautiful self-effacing manners had really not been helpful in the strange enforced intimacy. She had suggested tentatively once that he go back to the mainland, but he had been both angry and hurt. Iain had come out on his regular supply run and had stayed over. Quite suddenly, and in no apparent context, he had turned to Chen and said, 'My thesis was on "home", on love-of-place, *oikophilia* we called it. What makes a particular place or topography home, necessary to someone, and why. Just accept this is not yours, and you'll be fine.' There had been a sudden surprised pause, and then he had gone on, told them very briefly about his work, and finally said, 'As a psychologist I'd want to ask why people chose to research particular things. With me it became obvious. I learned I couldn't really live anywhere else except here. I completed the thesis, had a breakdown and came home. I've not been off the outer isles since. Hope I never have to.' He took a slug of whisky and added, 'Of course the really weird ones aren't people like me, with our own language, or own music and our own rather particular

11

landscape. I was kind of interested in the people who find "home" somewhere they have never been before, that they have no roots in, no story, might go all their lives and never find it, but they do – a sort of instant recognition of *here*.' And he gave her a straight, clean look. He had barely ever mentioned his past again.

Now he pours tea from a thermos; smiles, looks comfortable in his body, in his boat. The headland drops into the sea. Beyond it the island appears, whole, shapely, welcoming. She lifts the binoculars from her chest, holds them to her face and scans the air above the cliffs.

She is home.

They reverse the loading process, getting everything up onto the jetty and then Iain goes off in search of the trolley, and she walks over to the low building, walking round the inside, resting her hand on the long table, opening the window of her bedroom, checking. Then she goes back out. Iain is already at work stacking the boxes onto the trolley and she joins him.

It takes three loads to get everything into the centre; the smaller boxes on the table and others sitting around on the floor. She thinks Iain will leave now, but he does not. They start to sort everything out. Kitchen area, bedrooms, work space. Iain asks sometimes where he should put something.

He hefts up a small solid cardboard box marked 'FRAGILE'. It has been ripped open and the lid stuck down again.

'What about this?' he asks.

She glances up from her knees beside the sink where she is putting away several bottles of washing-up liquid, 'Oh, put it beside the computer for now. It's the sat navs.'

'The whats?'

'Satellite navigation thingies. But tiny. The idea is we put them on the skuas and then we can follow them, know where they are, all the time.'

'I thought that was what your computer chips did.' He

had always followed the work, in a mildly curious sort of way.

'Well they do, but only when the birds get back. You know, we have to find the individuals, get the chips back off them, download them. And even then they aren't that accurate. These new ones, we will be able to pin point them, now, at any given instant.'

'So...?'

'Well the European Fishery people who are paying for them think they can use them to see which fishing boats are dumping catch illegally, against the quota regulations. Skuas, you know, follow fishing boats; they're carrion feeders and it is much less effort for them to take dumped fish than go forcing gannets to give up theirs or just hoping for some dead ones to come bobbing along on the surface. Well obviously it works, because they sorted out dumping in the North Sea and so the skuas went to Portugal – and now we know they are making the effort to go all the way south to Africa. So the plan is that if they know exactly where the skuas are they can match that to where the individual boats are, because they have sat nav anyway, and then they can board and inspect... Skuas as policemen.'

'Hard to imagine them that way,' he says grinning. 'They're more like pirates.'

She grins back, but she is really interested in this and pushes on. 'And for me, from my own point of view, I'm not so interested in dumping, what I am interested in is migration patterns. And – do you remember – the chips work by recording the hours of sunshine, so you can tell the latitude the bird was at on a given date? But the thing is they can't tell you anything useful at the equinoxes.'

'Why?'

'If the days and nights are the same length across the whole hemisphere, you can't get a latitude reading, can you? Equi-nox. Equal nights – and days of course.'

He thinks about it and then smiles.

'That's fine for the Fishery people, but not for me,' she goes on. 'The vernal equinox is exactly when migratory sea birds are migrating. So, at the very moment I want to know most what they're up to, they disappear. Vanish somewhere between winter and summer. But these new things – they'll let me watch them, daily, in real time. They cost an arm and leg mind you – I could only get twelve – they were supposed to come last year, but they arrived too late.'

'Cool,' he says, putting the box on the table. 'Deep magic. Can I look?'

'Sure.' She does not look round, busy with her cupboard. It takes a few moments for his stillness and silence to register with her. She crosses the room to where he is standing, rigid, looking into the box. His right hand is shaking slightly, a just visible tremor.

There should be twelve little boxes in the bigger box. There are only eleven, and a tidy square well where one is missing. She stares at him. At last he draws a shuddering breath and says,

'You ringed him.'

She stares at him.

'You're spying on him. He won't like it. Helen, be careful.'

She goes on staring. Then blushes, looks away. She cannot pretend he has not spoken.

'How did you know?'

'Mine's a Selkie,' he says, 'a seal woman. Much more standard. Normal... well, relatively. But that's how I know.'

He seems to think that is enough, and she does not know how to ask the questions she wants to hear the answers to. After a few moments, she leaves the table, goes out the door and walks down to the tide line. There is a rack of kelp, bobbing close along the rocks. She looks at it.

She has spied on him and he will not like it.

She tries to feel embarrassed, but fails. She looks back towards the low corrugated iron roof of the field centre, sitting in its green grass bowl under the jagged rocks. After a bit Iain comes out of the door, walks down and stands beside her. Together they watch the gentle rocking of the tangled strands of seaweed. Eventually he says quietly,

'I'm sorry. I shouldn't have spoken.'

'No,' she said, 'you were kind. Thank you.' Then after a pause she smiles and says, 'It's all right,' and then 'it is all right.' And suddenly it is, it very much is. Her heart rises, singing in the wind. She turns towards him and very briefly, sweetly he hugs her. They go back into the Centre and continue with their chores.

Later, she starts to get fidgety. When he notices he says it is time for him to be going. She does not argue. She accompanies him to the jetty, but finds herself glancing up towards the cliff top.

'Don't worry,' Iain says, 'he won't have come in last night.'

'How do you know?'

'Not on the Sabbath,' he says blandly. 'He'll be an island boy.'

They both laugh.

'Thoir an aire dhut fhèin,' he says. 'I'll come out before the end of the week. Take care of yourself. Agus turas math dhut. Tha mi 'n dòchas gun còrd e riut.'

As soon as she has waved him off, while she can still hear the chug of the engine and pick out his head in the wheelhouse, she turns, zips her jacket and walks up beyond the buildings, following a worn track across the grass. She starts climbing, trying to ignore her winter lack of fitness. The path zigzags up the ever steeper hillside. After about fifteen minutes and panting, she breaks out onto the flat short grass at the top of the island and turns west towards the sunset. At the edge of the cliff she sits cross-legged staring down into the cove; the sharp rocks at the very bottom are white frilled with small breaking waves. The shelves where the gulls nest are still grey

15

with last year's mess. Below her she can see two shags flying low on the water and suddenly a gannet, powerful and lovely, sweeps across her line of vision. She sits very still and waits.

Something has changed. She has ringed him. He does not know and he will not like it. He must not find out.

The western sky is bright but there are clouds over the sun so she can see out towards America. There is nothing else before that.

He comes on the last breath of the day, on the turning of the tide. She sees him first against the light, in silhouette. He comes in straight and fast. She sits tall and stretches out her arms, only slightly wider than his wing span. He is huge and strong, blotting out the sea, the view, her thoughts, everything. He crashes down on her, his webbed feet splaying, grinding into her thighs; his massive beak ramming into her neck, bruising painfully, unbearable, necessary, joyful. His beak is very hard; his feathers thick and soft; his body undernourished but fierce against her breasts — wiry, tough, greedy after his long journey. She folds herself around him. He struggles and then softens. He is so beautiful.

'Bonxie,' she croons.

'M'eudail, tha mi dhachaigh,' he says, 'dhachaigh bhon mhuir.'

She is like a gannet, lovely, graceful, strong. He will harry her, kidnap her, force her to regorge, vomit up her hard won freedom in the real world. She will scarcely be safe.

She does not care.

'Tha e dhachaigh.' She is home. They are together.

He is a fisherman of souls. Her Bonxie boy.

Afterword:

Bonxie Migration, a Quick Tour

Prof. Robert Furness

'BONXIE' IS AN old Norse word supposedly meaning a 'fat untidy old woman'. This Shetland name is now widely used for the big brown aggressive seabird also known in English as the Great Skua, *Stercorariusskua*. Its scientific name is not very complimentary either – *Stercorarius* means 'dung-eating', based on the observation that these mean birds chase and attack other seabirds and catch and swallow what they drop in fright. What they drop is actually their food, vomited in terror, but the unfortunate name has stuck. Bonxies are rare, breeding in only a few remote places in the North Atlantic. I was first introduced to bonxies as a schoolboy when my biology teacher took me on a scientific expedition to ring seabirds on the remotest inhabited island in Britain, Foula – an experience that was to change my life. I was fascinated by these charismatic birds and awestruck at the opportunity to spend months studying them on remote islands. I have been studying bonxies throughout my career as a university scientist, and have sent dozens of my students up to Shetland, Orkney and the Western Isles to continue this research.

Bonxies are only found at their remote breeding colonies from April to August, spending the rest of the year at sea. As a young student, I ringed thousands of bonxie chicks, with the aim of finding out where they go from the end of the summer until the following spring. Ringing told us that they spend the winter off the coasts of Spain, Portugal, and even as far south as West Africa. Ringing also told us that bonxies don't breed until they're about four to seven years old, and as immatures they may wander as far as Brazil in

17

winter or Greenland in summer, though if they survive, most return to breed in the colony where they were born. However, over 90% of all the ringed birds never get recovered, so our picture of their migrations is based on a possibly biased sample of recovered birds, often those found dead on a beach, or drowned in a fishing boat's nets.

Recent technological developments have allowed us to study bird migrations more accurately. Satellite tracking of the largest of seabirds became possible in the 1990s, when transmitters powerful enough to send signals to orbiting satellites became small and light enough to be put onto albatrosses. Unfortunately, though, these satellite transmitters are still too big to be used on most seabirds, and are very expensive. However, after some very clever theoretical work, small data loggers were developed that could simply measure light levels and store the data, and which are small enough to be attached to the leg ring of a seabird. If you can catch the same bird a year later (and fortunately most seabirds live for many years and nest in exactly the same place each year, so this isn't as impossible as it sounds) then you can download the light intensity data, from which you can work out the latitude and longitude that the bird was at, twice each day. This works because day length varies with latitude (except during the equinox), and the times of sunrise and sunset vary with longitude. Geolocation by this method isn't very accurate, but it can tell you if your bonxie spent the winter in the Bay of Biscay, or the western Mediterranean, or went to West Africa. The latest gizmo to come onto the market is a data logger that uses GPS satellites to record a bird's position to within a few metres, and which then automatically downloads the information to a computer whenever the bird comes within a few kilometres of a base station. So now you don't even need to recapture your bird to get the data back.

These devices are providing new insight into bird migrations, and other aspects of bonxie ecology. Their use of waste fish thrown away by fishermen is of particular interest.

Trawl fisheries often generate huge quantities of 'discards', and bonxies follow fishing boats to scavenge on these discarded moribund fish. We think their migration patterns may be changing to take advantage of newly developing trawl fisheries. Geolocators show that increasing numbers of bonxies from Shetland are migrating all the way to West Africa, whereas they rarely used to venture so far south. Longer migrations are the opposite of what might be expected as a consequence of global warming, but make perfect sense in the context of declining trawl fisheries in the North Sea and off Iberia, and rapidly growing trawl fisheries on the West African continental shelf.

Scientists have put geolocators on bonxies breeding in Iceland, and on Bear Island in the Svalbard group, and have shown that birds from those colonies often migrate to spend the winter off Canada, rather than off Europe and Africa like Scottish bonxies. Such differences could be due to genetic differences between the populations, but bonxies only started to breed on Bear Island a few decades ago, and several of the birds that colonised Bear Island had been ringed as chicks in Scotland, suggesting that their different migration habits are cultural, rather than genetic. Our current research, however, has shown that the levels of persistent organic pollutants differ between birds that winter off Africa, off Europe, and off Canada, so where birds spend the winter may affect their health.

The latest logger development has been the production of devices that use the GPS network to locate the position of birds to within a few meters, and then store the data, subsequently to download it to a base station when the bird comes within a kilometre or so. These very accurate loggers not only measure position but also height above sea level, and are now helping to identify collision risks for seabirds flying through areas with offshore wind farms. The renewables industry is currently a major driver of seabird research, with a particular requirement to know whether birds liable to be killed by collisions at offshore wind farms come from European Special Protection Areas and hence are strongly protected (essentially making it illegal for wind farms to kill these protected birds in significant numbers). At this early stage of offshore wind farm development there is some evidence that seabirds (at least eider ducks) are pretty good at avoiding wind turbines at sea, but with rapidly increasing numbers of offshore wind farms the theoretical impact these could have on seabirds is not trivial given the low natural mortality rates of seabirds, their late maturity and low reproductive rate. There is a real possibility that future developments of offshore wind farms could be constrained by seabird conservation concerns.

In her story, Sara has suggested that bonxies could be used to monitor illegal discarding by fishermen. This would be quite a step for the European Commission to take, but wouldn't be impossible. Bonxies regurgitate pellets that contain the bits of their food that they can't easily digest, including fish otoliths. Otoliths are bone-like structures in the fish's skull that they use to sense their movement. Otoliths vary in shape between fish species, so you can collect bonxie pellets, pick out the otoliths and work out what they've been eating, down to the size and species of fish. Discards from trawl fisheries are bottom-living fish like cod and haddock, which birds that feed at the surface of the water, like bonxies, couldn't catch naturally, so any of these fish in the bonxie diet must come from fishing discards. We found that breeding bonxies feed on whatever fish happen to be in the trawl fishery discards in a particular year, and that bonxies only bother to attack and kill smaller seabirds when the fishery generates few discards. Even the presence of bonxies behind fishing boats indicates that discarding is taking place, because the birds wouldn't bother to follow boats if they weren't getting some food in return. So bonxies could yet have a role to play in monitoring compliance with discarding regulations in the (improved) common fisheries policy of the future.

How bonxies will cope with future reductions in discarding by fisheries if fishery management practices are cleaned up is less clear, but it remains a fascinating research topic for a biologist keen to spend time on remote islands studying birds with attitude.

A Geological History of Feminism

'WHO'S THIS?' TISH handed her aunt another black and white snapshot. She was supposed to be doing a summer project for her History A Level. Family history; research techniques; something like that. Her mother had sent her off to her Aunt Ann's. Both of them had rather resented this at first. Tish had had other plans for the summer. Ann knew it was one of those kindly things her sister-in-law, who was a good woman, would do, whether or not she herself wanted such family tenderness and care. But stuck together for a wet summer week they both found themselves having an annoyingly agreeable time. They liked each other. It was a bit of a surprise.

The photograph, slightly yellowed now, was taken from above, and showed, with inevitable foreshortening, a yacht tied up to a quay in bright sunshine and a tall, lean woman with short hair standing on the deck; she was looking up towards the camera and laughing.

Ann glanced at the photograph and smiled, 'That's Elsie,' she said.

'She's gorgeous.'

'Not bad; better under full sail, I always thought; I never liked the way her bow stood up.'

'No, not the boat. I meant the woman.'

'Oh. That's me.'

Ann looked at the picture again; in it the woman was wearing a sleeveless T-shirt and a pair of shorts and was

23

indeed somewhat gorgeous. Tish looked embarrassed, and Ann knew she had nearly said, 'You've changed;' polite teenagers got embarrassed by that sort of thought, even when they didn't speak it. Especially if it were true.

Tish rushed for something more polite. 'Where were you?'

'Florida Keys.' There was a tiny hesitation and then she could not resist it. 'I'd just sailed her solo across the Atlantic.'

Tish was Jeremy's daughter – she knew what that meant. 'Non-stop?' she asked, awed.

'Oh, no; I went the scenic route – Spain, the Canaries, the Bahamas. I wasn't in any hurry.' Tish was looking at her, almost speculatively, so she said briskly, 'OK. What's next?' and put the photo face down onto the pile.

Later, they took Charlotte Sophia, Ann's miniature dachshund, for her walk along the beach. The sea was bright and gentle, stretching away into the sunshine. Under the stripy cliff where the layers of rock had been tipped nearly vertical by some ancient movement of the Earth, Tish stopped. She stood quite still for a while and then said,

'Aunt Ann, why didn't I know? About the Atlantic? Why hasn't Daddy told me?'

Ann had thought all afternoon that she would ask; she had even thought about how she would answer.

'Let's just say he wasn't very happy about it.'

'But why? I mean, why not?'

'Well for one thing, I stole his boat.'

Tish surprised her by giggling. It gave her a rush of confidence, bubbling up as a hot wicked joy she had not felt for years.

'Perhaps I'd better tell you about it.'

'Perhaps you had,' said Tish, sounding very like her mother.

'I was furious with him.' She paused. 'It's quite a long story really – I don't know what he has told you... you know

24

our father died just before he was born and your dad was six years younger than me, and your grandmother couldn't really cope, so I grew up feeling responsible for him. Big sister, little brother. But we were all right really because her brother, I mean your grandmother's brother, your great-uncle Tony, sort of helped and took care of us for her. He was rather rich and he never married and he took us on. He was lovely actually, very generous and just there, around without interfering. He gave us lots of things, like sailing. He was very keen and taught us both that; that's where it comes from, for both your father and me. Anyway, he was a geologist and after the War he worked in the US with Hess on Ocean Floor Topography.'

'What's that?'

'Oh. That's... well, because of the War... one odd thing about wars is how they develop technology; things that didn't get invented or discovered or developed for good reasons, get done for war; it really is not fair. Like flying in the First World War. I bet you that if we had a war so that we couldn't get oil or were frightened we wouldn't, they'd solve the sustainability problems quick as a flash. It's depressing.'

'Aunt Ann. About Daddy.'

Perhaps Freud was right about fathers and daughters; Tish and Jeremy. Herself and Uncle Tony? Never mind. 'Sorry,' she said, 'Well during the war they had developed sonar and other ways of imaging, mapping, seeing if you like, the sea floor and that gave people like Hess and then Tuzo Wilson and others...and yes this does have to do with why I stole Elsie from your father... it gave them some really exciting ideas and in the 1960s they were coming up with a brilliant new answer to a question that people had been asking since Francis Bacon in the seventeenth century: why it looks as though America and Africa and Europe fit into each other like jigsaw puzzle pieces.

'So, Uncle Tony would take us out in Elsie – she was his boat first – sailing round Aran or out to the Islands, and later we went to Maine once with him and over to Scandinavia and he gave us dinghies and taught us and – this is the point – all the time, he was telling us all this stuff, all these new ideas and how they explained the things we could see; the rocks and the islands and the maps. It was what you'd call cutting edge. Now you might call it a paradigm shift. Once everyone thought the earth itself was stable; there might be movements at the top – historical movements or weather movements, and it was all spinning through space of course, but... but it was all fixed. It was in the language, you know, terra firma and keeping your feet on the ground and things being rock solid. But then of course it didn't feel like a paradigm shift, no one knew just how much it would change things. It felt new and exciting. It was now, if you know what I mean – not like Galileo, or Darwin or even Einstein, but now. It was a brand new big idea. It changed everything for me – just the idea that things do not stay the same, that slowly, slowly they move and change; once there was one huge continent and one day there will be again and nothing is quite stable, nothing is fixed.

'So then I went to university and studied geology because I adored your great-uncle and thought it was really exciting. Women didn't do that sort of thing much in those days and I think it amused Uncle Tony in a way, but he was supportive and kind and helpful. And I did pretty well and I planned to go on and do a doctorate only I needed to go to Canada to do it, because that's where Professor Wilson was; and Uncle Tony promised me he'd pay for it. And then he died and he left all his money and everything to Jeremy, to your father. He was only 18.'

Tish looked up, startled.

'Yes I know, but that's what people did in those days... It wasn't fair, but it was quite normal. And then, well probably if your dad had been a bit older, or he'd had a father or our mother hadn't been so... so wet... or... perhaps if I hadn't been his bossy big sister all his life and now he had some power...

or... I don't know, Tish, I just don't know.

'Anyway, of course he owned Elsie and we thought it would be fun to sail her across the Atlantic together before he started university. Like a gap year. So we got her all ready in Falmouth, and then the night before we were supposed to sail we had an enormous fight. The thing was he wouldn't give me the money to go to Canada and do my research. He wouldn't even lend it to me. It wasn't about the money, you know; he's very generous with money, your father, he always has been. He wasn't being mean or greedy. He was being... he thought he was being grown-up and I thought he was being unfair; and actually I still do. He said it wouldn't be right for your grandmother if I went off to Canada, that she needed someone to look after her and that someone was me. He said I didn't need a doctorate and that I shouldn't be so selfish. He said geology wasn't ladylike.'

'Daddy? Daddy said that?'

'It was a long time ago, Tish. Things change. Continents. Oceans. Even your father.

'But I was livid. So the next morning I left him a note saying if he wanted to meet me in Florida we could bring her back together and I just went down to the harbour, slipped anchor and took her out on the early tide and went solo. So you see, he did have something to be not very happy about.'

There was a long pause, then Tish said consolingly, 'You didn't steal her.'

'Big borrow though,' Ann said smiling.

'More like twocking.'

'More like what?'

'Twocking – Taking Without Owner's Consent. It's what joy riders do... you know, to people's cars.'

'Well if it was my car it would feel like stealing.' She tried to sound auntly.

'Don't sound so auntly,' said Tish.

They called Charlotte Sophia from her busy snuffling along the tide line and turned to go home.

They walked silently; Ann watched Tish trying to absorb this new gorgeous aunt who stole someone's boat and sailed alone across the Atlantic. She was not yet ready even to try to absorb a father who did not share his good fortune nor an aunt who had run to fat and become a geography teacher. They were nearly back at the cottage before Tish got her head around the story. She looked up suddenly and asked, 'Was it fun?'

'Oh yes,' said Ann, 'it was fun.'

She turned and looked over her shoulder at the sea again, reaching away southwards in the sunset. 'It was more than fun, it was wonderful.' She crouched down to clip Charlotte Sophia's lead onto her collar to cross the road and said again, 'it was wonderful.' And then, 'It changed my life.'

It hadn't been wonderful at first of course. She had been so furiously angry and then inevitably guilty. Several times in the very early days she had thought she would have to turn round, go back, apologise; several other times she had caught herself piling on too much sail, edging too close to the wind, running away. Fretful down into the Bay of Biscay and then she had caught her first storm and she had simply been frightened. For about four hours she had been terrified and then, in a short lull, she had realised that it was nothing like as bad as the storm she had ridden out alone and happily off St. Kilda two summers ago, when along with the waves and the wind and Elsie's moaning and shrieking, there had been currents and tides and sharp, dangerous rocks waiting to rip the boat apart and casually kill her. Out here there was space enough for error and she had not made any errors. She hove to and waited it out. Later, when the rain stopped and the wind dropped and the sun shone, she heard Elsie giggling; the water under her bow often sounded like running laughter and it made Ann laugh with her and they ran on southwards, happy, confident and at one. Elsie appeared to know who her true owner was.

Even so she did not come ashore in Tenerife as they had

planned. Some vision of a furious Jeremy and a ferocious, incomprehensible Spanish-speaking Harbour Master arresting her for unladylike behaviour haunted her dreams the night the craggy volcano lifted itself over the horizon. She sailed on and dropped anchor at a small port on Las Palmas, where she stayed only to take on fresh water. Even there, she excited groups of children hovering on the quay and squealing 'chocha, chocha' accompanied by gestures of both disbelief and sexual mockery.

It was after she left the archipelago behind her and sailed west into the open ocean that it started to be wonderful.

Once she was out of sight of land, really out of sight, days beyond any dark smudge or lifted profile breaking the horizon line, so far out that it would be as hard to go back as to go on, her mind flew free, freer than she had ever felt before. There was her and Elsie and the enormous unbroken heft and fall of wave and wind. There were daily duties and delights. There was a deep sense of physical competence and confidence. Life smoothed into a rhythm that was very pure, very joyful; she forgot to be either angry or frightened. The weather stayed calm and she made gentle, steady progress through the blue seas. It was so huge and solitary that she could hear herself think – and something deeper than think, she could feel herself feel.

And one dawn, so bright that the rising sun pushed a shadow-Elsie through the waves in front of them and the solid, real Elsie seemed to be chasing it, she had felt a deep surge of energy, more powerful and precise than she had ever felt before. It pushed her up and forward, making her want to sing, to cry out for the beauty and freshness and loveliness of the future. Later, peering down over the charts on the cabin table, she knew what it was. She was sailing over the mid-Atlantic ridge and deep, deep below her, through first blue, then green and down into black water, down below where no one had ever been or could ever go, there was new liquid rock welling up, pouring out, exploding into the cold dark, and crawling east and west either side of the ridge, forming a new, thin dynamic crust, pushing the Americas away from Africa and Europe, changing everything, changing the world. A plate boundary where new rocks are born out of the cauldron below.

She patted Charlotte Sophia and stood up, surprisingly gracefully. She grinned at Tish and said again, 'Yes. It was wonderful. It changed my life.'

Later, when they were back in the cottage kitchen, Ann knew that was not enough. She needed to explain and she sensed that Tish needed to hear the explanation. She opened a packet of shortbread and, not looking at her niece, said, 'It wasn't just wonderful, Tish; it was important.' Then she did look at her.

'When I sailed Elsie across, I wasn't the first, or the fastest or anything like that, and just the next year Robin Knox Johnston sailed solo non-stop right round the world, but it was still a big deal. It was a big deal out there – it was not a thing that many women did and I was pretty young to do it. But it was a big deal inside as well; it changed me forever. Your father flew out to Florida and met me, but we didn't sail her back together; we couldn't. It wasn't just because he was angry, which I suppose he sort of had a right to be, but he was... perhaps jealous is the easiest word. There was a seismic shift in our relationship, deep down. So we both just knew he couldn't be The Captain any more. He had always been the captain and I was the crew and we'd never even thought about it, which given that I was much older must seem odd to you, but that was how it was. Now we weren't comfortable in the boat together. And you shouldn't go blue water sailing if you aren't comfortable. We didn't really talk about it. But he didn't do the obvious thing – he didn't come back solo himself. I wonder if he was scared or if he was just too young and had the sense to know it. After a bit, he found some mates and they sailed her home –

impressively fast I should add. And I beach-bummed around for a bit and then crewed back in a big posh yacht.'

After a pause, she changed tack. 'Tish, what do you think about the 60s?'

'I don't know; I don't think I do much.' Tish seemed a bit thrown. Ann almost smiled – more of a gibe than a simple change of tack then. 'The Beatles of course, and all that Panda make-up.' Perhaps it was the reference to beach-bumming that triggered something. 'And hippies; drugs.' Ann might as well have asked what she thought about Roman Britain. Tish sounded slightly aggressive when she asked, 'Is there a right answer here?'

'No. Well, to be honest, yes, actually. Everyone laughs at the 60s now, or worse. Since Thatcher it's been ok, or more than ok, to be dismissive, even to blame us – that it was all silly at best or even dangerous, bad, or like your father said – selfish. But I go on believing that something happened, something beautiful and important and that it changed everything. Or promised to; but a real promise, a covenant. I see it like... after I came back to England everything seemed to have changed, or rather to be changing. It was very exciting, to me. And then there was feminism.'

'Were you a women's libber, then?'

She could wish Tish didn't sound either quite so surprised, or quite so near to a sneer. 'I am a feminist and therefore was an active member of the Women's Liberation Movement. Yes. Definitely.'

'Oh.' After only a fairly short pause Tish added, 'Sorry.'

'It's ok. But, for me, for us, 1968 was sort of Year One. And... well one of the things that the Women's Movement was trying to do, lots of historians and psychologists and those people, they needed to prove that sexism wasn't a constant, that it could be different because it used to be different. The difficulty, though we did not know it then, was we didn't have enough scientists. They had been clever to keep women out of science, because what science learned in the twentieth century, what I had learned about tectonic plates, what was the real new thing was knowing that things could change, could really change – that there wasn't just relativity and sub-nuclear randomness, there was hard, material, real, physical, actual change. New things happened. The same old materials could change into entirely new things. It was all dynamic.'

Suddenly it seemed urgent, terribly important that Tish should understand. She tried to sound lighter, more jokey.

'When I was sailing across I felt I could feel the Mid-Atlantic Ridge, all that new lava welling up, those hot shallow earthquakes and movement; all that energy and power. As a matter of fact when lava cools fast in water it forms itself into what are called pillow rocks, so I might just have gone to sleep and become a true hippy beach-bum. But, maybe because I couldn't sail with your father any longer, or because he really had rubbed my face in it, in a very crude sort of sexism, I wanted to be at the destructive plate boundary, pushing, shoving, changing the old world into a different shape, making something new. It was hard work and it was very exciting.'

She tried to describe that excitement – that sense of virtue and delight coming together, so that she did not even want to do a doctorate on their terms and she could and did forgive Jeremy because he had handed her joy on a plate, even if that plate had been so hot that it had scalded her fingers. She tried to make that excitement palpable, understandable to Tish. She wanted to share it and could not tell if she succeeded.

But later, sitting at the table after supper, Tish suddenly reverted to the subject.

'So, what went wrong? I mean for feminism – why did you give up?'

'We didn't give up, Tish, we were ground down, pushed under, subducted.' She looked terribly sad for a brief moment and then grinned. 'Do you know what happens when a thin, dense oceanic plate meets an ancient, buoyant continental plate?'

'Mountains?' Tish tried tentatively. 'Like the Himalayas. And the Alps.'

'Good girl. Yes, that's one effect. But I was thinking of something else. Only be careful – this is just an analogy, an image; and in one way I shouldn't use science like that, because I'll have to cheat a bit, but I'm going to anyway. These oceanic plates are thin, but they are very dense. When they start shoving at the old thicker, but more lightweight, more buoyant, continental plates, you get something called a "destructive plate boundary". Eventually the continental plate bobs up and over the new plate, and because it is heavier the new plate gets pushed under... or it starts plunging down under the thicker but more buoyant continental plate. It goes down deeper and deeper and it heats up and melts. Disintegrates. It gets destroyed. And then it is gone.'

'But that's so sad.'

'No not really. Because... well, two becauses.

'The first because is what happens as they subduct, as they go down. They create earthquakes – some of these will be near the surface and will shake the continental plate and that can make waves, as one says, like tsunamis and other really violent and efficient disturbances; and some are so deep we never feel them on the surface, but they are there and later, billennia later, they will have changed things, unseen, unnoticed, irreversibly. And the new plates can push up mountains, as you said, like the Andes for example; and also make volcanoes, sometime much further, deeper into the continental plate, throwing up new stuff sort of behind the enemy's lines. And they nibble at the edges of the plate and pull chunks of the old plate down with them, gnawing away and making inroads, fissures along the edges. So the oceanic plates can't destroy continental plates, which is probably a relief, but they can change and move them. They do change and move them.'

Tish interrupted, '*Eppur se muove.*'

'What?'

'That's what Galileo said when he signed that thing saying he had been wrong. It means, "It bloody well does move."'

What extraordinary things teenagers knew and did not know. 'Yes, but this time much nearer home.'

'And the other because?' Tish had clearly been paying attention.

'Ah. Well there's the oceanic plate being pushed down and down; it's making earthquakes and volcanoes as it goes – forcing the continents apart, changing them, remaking the topography and even the weather. Eventually it plunges down deep enough to break up and melt because the deeper you go the hotter it gets. So the rock melts and then that hot stew of materials is sort of stirred around by convection currents and so – this is why it isn't sad, although this isn't always easy to remember – one day it will well up again, come back to the *constructive* plate boundary, explode out and start pushing again. There are more dynamic periods and less dynamic ones, but all the time, inch by inch the push goes on, and the continents move and change.'

'So, sort of like, first women get the vote, then there's a bit of a lull and then you get Women's Lib – Liberation, sorry.'

'Well done. Yes. Though of course you have to be very patient – it's very, very slow. The continents move, perhaps, at about the speed that finger nails grow.'

Tish looked at her own fingernails and smiled very sweetly. 'I'd better stop biting mine then. I'll tell you something funny, Aunt Ann. At least I think you'll find it funny. Daddy is really harassing Amy now, because she doesn't want to do a graduate degree.'

Ann laughed, 'I think your big sister will prove a very dynamic Destructive Plate Boundary. I wonder if your father is aware, remembers. But you see, things change.'

'Yes, but him thinking he has the right to decide doesn't change.'

'Oh dear. No, that's true. I'm afraid it comes back to patience. Very trying.'

'I think I prefer volcanoes.' Tish grinned fiercely.

Two days later, Ann drove Tish to the station. They arrived a little early and sat in the car, comfortable with each other, pleased with what might be a new and real friendship or an old and sweet connection, and only patience was needed to show which. After a little, easy silence, Tish said:

'Aunt Ann, you know Alison Utley?'

Ann knew she did not mean *Little Grey Rabbit* and probably did not even know those books. Alison Utley was Jeremy's cruising yacht, the successor to Beatrix Potter. Something about childhood nostalgia she presumed. So she said, 'Yes,' without cavil.

'Do you think, if I found an experienced woman to crew for me, that a bit of Twocking might be in order next Easter?'

Ann looked at her abruptly. 'We are not crossing the Atlantic.'

'No? Well, you were pretty quick weren't you? How about the Norwegian fjords to start with?'

'My poor brother.'

'Just a little earthquake, you know.'

'Tish!'

'Seems to me that it's time we gave the continent another shove.'

'You'll miss your train. Go.'

They kissed and, humping her backpack, Tish legged it across the car park and vanished into the station.

Ann laughed and drove home.

Afterword:

Tectonics on a Plate

Dr. Linda Kirstein

PLATE TECTONIC THEORY has revolutionised vast areas of the geosciences since its first publication in the 1960s. The theory unifies several aspects of geology and particularly provides a framework for interpreting major features of the Earth's surface. The theory emerged following the culmination of centuries of observations, fundamental changes in philosophy that recognised natural forcing of Earth systems and, finally, technical advances and instrumentation that allowed, for example, the ocean floor to be imaged. The theory forms a cornerstone in our study of the Earth and other planets but its implications – for example, how the uplift of mountains influences atmospheric circulation and climate – continue to be discovered. To understand plate tectonics as presented today requires a brief summary of its development, recognition of individual genius in the early proponents of various contributing theories, and the consequent evolutionary direction of ideas over time. A very brief summary of key moments is provided here for context to the story.

Since the sixteenth century the similarity of the coastlines of continents to pieces of a large jigsaw puzzle has been commented upon, especially the way Africa and South America appear to fit together. It was not until the 19th century and the concept of uniformitarianism (the present is the key to the past) that the idea of natural driving forces shaping the Earth's surface was advocated, particularly by James Hutton and Archibald Geikie. In the early twentieth century, Frank Taylor and also Alfred Wegener controversially proposed that the continents were drifting apart and that, pre-drift, they fitted together. Observations such as the continuity of geological formations, the separation of ancient fossil faunal provinces, glaciation in regions now at the equator and desert dune deposits in the northern hemisphere all contributed to the continental drift theory. And importantly the Earth's surface was no longer static!

In the decades that followed, mechanisms to cause continental drift were advocated including a suggestion by Arthur Holmes that the motion of the crust was related to convection currents in the mantle formed by heat transfer due to radioactive decay.

Until the 1950s geological observations and resultant models were based on our knowledge of the continents, but the two thirds of the Earth's surface that lay beneath the ocean remained relatively unknown. This all changed with the advent of World War II and the war at sea. Technological developments during the war, particularly echo-sounding devices that were used to calculate ocean depths, ultimately allowed a survey of the ocean floor to be completed during the 1950s. This work was spearheaded by Harry Hess who collected data across vast tracks of the Pacific Ocean. He noted the ocean floor had a highly variable topography with small mountains in particular locations. Later, large mountain chains thousands of kilometres long, hundreds of kilometres wide and more than 4km high in places were imaged. These were termed mid-ocean ridges because of their location in the middle of the oceans. In 1961 Robert Dietz and colleagues proposed the theory of sea floor spreading in which it was suggested that mid-ocean ridges were sites where new oceanic crust was constantly being produced and moved away – a magmatic conveyor belt! This was a major step towards developing the current theory of plate tectonics – mid-ocean ridges were sites where new magma reached the surface and rigid plates split apart.

Meanwhile, during the 1950s, the measurement of remanent palaeomagnetism in continental rocks (a technique that relies on the fact that certain minerals in rocks, particularly those that are rich in iron, record the direction and intensity of the Earth's magnetic field at the time of formation) was combined with dating of rock formations by either palaeontology or radiometric methods to demonstrate the relative movements of different continents over geological time. Furthermore, surveys in the oceans using magnetometers adapted from World War II technology began recording magnetic anomalies which were ordered and appeared as magnetic 'stripes'. What were these stripes and why were they symmetrical about the mid ocean ridges? Frederick Vine and Drummond Matthews proposed that the 'stripes' were recordings of changes in the Earth's magnetic field (from normal to reverse polarity) with time – a tape recorder of Earth's magmatic activity. Tuzo Wilson and colleagues, recognising the significance of Hess's work on sea floor spreading, argued that if rigid continents were moving as a function of the creation of new oceanic crust at mid ocean ridges, then the Earth must be either expanding in size or there must be sites where oceanic crust is being destroyed. The imaging of bathymetric depressions, that have intense earthquakes and volcanism associated with them, confirmed the existence of destructive margins. The forces exerted as plates are dragged down into the mantle were acknowledged as important drivers of plate motion. The theory of plate tectonics was born.

Although the theory of plate tectonics is widely accepted within the geosciences community, it is not often clear how much the public know about this fundamental theory of plate motion that influences daily life and is essential to understanding the Earth as an integrated system. When I was asked to talk to Sara about the general field of tectonics it was suggested that she had 'no pre-conceptions or pre-planned ideas with respect to what area of tectonics she wants to write about, she just wants to learn, and inspiration will come from that.' Hers *was* an open mind, and as anyone knows when faced with a blank piece of paper the hardest part is knowing where to start – having at least a spatial or temporal scale would have been useful. When this conversation began, Eyjafjallajökull had yet to erupt but there had been plenty of news coverage of devastating earthquakes around the globe including L'Aquila in Italy and also Sumatra – both clearly related to plate tectonic activity. It occurred to me that a basic introduction to plate tectonic theory, which continues to evolve as we image and understand geological processes better, was a good place to start, and potentially Sara could direct me through questioning to something that particularly intrigued her. As a result Sara received eight hours of pre-honours lectures on Earth dynamics in just 40 minutes. It was clear that some of the material was not new to her but a lot of it was and it was the energy associated with plate boundaries that intrigued her most. The words 'divergent' and 'constructive' are used to describe mid–ocean ridge systems as one plate moves away from the other, while 'convergent' and 'destructive' describe sites of plate subduction and/or collision. Transform zones, where plates slide past each other without addition or destruction of material were less exciting, which is interesting as these are regions that are least understood by geoscientists.

In Sara's story key aspects of the evolution of plate tectonic theory are incorporated with ease, as she weaves a story emphasising how much change the world experienced in one decade – the 1960s – and which continues to have repercussions today. The energy she associates with crust formation and destruction, and the emotional associations she makes with the rock cycle – creation, destruction, transformation, renewal – is extremely interesting and manages to humanise a process that I had previously considered in a detached manner. Her choice of Tuzo Wilson as the leading scientist of the day fits well as it was his experience, his interaction with Cambridge scientists and ultimately his ability to put the global evidence that emerged in the 1960s together that helped develop the plate tectonic theory. Sara's integration of plate tectonics clearly demonstrates an enthusiasm for understanding how elements that span variable temporal, and spatial scales shape our lives. Working with a writer has been an illuminating experience and I am glad I have taken the opportunity to work with Sara, it really was rewarding and incisive.

Seeing Double

HIS MOTHER HAD died when he was born. His mother had been young and at the end of a long and very hard labour, made more exhausting by the size of the baby's head. The midwife had acted promptly, gathering in the baby and carrying it away. She had washed and dressed it, before bringing it back to the mother, with a delicate lawn and lace bonnet framing its sweet little face. The mother had taken the child in her arms and smiled, though wearily; but she had made no apparent attempt to count its toes, fingers, eyes and mouths, and after a moment the midwife had turned away to her immediate duties. When she turned back the mother was dead; her face was frozen in a strange rictus, which might have been the consequence of a sudden sharp pain or might have been terror. The midwife, a woman of sturdy good sense and addicted to neither gin nor gossip, deftly massaged the mother's face back into a more seemly expression and closed her large blue eyes forever.

His father, a hero of the nation, loved, admired and honoured, but now retired to his family home in the mountains, grew gentle and sad. He spent most of his time walking in the high hills above the forest or in his library, where he was slowly but steadily compiling a taxonomy of the local flora and fauna. He took tender but perhaps slightly distanced care of his only son. He created a pleasure palace for the child – his own small suite of rooms, opening through large, airy glass doorways onto a pleasant, shaded portico and beyond that, a delightful, secluded garden with high walls, climbable trees and a pool designed for swimming in. At considerable expense, and to the irritation of the local community, he employed the midwife as a permanent nanny and found a blind but nimble servant to assist her.

The child grew, grew strong and straight and healthy. When he was old enough, his father would sometimes take him up into the forests and the mountains beyond the forests where he learned the names of all the butterflies and many of the flowers. Sometimes at night they would climb together onto the roof of the house and watch the stars, and his father taught him to trace and see the patterns of the noble constellations and told him the ancient Greek stories that gave the patterns their names.

The Christmas that he was eight, his father gave him a train set and together they built and developed it. When it grew too extensive for the nursery floor, his father opened up the attics and they created a whole little world there, with electric signals and tiny model towns; and model mountains with tunnels through them, so that the boy could wait in eager anticipation for the engine to emerge from the darkness and sound its miniature horn. They made and remade ever more complicated timetables and were anxious that the trains should run on time, and not crash into each other at the points.

Each evening, after his bath, and when he was all clean and warm and ready for bed, his father would come to tuck him up and give him his good night kisses, one on each cheek and one very gentle special one on the back of his head. Then his father would pull up the hood of his pyjamas, tie the strings and say, 'God bless and keep you, little dark eyes,' and the boy would snuggle down, scarcely conscious of his own happiness.

He was twelve when he found out. One morning, Nanny woke up sick – not very sick, but with a feverish headache and heavy eyes. When she did not go to the kitchen to collect the breakfast, the housekeeper foolishly sent one of the younger maids through with the tray. The boy was already up, hungry and eager, though, of course, properly concerned about Nanny. He was sitting cross-legged on the sofa reading a book. The maid plonked the tray down on the little table by the window and then stood there, fidgeting. The boy did not often see people other than Daddy and Nanny and the blind servant, and he was not sure how to behave. He smiled at the girl. He had a very sweet smile, like his father's but younger and more carefree. She smiled back. She was not much older than he was and the differences between them, obvious to grown ups, were nearly invisible to them.

He said, 'Hello.'

She bobbed a sort of half-curtsey and said, 'Hello' back.

There was a pause, in which he smiled some more and she fidgeted some more.

But in the end she could not resist. For fourteen years she had heard the talk and the secret murmurs, because no respect or even love for their Squire is going to keep his tenantry from gossip about him and his, from speculation and a mild-mannered sort of malice. She was curious on her own behalf, and more tempted yet by the stir she would create in the servants' hall at dinner. And he looked so sweet, with his huge dark eyes and a smile like his father's. And she might never have another chance.

'Go on,' she said, 'show us.'

He almost turned his book towards her, assuming she wanted to see the picture, but there was something, something else; even with his negligible social skills he knew there was something else.

'Show you what?' he asked, but still pleasantly, almost in his father's kindly style, which unfortunately made her bolder.

'You know,' she said, 'it.'

The new pause was longer; he really did not know and she, better attuned, as all servants are, to the nuances of social meaning, realised that he really did not know. She had gone too far. She was embarrassed. But her shame made her even bolder.

'You know,' she said again, 'the face, the other face; the back of your head.'

Instinctively he lifted his hand to the back of his head. Through the soft flannelette of his pyjama hood, he felt the back of his head lumpy, then moving. His hand was frozen for a moment. Then he felt something bite sharply into the fleshy pad at the bottom of his thumb.

He screamed.

Suddenly Nanny was standing in the door, her hair down, grey and straggling as neither of them had ever seen it, her face flushed with her fever and fury.

'Be quiet,' she said in a commanding tone, and then losing her grip on her anger. 'Be quiet, you evil, wicked girl. Go away. Go away.'

Sobbing, the little maid ran from the room and the boy and his nanny listened to her clogs go rattling down the passage.

'Nanny?' he said, and had she been well and wakeful it might yet have been alright; she might have given him a cuddle and he would have shown her his hand and she could have magicked a pin out of his pyjama hood and told him she was a silly old nanny for leaving it there. But the headache was stronger than her wisdom and all she wanted was her bed.

'It was nothing, darling,' she said quickly, 'nothing at all. Just a silly girl. A very naughty little girl, probably trying to be funny. We won't be seeing her again. Now eat up your breakfast and go and play in the garden.'

He ate up his breakfast and went into the garden but not to play. He had so seldom been lied to directly that he did not understand it. Thought and speech were one in his closed world. But he knew, he knew that Nanny had made a deliberate gap between her thoughts and her words. He went into the garden, but not to play. There was playing, which was not relevant; there was hearing, which was not trustworthy; there was seeing which was not possible. There was touching and feeling. He looked at the little red mark at the base of his thumb, which was beginning to bruise and very tentatively, very, very carefully, using only his fingertips and ready for sudden attack he began to explore the back of his head.

After an hour he knew. And knowing, he knew that he had always known. There was another face: he could feel its nose through the flannelette of his hood, shorter perhaps than his own, though hard to tell, but with two indentations for nostrils, certainly; he could feel its lips, though carefully with the flat of his hand so as not to get bitten again. He knew already it had teeth. He thought he could feel the hinge of its jaw moving just behind his ears.

He could not untie the string of his hood, but after some effort he worked it loose enough to pull it back from his head. He placed his two hands delicately on the back of his head, either side of its nose, and could feel the hollow underneath his palms. He waited and felt a flutter, like a butterfly's footfall. It was blinking. He pulled his hood back on and wriggled the knot tight. He went inside and sat on the sofa again and chanted his times tables, all the way from one-two-is-two to twelve-twelves-are-one-hundred-and-forty-four over and over again, all day long.

Later on, just as the day began to fade, he left his room very quietly so as not to disturb Nanny and went along the passage to find his father. After he had passed the bottom of the stairs that went up to the attic, he did not really know the way. He opened various doors into various rooms all heavy with dust and cold. A huge cold dining room with twelve empty chairs and faded red velvet curtains; a room with an even bigger table covered in green cloth; there were no chairs and the edge of the table was turned up – he did not know what it was for. There was a long passage, a huge hall almost dark, and a room with little uncomfortable sofas and lots of little tables with lots of little things on them – that room was lighter, with long windows looking out over the shaggy field that his father called 'the lawn'; he had only ever seen it from high up on the hillside. That room seemed a strange thing to him because it was both beautiful and pretty. He had not known that something could be both. But his father was not there.

He came to a door with light coming out underneath it. He opened it very softly. The room was warm and clean and wonderfully untidy, with precarious piles of paper and books stacked up or lying on the floor, as Nanny never let him leave his. His father was sitting with his back to the boy; his bald head inclined forward over a large desk. The boy could see that he was writing. He watched him, watched the smooth back of his skull and the slight movement of his elbow.

His father was unaware of him. After quite a long while the boy said, 'Daddy.'

His father raised his head, apparently without shock or surprise and said, 'Hello, what are you doing here? I was just going to come for you. It must have been a boring day for you with Nanny *hors de combat*.' He often had to guess what his father meant, and it did not worry him. 'But you must learn not to be impatient.'

'I am not impatient,' he said with dignity. 'I have come to ask you something of grave importance.'

'And what is that?' His father smiled at the formality of the announcement.

'I need to ask you why there is someone else on the back of my head.'

The boy was aware that the warm peace of the study was broken. It made him wary – his father was a hero of the nation and should not be afraid of anything. He said nothing, awkward now. After a pause his father said, 'How did you find out?' He sounded weary.

'It bit me.' The boy walked towards the desk holding out his hand.

He was almost too big to climb into his father's lap but the older man held him close, kissing the small bruise. He sagged there for a while, exhausted by the long, slow day. But it was not enough.

'But why, Daddy?'

'I don't know,' his father said, 'no one knows. It is a strange and mysterious thing.'

'Couldn't you take it away?'

'No, no, I'm afraid not. But it is not a someone, it is a part of you.' The boy could hear a troubling, insistent urgency in his father's voice; and he thought it might be fear. So his father was afraid of something. The boy's world shivered, threatened. Perhaps it was his own fear that made him daring, because even as he asked, he knew it was a dangerous question. He asked, 'Is it what killed my mummy?'

'No.' But the no was too loud, too strong, too resolute. It was like Nanny's 'naughty girl'; it was true but not true; the speaker chose it to be true although there were other choices which the speaker did not choose. Grown-ups, he learned far too suddenly, spoke with double voices, cunningly, so that true and not true weren't like white and black, like either-or, like plus and minus; they were like the bogs on the hill side, shifty, invisible and dangerous.

His father's revulsion from the boy's deformity was very strong. Because he was a man of self-discipline rather than courage, he would never admit this even to himself; this was why, each evening, he obliged his often reluctant lips to kiss the secret face so tenderly. This was why, too, he missed the boy's curiosity and tried to offer him consolation instead of information.

'Look,' he said, 'have I ever shown you a picture of your mother?' He turned the boy's head very gently towards a miniature set up on a filigree easel on his desk. She smiled there, all pink and blonde and blue-eyed. She was pretty. But it was a picture, a painting; the boy knew that paintings did not always look like the thing they were paintings of. He

47

could never be sure. And he did not much care; he had other things on his mind. But he understood that his father had let him into a secret place of his own and deserved some sort of thanks. He tried, slightly experimentally, to say the right thing, to do that grown-up speaking which makes a gap between the feelings and the thoughts and the words.

'I don't look much like her, do I Daddy?'

He had got it right. He felt his father smiling. 'No, you look more like me, and bad luck to you, except that men should never be that pretty.' Their dark eyes met in what the father thought was a sweet moment of male complicity and bonding. And a little later they went upstairs, hand in hand, to play with their train set.

But the day had been too difficult and his need had not been met. What he had learned was not about the other face, but about the way grown-ups did not want to talk about the other face. There was something dark and horrible about it. They were ashamed. They wanted him to keep it secret with them and from them.

But alone, alone in the darkness of night, and the deeper darkness of its invisibility, with delicate and attentive fingers, he began to explore the back of his head. He learned that what hurt it, hurt him, so he had to treat it tenderly; he learned that it blinked when he blinked, but did not smile when he smiled, or weep when he wept; he learned that its nose never dribbled, but if he pinched its nostrils closed, it did not breathe through its mouth, but he became breathless; he learned that he could make it happy or angry, but that it seldom bothered to be sad.

In the end, fingers were not enough. He needed to see. He could not ask.

It took him nearly two years to work it out. Then one day while the blind servant was in charge, he stole into Nanny's bedroom and borrowed the mirror from her dressing table. He took it into the bathroom and began to experiment. His father had by now taught him both some physics and how to play billiards. There had to be a way of angling the light, like angling a delicate in-off with the ivory billiard balls. If he looked in a mirror into another mirror at the right angle, he calculated that perhaps it might be possible. It was awkward. The bathroom was not designed for the purpose and its mirror was fixed to the wall.

Then, almost unexpectedly, with Nanny's mirror propped a little precariously on a tooth-mug on the windowsill, he turned his head a little and he saw what it was he was trying to see. The face was paler than his face and had no proper chin so that the mouth was angled slightly too much downwards; but he could see that its nose was very like his and its eyelashes were longer. It was prettier than he was, and it was not a painting or a picture; it was real. It opened its eyes and they were blue, as blue as the summer sky, as blue as his mother's were in her painting. Its eyes met his and it smiled, a cunning, triumphant smile. It was not an it, but a She.

All women have double mouths, he thought and then he thought that he did not know where the thought had come from.

After that he could hear her voice. She whispered to him. She used his brain to think her thoughts. She used his breath to be alive. He was never alone. And he could not tell anyone.

Sometimes it was fun – She was his friend and he had never had a friend before. They played games together, and usually he won because their feet and hands were under his management; but when he tried to run away She would come with him, following close behind, though looking in the other direction, and he could never get away.

Sometimes it was not fun – She thought thoughts he did not want to think; She said words he did not want to hear and he could never get away.

He could not have any secrets. He made his life a secret from Daddy and Nanny, but they were not real secrets because She always knew and he could never get away.

Adolescence. That was what Daddy and Nanny called it, affectionately usually, even proudly. But She called Daddy 'Papa' in a sweet little voice, which Daddy would have loved if he could have heard it; and She was mean about Nanny and refused to understand how much he needed and loved her. She complained when he wore a hat; She would wriggle and protest if he tried to lie on his back, to sleep or to look at the sky; She loved the light, and the sunshine, to which he did not like to expose her.

She hated it when he masturbated. His fingers, now well practised in delicate explorations, had new plans of their own; plans which sometimes he found appalling and sometimes found intriguing and occasionally found absolutely the most fascinating and delightful and demanding and consuming ideas in the whole wide world. She would distract him with loud noises, silly giggles, filthy words and a scathing contempt at his ineptitude, both physical and manual. He was to her both pathetic and disgusting. She was always there, and he could never get away. She had to be kept secret but he was allowed no other secrets, or privacy or silence.

When he was seventeen he fell in love. A new maid came who sang like a bird in the early morning and was soft and round with dimply cheeks, big breasts, orange hair and a merry smile. He never spoke to her, but he watched and yearned and dreamed and hoped. He wanted without knowing what he wanted. Sweet first love, or first lust without knowing the difference. But She was having none of it. She was jealous and mean and set up a shrieking in his head. Over and over again she shouted, 'Freak, freak, freak. That one will never love you – she'll only want to see me.'

When he tried shouting 'Freak' back at her like a little boy, she giggled spitefully and said, 'No, no. I don't exist. I am just the freak in you. I don't have a me. I have a you. I'm not a someone. I'm a part of you. Ask Papa.'

She said, 'That little trollop won't love you; she won't

spread her legs with a Lady watching.'

'Never?' he asked her plaintively.

'Never,' She said with undisguised glee.

'I'll kill you,' he threatened.

'You can't,' she said. 'You can never get away.'

So one evening, just as the day began to fade, he left his rooms very quietly so as not to disturb Nanny and went along the passage, but not to find his father. As he passed the bottom of the stairs that went up the attic he remembered the train set with which he and his father had not played for years. It was not enough. He opened various doors into various rooms all heavy with dust and cold. Then he went downstairs to the gun room, wrote a short note for his father and shot Her through the mouth; his mouth because he couldn't get the shot gun into the back of his head.

Afterword:

Poor Edward

Prof. Jamie Davies

THIS STORY MAY be seen, in some ways, as a prose companion to Tom Waits' beautiful song 'Poor Edward': the heroes of both have the same problem: an unwanted female face on the back of the head, with its own malevolent personality. Both the song and the story end with combined sororicide and suicide.

The myth of two-faced individuals is at least as old as Janus: how plausible is it that someone like the boy in the story could really exist? The dusty jars of the world's anatomical museums show that, although human development is usually robust, when it goes wrong it can do so in many bizarre ways. In the jars of our own small museum in Edinburgh, we have several foetuses whose anatomy echoes the monsters and gods of mythology: there are 'mermaids' with joined lower limbs, cyclops faces with one central eye, multi-headed foetuses like Cerberus, and many-armed ones like Kali. Three known foetal abnormalities can give rise to a human who, Janus-like, has two faces. One, *fetus in fetu*, arises when the smaller of two foetuses is trapped in the closing body folds of its twin. Usually, it is enveloped completely but can sometimes protrude, occasionally presenting its face. This type of abnormality would not, however, result in the joined airways implied by details in the story, so can be rejected as a cause. A second abnormality, *cephalothoracopagus syncephalus*, has two faces on the opposite sides of one head, but the faces each point sideways and there are two distinct bodies: this is nothing like the anatomy described in the story. The third possiblity, *monocephalus diprosopus tetraophthalmos*, is the closest match.

Monocephalus diprosopus tetraophthalmos (MDT) – literally 'one head, two faces, four eyes' – is a very rare condition: only about 40 cases have ever been described in world medical literature. In *MDT*, the faces are normally at about 90 degrees to one another, each facing about 45 degrees to forwards, rather than one being at the back of the head as in the story (a web search will bring up good images, but most of these are of stillbirths and are best avoided by the squeamish). *MDT* is an extreme type of conjoined twinning, an event more typically associated with the birth of two clearly identifiable separate people who are joined together somewhere along the trunk and may share organs. Despite the roots of the word 'conjoined', the shared anatomy is generally thought to arise not by fusion of two initially separate individuals but rather by an incomplete separation of one embryo into two identical twins.

Early in normal development, there is a stage at which human embryos exist as a two-layered flat disc. Signals from the bottom of the disc cause cells in the top disc to define a single straight line across most of the disc: this is the primitive streak and corresponds to the future head-tail axis of the body. Sometimes, instability in the signalling causes the formation of two parallel lines, rather than just one: these will become the axes of two identical twins. If these are far apart, each will have enough tissue around it to make an independent body. If they are close together, they each try to use the cells between them to make ventral organs, which is what these cells would normally make, and end up sharing these organs and remaining joined. Occasionally, the line forms as a Y shape, making a foetus with two heads and necks but one body. This is quite common in reptiles, many of which live to adulthood. In humans, it is rare and usually lethal, although at least one pair of such twins have reached adulthood. When the junction of the Y is even higher, only the highest parts of the head, such as the face, are duplicated and everything else is shared. This is assumed to be the cause of *MDT*, although there is a lot of guesswork involved as these cases are diagnosed only after the critical events have happened.

People born with *MDT* usually suffer a range of serious internal abnormalities, particularly of the developing brain, heart, gut and airways. Most conjoined twins die before or within a few weeks of birth but some do live. Abnormalities in the nervous system can have a severe impact on intelligence. One of the features of the story that would be hardest to accommodate within our current understanding is the normal mental development of its hero. In the story, his vision, hearing and intelligence are normal, suggesting his forward-facing face has proper connection to a normal brain. The backward-face also has a will (it bites), it can communicate low level pain into the boy's brain ('what hurt it, hurt him'), it can see independently so must have an entirely independent visual cortex and higher brain, and finally it can think independently using the boy's brain. The boy having a normal brain could perhaps be achieved if the extra face made no significant connections to any brain tissue, or if were on a completely separate head. The two-faces, two-personalities, two-visions yet one brain idea is very challenging. It would, if it really were to exist, no doubt tell us a great deal about consciousness.

The story highlights a difference in eye colour between the two faces (the forward face is 'little dark eyes', the reverse one has eyes 'blue as the summer sky'). Eye colour is determined genetically, so should be the same in conjoined twins (which develop from the same embryo). Rare humans do exist, though, who have two eyes of different colours (*heterochromia iridum*). One explanation is that some of the cells in the embryos that made these people mutated early in development, and now express the pigment melanin to a different extent. We will return to the possibility of some cells having mutated below.

One of the most striking ideas in the story, an idea that also appears in Waits' 'Poor Edward', is that the rearward face is female. This is even more difficult to explain than the eye colour. In humans and other eutherian mammals, the sexual development of most of the body (everything except for the gonads) is controlled by hormones. Early in development, cells in an as-yet undecided gonad try to switch on a gene on the Y chromosome. If the chromosome is present, the gene switches on and sets off a cascade of events that causes the gonad to become a testis, while if there is no Y chromosome an alternative pathway makes the gonad an ovary. If the gonad is a testis, it secretes two hormones (testosterone and AMH), and these cause the rest of the body to follow the male route. Without these hormones, the body becomes female. In the story, both faces, and whatever brain structures are connected to them, will have received the same hormones: if the front face is male (and the story clearly implies that normal male sexual development has taken place before and after puberty), the rearward one ought to be male too. Is there any way that a face, or any other part of the body, can be female when there are testes secreting testosterone? There is one: inactivating mutation of genes that encode the testosterone receptor leaves the body's cells 'blind' to the presence of testosterone. People who have this mutation develop outwardly female bodies (androgen insensitivity syndrome, AIS). If the hero had only one functioning gene for a testosterone receptor, and if even this was inactivated in a freak mutation that affected only the cells that went on to form the other face, then that face could have developed as female because its cells would be unaware of the maleness of the body in which they are embedded. If we add in a simultaneous, doubly-freak mutation of eye colour genes, we get to the required phenotype.

Mythology, science fiction stories, and the gruesome contents of anatomical museums can all provoke deep questions about what it is to be human; questions about identity, free will, uniqueness, individuality and togetherness. Science and philosophy often progress by consideration of cases so extreme we no longer expect common sense to be a guide, so we have to think. 'Seeing Double' uses a congenital abnormality of human development to explore what it would really be like to achieve what many people think is their heart's desire – to live as an inseparable couple, to be one of two people living as one. Like all of the best science fiction, it makes us see our lives, hopes and dreams from a new and enlightening angle.

On Sneezing
an Uncertain Sneeze

ON A RELATIVELY random basis Einstein is invited by the Old Man to come and play craps with him. It annoys Einstein that the Old Man's hair is even more wild and eccentric than his own. Otherwise he rather enjoys these sessions, except when Niels Bohr and Werner Heisenberg come to watch. Although they do not jeer, because, up there, there is perfect charity, he knows that they would like to and they would be justified in doing so. Occasionally, usually when the Old Man is on a winning streak, his doubts raise their heads again. Once he picked up the dice, peered at them closely and said, 'They're loaded, aren't they?'

'Albert,' said the Old Man, gentle but reproving.

'How can you stand the uncertainty?'

'I like it,' said the Old Man. 'I wanted there to be a fundamental limit to logical scientific observation. I built it in.'

My dear Lis,

Congratulations. I was so thrilled for you – a real proper significant prize (to say nothing of the cheque). It would be impertinent of me to say 'and thoroughly deserved' because what do I know about contemporary poetry? But I am sure it was. I swell with pride at the dedication, although I've been doing that since it was published. Extra pride, let's say, and I saw online what you said in your acceptance speech and do know enough to say 'thoroughly undeserved'. But I am going to accept any reflected glory that comes my way and immediately put the URL and full quote onto my Impact list and my department will be pleased with me. And it is undeniably pleasing to us all to have the eminent judges talk about 'forging a new resonant poetic, beyond the sacralising of nature, out of the mysterious ore of quantum mechanics.' I glow at the idea of being culturally resonant instead of nerdy and weird! And, of course, I agree with them entirely!

I'd come to town, bearing champagne and take you out to dinner – and will soon – but at the moment I'm a bit tied down here on Granny duties. Lou honestly did have to go to Singapore (the 'honestly' is probably to persuade me not you!) so I'm with Laura for the week, and actually not grumbling at all because, as you know, I completely adore her. However, the poor thing is having a pretty nasty time with hay-fever – all puffy eyes, virulent sneezing attacks and general grotty misery. Lou is convinced this is caused by all the uncertainty Harry's carrying-on is creating; so that Laura doesn't know what precisely is going on, where she's at or what will happen next. I personally think a little more house-cleaning and a little less psychology would be more effective, but that is the sort of thing you learn very quickly not to say once you are a grandmother. (You learn not to say quite a lot of things – including the fact that even if it is all Harry's fault, and frankly I don't think it is, Lou shouldn't be lumbering Laura with any of it. I think they are both behaving appallingly; and it is probably not such a bad idea for Lou to go to Singapore for ten days and give the poor wee thing a break.)

Anyway, I've kept her home from school for the last couple of days, which may be partly self-indulgence. We've had rather good fun despite the sneezes, which we now call *sternutation* as I am a scientist and she is just at the age where she loves long words – especially ones her grandmother comes up with. Do you think that could become culturally resonant? And we've spent merry hours looking at slow motion sneezes on YouTube – disgusting and totally riveting. 40,000 droplets per sneeze spraying out at up to 115 mph and spreading for up to three yards – yuck. But did you know the young still believe that if you sneeze with your eyes open they will pop out? Unfortunately, the two of us failed to verify or falsify this hypothesis. We just couldn't do it.

Anyhow, this is just a sort of a run-up to telling you how I made a complete fool of myself in relation to all this which will make you laugh, and you are probably the one person who would understand it. I was in the kitchen and Laura was drawing at the table, with that extraordinary concentration that the young can achieve – no multi-tasking for them, a kind of purity of attention that I long for and envy and admire. And after a bit she comes in and says:

'This is for you, Granny,' (I do wish she could call me Nell like everyone else does, 'Granny' is a bit discouraging somehow, but that is another thing you learn not to say) and she presents me with a picture – like this:

Well! You can imagine – Grandmother in Ecstasy (like Bernini but with more wrinkles). My little one has drawn a charge-cloud picture of the atom. Knowledge of angels – or an unusually impressive primary school teacher of course, but I do not think that at the time; I think 'natural genius.' I am also of course flattered because if this is what she has chosen to give me, she has taken on board the idea that her own grandmother is a quantum physicist and she at least finds this perfectly natural and proper. So I ooh and ah without any difficulty and then sort of go off on one – launch into a history of the atom: Dalton's billiard balls, Thomson's plum pudding, Rutherford's empty spaces (with little minus-dashes for the electrons), Bohr's planetary model...

(No, I am not sending my sketches! I can't draw and the Bohr orbits looked a good deal more wavelike than he would have cared for.)

So, I am warbling on happily and would probably have tried to draw little pictures of Planck's quanta or something next (there's a challenge for you, Lis!) when I finally notice that Laura is not quite with me on this. Indeed she is looking distinctly baffled and bemused. Not to say miffed.

'What's the matter, darling?' I ask, not yet put out because, after all, many people a good bit older than she is really do not get it. I suspect I was poised for some seriously tricky questions: 'Can there be an inevitable probability? What are those naughty neutrinos up to? How can we be certain it *is* uncertain?' (Your sort of questions really.)

But she looks at me with a sort of sad exasperation and says, 'Granny, it is not a science thing.'

'Oh,' I say, falling off my little cloud, 'what is it a picture of?'

'It's not a picture,' she says with dignity, 'it's a di-ag-gram. It is of me sneezing. The black blob in the middle is me, and all the little bits are the germs and pollens and snots.'

My dumb is founded; my crest is fallen. I feel a complete idiot. I comfort myself with the high minded thought that this proves relativity: the position of the observer affects the observation; and also with the hope that it will make you laugh.

Lots more congratulations and warm love,
Nell

p.s. I told Laura I would ask how you would spell the noise a sneeze makes because we both think 'atishoo' isn't very good – and you are the poet.

Dearest Nell,

Many thanks for yours. I've adjourned temporarily to Devon, with Sally, so couldn't have made dinner in the next couple of weeks anyway – it will keep though and I will hold you to it. I'm reading at the South Bank in September and plan a little party, so you can come to that if we don't catch up in the flesh before then. But I hope we will.

I'm really replying so promptly though because of your grandmother story. (I sort of like 'Granny' myself – although I am not one – because I like it when names mark a particular relationship. Mummy, Granny, domestic nicknames that the world in general don't know or use. People used to have Christian names for that and now the bloody utility companies write 'Lis' or 'Nell.')

Sorry, digression. The point is that wee Laura is more of a genius than you apparently realise! Or rather perhaps there are more frames of reference than you give credit for. 'What we observe is not nature itself, but nature exposed to our method of questioning.' (Schrödinger, by the way, not me!) Because, as you seem not to be aware, Heisenberg discovered (described? Formalised? Invented?) the Uncertainty Principle because of hay-fever! In the light of Laura's diagram I want to say 'because of sneezing,' but probably shouldn't risk the perils of such definite causality.

Seriously. You know Heisenberg and Schrödinger really did not get on – scientifically and I suspect personally. Even before Schrödinger trashed Heisenberg's Matrix theory, H was really unhappy about the inflexibility of Schrödinger's maths. There's a nice quote in a later letter to Pauli: 'The more I think about the physical portion of Schrödinger's theory, the more repulsive I find it... Schrödinger writes that the visualisability of his theory "is probably not quite right." In other words it's crap.' (Very pleasing to the poet in me!) He could see there was a problem in the maths about measuring basic physical variables like position and momentum or energy and time. He was sure this was not the fault of the experimenter but inherent in the atoms themselves. But he did not know how to express that. So he and Bohr go stomping about in the woods trying to talk it through and what happens is it brings on a savage attack of hay-fever. I'm not going to enter the psychology versus allergy issue – sorry.

So he goes off to Helgoland to recover. Helgoland, in case you don't know, is an island in the south east corner of the North Sea, which is a pretty odd place geologically and historically and even linguistically, but the point here is that it is freakily pollen free, so Germans with allergies used to go there – antihistamines were not invented until the 1930s.

And in Helgoland we assume that he stops sneezing so he can concentrate and his eyes stop seeping so he can see and – Lo – he defines the Uncertainty Principle (although his preferred term was 'imprecision'). It's only a teeny tiny step for the poet to see why it is like a sneeze. Clever Laura. Perhaps we should all develop allergic rhinitis and become more richly creative.

Not probably creative enough though, alas, to generate a decent onomatopoeic representation of the common or garden sneeze. Tell Laura I tried to the point of inhaling pepper – but it is quite a long process, the full sneeze, involving gasps, head movements and a sort of poised waiting while the outcome has both a probability of 'one' and is completely immeasurable – you just don't know what will happen. They attribute the powerful nature of a sneeze to the fact that so many physical organs are involved – lungs and eyelids and chest muscles and face and throat, and apparently people can even dislocate their vertebrae sneezing! 'Atishoo' is not bad really, but should perhaps have some blank page space around it and a couple of prefixed huh or ha markers, aspirants. As in:

H   h   ha huh   haaah   h–atishoo.

I don't think this will catch on.

I love the Uncertainty Principle by the way. 'In the sharp formulation of the law of causality – "if we know the present *exactly*, we can calculate the future" – It is not the conclusion that is wrong but the premise.' (That's Heisenberg himself by the way.) One thing I simply do not understand is why fundies – and not just them, all sorts of theists and deists and religionists – so hate quantum stuff. It seems much more intelligent and divine to me than 'intelligent design'. (Pah!) I feel it must be how God works, how God is, (assuming there is a god). I try to avoid the word 'magic' when talking to you scientists because I do understand why you don't like it, but left to myself I'd call it 'quantum magic' rather than 'mechanics'. I don't think that will catch on either – though it would make a great title for my next collection!

I've promised Sally I'll weed her herbaceous border while she's at the office, so I had better run.

Thanks and love, as always,

Lis.

Up there, of course, unlike in Helgoland, there is a great deal of pollen: all those lilies and roses and the February hazel catkins coating everything with gold dust. But because, up there, everything is perfect, there is no hay-fever. This is, naturally, a deep relief to Werner and he wanders around sniffing appreciatively and joyfully. But just sometimes he misses that moment when velocity and position blur, when energy and time slip away into the uncertain immeasurable, when the charge-cloud thickens towards 'one' at the back of his nose and… Then, there is a high probability, though it is never certain, that the Old Man will come by and offer him a pinch of snuff. And he will take it and inhale and (obviously in an entirely unphysical way) his soft palate and uvula will depress while the back of his tongue elevates and partially closes the passage to his mouth so that air ejected from his lungs may be expelled through his nose.

He will sneeze. A full, perfect, satisfying sneeze, although the force and extent of the expulsion of air cannot be precisely predicted or measured.

He will sneeze; the Old Man will laugh.

Afterword:

Three Years That Changed Physics Forever

Prof. Jim Al-Khalili

TODAY, WE LOOK back on the period 1925–1927 as one of the most important in the history of science. Over a period of just three years, physics was turned on its head, making even the achievements of Einstein two decades earlier seem tame by comparison. The orchestrator of this revolution was the great Dane, Niels Bohr, who had received the 1922 Nobel Prize 'for his services in the investigation of the structure of atoms, and the radiation emitted from them'. By this time, however, a number of young European physicists were just completing their PhDs and beginning to question whether Bohr's theory of quantised electron orbits in atoms was really the last word. The three grand masters of atomic theory at the time were Bohr in Copenhagen, Arnold Sommerfeld in Munich and Max Born in Göttingen. But it was their young students who were to make the greater impact.

Before 1925, physicists were aware that a major problem with Bohr's atomic theory, involving electrons in fixed orbits around atomic nuclei, was that it was unable to explain how two electrons in the same atom interact with each other. Bohr's equations worked just fine for the hydrogen atom, which contained just one electron, but the atomic structure of the next element up, helium, with two electrons, could not be described. One of the young brat pack, the Austrian genius Wolfgang Pauli, characterised the desperate situation in a letter to a colleague in May 1925:

Physics at the moment is again very muddled; in any case, for me it is too complicated, and I wish I were a film comedian or something of that sort and had never heard about physics.

The first breakthrough was to come from Werner Heisenberg, a young German working in Göttingen who in spite of his brilliance almost failed his PhD examination in 1923. While recovering from a bout of hay fever on the German island of Helgoland during the summer of 1925, he made a major breakthrough in formulating a new mathematical theory. At the same time, back in Göttingen, Max Born and his young assistant, Pascual Jordan, had submitted a paper entitled 'On Quantum Mechanics' in which they suggested that the '*the true laws of nature should involve only such quantities that can be observed.*' As soon as Heisenberg returned to Göttingen and digested their work, he incorporated his new ideas into it. What it meant, he argued, (and I'm sparing you the technical details) was that Bohr's atomic theory could not be correct since it relied on quantities that could never be experimentally observed and measured, namely the electron orbits. His theory stated that only those quantities that can be measured directly, such as the electrons' energies, have any physical meaning. Everything else is just maths.

By September of that year, Heisenberg, Born and Jordan had completed their new theory of quantum 'mechanics'. Their idea relied on a rather strange set of mathematical relations; basically, that the product of two quantities, say A times B, was not necessarily equal to B times A. Of course, with ordinary numbers this is silly: obviously, 3 x 4 is the same as 4 x 3; the answer is 12 in both cases. But the quantities in their quantum theory followed a different multiplication rule – one already well-known to mathematicians and that was obeyed by quantities called matrices (essentially grids of numbers). Very soon, this new theory became known as matrix mechanics. It was attributed to Heisenberg, but in truth the contributions of Born and Jordan should not be underestimated. The three's voluminous paper 'On Quantum

Mechanics II' was published February 1926.

At the same time, in January 1926, the Austrian physicist Erwin Schrödinger submitted his first paper outlining an alternative theory. His atomic theory started from the idea of electrons not as tiny localised particles orbiting the nucleus like planets around the sun but as waves of energy. His version became known as wave mechanics. He had based his idea on an earlier one by the French nobleman Louis de Broglie. However, unlike de Broglie who imagined all particles being carried by their associated waves, Schrödinger dispensed with the idea of matter particles, such as electrons in atoms, altogether and instead claimed that only the waves were real. Crucially however, Schrödinger's approach yielded exactly the same results as those of Heisenberg.

Schrödinger's wave mechanics and his now-famous equation were an instant success. His approach was seen by most physicists as simpler to deal with than Heisenberg's rather abstract matrix formalism. This frustrated Heisenberg immensely, who by this time was working with Niels Bohr in Copenhagen, but at least he had the support of Bohr and Pauli.

It is commonly believed that Paul Dirac was the first person to resolve the issue by showing that the Schrödinger and Heisenberg theories were equivalent (like saying the same thing in two languages). In fact, it was Pauli who was the first to prove this, in a letter that was never published and which only appeared in print many years later.

In the spring of 1927, Heisenberg published his famous Uncertainty Principle, which showed that there is a certain unavoidable limit to the amount of information we can have about a quantum system. For instance, we can never know the precise location of an atom and how fast it is moving at the same time. What is not often appreciated is that the Uncertainty Principle relied crucially on Schrödinger's wave mechanics ideas.

Today, it is fair to say that physics students are taught the Schrödinger approach to quantum mechanics because it is more intuitive, whereas practising theoretical physicists like me tend to use a combination of both matrix and wave mechanics. The quantum world is strange enough as it is and we must use whatever tools are most convenient for us to make sense of it.

Heisenberg won the Nobel Prize for physics in 1932, Schrödinger shared the 1933 Prize with Paul Dirac, while Pauli had to wait till 1945 for his. We have never seen the likes of these geniuses since.

How the Humans
Learned to Speak

LONG, LONG AGO, oh best beloved, the primapes came down from the trees and out of the jungle. They could walk by then, and they had clever thumbs and could make good use of sticks and stones, for breaking bones, unlike words which they had not thought of yet.

They came down onto the ground and left the jungle and travelled east by north munching nutritious seeds and fruit all the way until they came to the great gold-green grassy savannah plain all set about with acacia scrub, where you can see for a very long way (especially if you are bipedal). There they settled down among some Mukusi trees, not too far from a reasonably reliable river and as far as possible from any termite heaps, and they got on with their daily business of hunting, gathering and breeding.

And also evolving, and this last, oh best beloved, is the most important of all.

As you go through life you may meet some strange people who will tell you that evolving does not happen, but they are wrong. And you will know they are wrong because I am telling you a very important story about it, so it has to be true.

Unlike hunting and gathering and learning your four times table, evolving takes a very long time. But there was all the time in the world, and by the point that we get to this story they had done several billion years of work on it, although they still looked much like their ancestors who had come down from the trees and out of the jungle and onto the great gold-green grassy savannah plain all set about with acacia scrub. Their fur had mostly been abandoned, and their brains and their buttocks were bigger (though I should not mention this latter, oh best beloved, lest some teacher should think this story improper and not let you read it, which would be a serious and shameful shame). But despite appearances, and you should never judge by appearances as the foolish do, they had changed. First of all, they no longer had to be spatially aware in three dimensions, as they did when they swung through the trees like their pendulous cousins, the orang-utan and the gorillas, and this meant that they could get rid of a whole lot of frontal lobe brain cells and connections (though very, very slowly as I have told you) and *this* meant there was space for their neocortex to grow – and the size of a neocortex is a thing of special significance and importance because the bigger it is the more friends you can have.

And out there on the great gold-green grassy savannah plain all set about with acacia scrub, more friends gave these primapes an evolutionary advantage, which is a very good thing to have if you can get it and a terminally bad thing to be without if you can't. For the more friends you have, the much more easier is it to do hunting and gathering (to say nothing of tending babies with big brains and managing fires and throwing stones at running animals with an effective degree of efficiency (which means lethalness as the military establishment has explained and explained ever since) and developing resource-and-sagacity and very most particularly not getting gobbled up by bigger and fiercer animals as you clamber your way to the top of the food chain). And the primapes got more neocortex and so they got more friends and they flourished and waxed as fat as butter – which incidentally, like words, had not been invented yet.

But then there was a pause, hiatus or interval. Because, you see, before the primapes left the jungle and travelled east by north munching nutritious seeds and fruit all the way until they came to the great gold-green grassy savannah plain all set about with acacia scrub, they had small neocortices and not so many friends, and they maintained and consolidated (which means to make them hard and firm and useful) those friendships by stroking and touching each other, in slow gentle rhythms. This is called grooming, which is not exactly the same as social grooming is now, although there are points of similarity so be very careful. And they groomed each other like this for hours, because grooming releases endorphins. And endorphins, oh best beloved, just in case you – like the Elephant's Child – have insatiable curiosity, are endogenous opioid peptides and they are excellent things to have released because they make you feel fabulously friendy and lavishly loveish towards whoever gave them to you, so you stay friends.

But it takes a long time for every primape to groom every other primape in the same gang, and they have to take it in turns and share, and we all know how hard that is, don't we? So, when the neocortex got bigger and the number of friends got bigger there was a problem. The best number of friends for hunting and gathering (to say nothing of all those other things I told you about before when I hope you were paying attention) was too many for the grooming and bonding. And that was the hiatus, or pause or interval.

But by now they were primapes of resource and sagacity, and after a very long time – because evolving takes a very long time – they learned how to laugh. And, as you may already have learned from experience, oh best beloved, if you laugh big laughs, all the way out until your breath fails, it makes you feel fabulously friendy and lavishly loveish towards whoever you are laughing with. And this, although you may not know it, is because laughing – like grooming – releases endorphins, which is a happy happenstance. And of course this solved the problem because two – or even three or four – primapes could laugh together all at the same time and without desisting from hunting and gathering (to say nothing of all those other things I told you about before when I hope you were paying attention).

So now these primapes had lots of neocortex, lots of friends and lots of laughter and they dwelt on the great gold-green grassy savannah plain all set about with acacia scrub and they were very nearly human, but not quite.

Then disaster struck.

Nothing funny happened for weeks.

No over-ripe fruits fell on anyone's head; Alf, their bullying leader, did not have a single momentary lapse from bipedalism and expose his arse to a bee sting; no swaggering lioness mismanaged a killer pounce and skidded onto her nose; no leopard chased prim Aunty Taylless until she ran up a tree that turned out to be very, very thorny. Even the babies, usually a sure source of merriment in their clumsy cavorting and sweet little ways, had been calm and dozy in the sun and their mamas had been unusually attentive.

It began to get everyone down. And a group or troop of grumpy primapes, oh best beloved, is not a pretty sight. Think of yourselves and your friends when things are dull and boring and tempers begin to fray at the edges. It was like so. Except there were no rude words or bitchy conversations, because they had not invented words yet. There was nothing between sulking and violence. Sulking is stupefying and very boring and so the violence started: Happy and Lucky tried to do something distinctly nasty to Amananda. Something boyish and not at all funny. I will not tell you what exactly for this is an edifying tale, suitable for the nursery and for good little children at bed time, but believe me your teacher would report it to your parents if you tried anything of the sort. And Amananda's mama did what I hope yours would do in the same circumstances and there was a good deal of blood and great deal of ill feeling. And the next day it transpired that Happy and Lucky had gone rogue together and snuck off during the night; but that did not stop Amananda and her mama and an aunty, with her small child and a young male cousin, departing in deep dudgeon. Eight members is a lot for a troop to lose in one day. It made them all nerbulous and biteful.

That afternoon found Henry and Alice and Thomas slouched under a boabab tree full of perturbation and perplexity. (They did not really have those names because, as I have told you, no one had thought of language yet and without language you cannot have names. I have invented the names because when I went to writer-school they told me that readers need to be able to identify with the central characters and obviously a name or two helps with that, so I have put them in here.) They were the closest sort of bestest friends – because once your neocortex is big enough to have lots of friends it is also big enough to have an inner group of friendier friends. These three had five of the six things needed for bestest friendship, and you only need three to make it happen. They had a shared location which was the great gold-green grassy savannah plain all set about with acacia scrub. They had shared hobbies and interests, which were mainly sitting around laughing at Alf and Aunty Taylless and lionesses and so forth and also hunting and gathering and sleeping (and mating too but I am not going to put that in my story). They had a shared educational level, since all their mamas were social friends and had taught them the same things, which was not much. They had shared values, like laughter good, violence bad; Alf a bully and evolution very slow, but desirable nonetheless. They had a shared sense of humour. The one they were missing of course was a shared language – because language had not been invented yet.

But it is about to be, as you will know, oh best beloved, if you were paying attention when you read the title of this story.

So – there they were slouched under a boabab tree full of perturbation and perplexity, because nothing funny had happened for weeks and they were suffering from withdrawal.

73

They did try to make each other laugh. They attempted to growl like leopards, so that they could creep up behind Aunty Tayless and scare her up a thorny acacia tree, but they could not even convince themselves that they sounded frightening. They imitated Alf's silly walk; they invented three-melon juggling; and finally, desperate, they spent a hot hour stretching a vine out tight between two trees in the hope that it might trip up a hunting lioness, but no lionesses happened to be hunting just there in the hot, high sunshine. None of these activities were funny.

They crouched and slouched, they itched and twitched, they slumped and grumped, they even tried some old fashioned grooming, but they had neither the patience nor the skill after all those millennia. The boys were cross and at a loss, but Alice who was a primape of infinite resource and sagacity sat quite still with her face screwed up and all her neurons firing. And as the sun was setting over the great gold-green grassy savannah plain all set about with the long shadows of acacia scrub, she stood up and walked away and disappeared behind a patch of scrub. Henry and Thomas waited. After a while they could hear some particularly peculiar noises. They waited. They waited. And they waited.

Until just after the sun had finally slipped down behind the far away but final edge of the great gold-green grassy savannah plain all set about with acacia scrub, Alice returned. She performed a posture; she inhaled a big breath and she said,

'Once upon a time there was an orang-utan, a gorilla and a chimpanzee...'

There was a pause. Henry and Thomas looked at each other quizzically. They looked at Alice, baffled, bemused and befogged.

And then they got it.

Alice was making a joke. There was language, and language meant you could make something fabulous funny even if nothing fortuitously funny had happened for weeks.

74

They drew in their breaths, puffed up their cheeks and they laughed. They laughed long and they laughed loud. They howled, roared, shouted, shrieked, snorted, cackled, doubled up and guffawed (and 22 other synonyms which you can fill in for yourselves). They rolled about and wet themselves with laughter, and the endorphins flooded in and they felt fabulously friendy and lavishly loveish.

Then the boys tried it out.

(Don't get huffy and puffy with me, oh best beloved, for giving the big break through to Alice rather than Henry or Thomas, because the wise scientists have told us that girls are quicker at language than boys.)

By the time the yellow moon rose over the great gold-green grassy savannah plain all set about with acacia scrub they had discovered puns and *double entendres* and silly voices and epigrams and gags and parody and repartee and wisecracks and raillery and monkey-business (and 27 other synonyms which you can fill in for yourselves). And the whole troop of the primape group of them had come to see and to learn and had broken itself up into little huddles of three or four, the very best number for laughing, and the great gold-green grassy savannah plain echoed with triumphant merriment and mirth – and most disturbing it was to some passing zebras.

So now the primapes had jokes, and with them language which turned out to be useful for other purposes too and they stopped being primapes and became humans – though they did not get fully sapient for several more millennia, because evolution takes a very long time. And this important discovery meant their neocortices grew again, until they reached the size you have now, oh best beloved, so everyone could have even more friends. In fact it turned out that the precisely right number was 148, but they did not invent proper counting for a very long time, since sums never made anyone laugh, so they rounded it up to 150 as a working guide.

And has your neocortex grown as you sign up your two-thousandth Facebook friend? I doubt it, oh best beloved, I seriously doubt it. Partly because they are not real friends if you don't sit out with them under a baobab tree on the great gold-green grassy savannah plain all set about with acacia scrub. But mainly because evolving takes a very long time.

Afterword:

The Role of Dunbar's Number

Prof. Robin Dunbar

WE HUMANS, AS Sara observes, have had a long and tortuous history ever since our lineage parted company with that of the other African great apes some six million or so years ago. Our lineage might easily have died out at any number of points. As it happens, we didn't – or, at least, not all of us went extinct, since in all fairness a very large number of species in our lineage did go extinct, not least among them the famous Neanderthals. What did, however, characterise the history of this lineage of ours is a steadily increasing brain size – and that means a steadily increasing group size.

In monkeys and apes, the typical size of social group that each species has is closely related to the size of its brain – or, more particularly, the size of its neocortex (essentially, the smart part of our brain where we do our conscious thinking). Species that typically live in large social groups have large neocortices. In effect, the bigger the social group, the more complex the social world the animals live in, and the bigger the computer they need to keep track of all the confusing in's and out's of their complicated social lives. This is known as the social brain hypothesis.

The equation relating group size and neocortex size in monkeys and apes predicts a group size of about 150 for us humans, and this turns out to be an extremely common group size in many different walks of life from business organisation to the ideal size for church congregations. It also turns out to be the typical size of our personal social networks

– the number of people that we know and have genuine relationships with. This doesn't include acquaintances, but it does include all our extended family. In fact, even in modern societies, our extended family make up about half of our personal social networks. Family relationships turn out to be extremely stable and resistant to erosion even when we don't see them for years at a time. In contrast, friendships seem to degenerate very rapidly in the absence of frequent contact, and our social networks tend to have a relatively high turnover of friendships over time.

Of course, there is considerable variability across individuals in the size of their personal social networks – the average may be 150, but the range is probably from as low as 100 to as high as 250. Where you lie in this range turns out to be a consequence of the size of those bits of your brain that manage these relationships – with the most important bit being that right at the front just above the eyes. The bigger this bit is, the more friends you can juggle, and the bigger your social network.

Within this, however, other psychological traits also play a role. For example, extroverts tend to have larger social networks than introverts. However, because everyone seems to have the same amount of 'social capital' (the emotional component that you can invest in relationships), extroverts necessarily spread theirs more thinly than introverts do. The one goes for many shallower relationships, the other for fewer deeper ones.

Instant Light

IT IS A restless river, the Tees – it always has been. It comes dancing off the Whin Sill; hurling down the Cauldron Snout and the High Force and the Low Force; fretting away from the hills and skipping towards the sea; writhing like a serpent across the plain; and then, just when it might turn into an old and stately watercourse, it meets the tide and the new rhythms of ebb and flow, coming and going, disturb its new-found peace.

A restless river, and flowing through a restless history of Roman Legions, Viking invaders, Scottish armies, rebellious lords, dispossessed monks, hardy lead miners, iron smelters, ship builders, rope and sail and brick makers. All busy, all busy and on the move, coming up river with the tide or down river with the spate; all a fidget of energy, of longing, of hope and restlessness.

And at the point where the down-rushing river meets the up-coming sea is a small town into which people flow like the water: sailors and merchants and farmers and travellers. And they mix with the folk who live there permanently, as the salt water mixes with the fresh. A warm, yeasty mix, restless and changeable.

John Walker is restless too as he walks along the wide High Street in the autumn morning, with the fret coming in thick and damp and the new gas street lamps casting a sulphurous glow. He knows his neighbours think of him as a fussy little man; too nervous to be a surgeon; too prissy and private to find a wife. He knows too that they are wrong: beneath his neat coat tails and tightly curled wig he is all a

79

fidget of energy, of ambition, of longing and restlessness. And of wasted love.

It is one or all of these which has driven him out into the night, into the fog, and now he is coming home, tired from a long walk down by the river in the dark. He is nearly 45 years old; perhaps it is too late for him, he thinks, as he passes the smart new Shambles, opened earlier in the year, and it reminds him of Stevenson and the arrival of the *Locomotive* that summer. It is all new and he is old. Those are the coming men and he is the past.

Almost he fails to notice. Almost he passes by. Afterwards he does not know if it was sound or movement that caught him. But as he comes up the wide High Street something makes him glance down the dark chasm of the Ropery – the alley running westwards where the rope makers are allowed the long space they need for the un-spliced sheets that haul sails up the highest masts. For one pure and lovely moment he thinks he is seeing an angel – a wing-shaped dancing, whiter than the mist, flying in mid-air and his heart responds with a leaping surge of joy.

It only takes him a moment to work out what is really happening. Someone, after work the day before, has left the rope still suspended between the iron wheels (and already his mind forms a peevish tut-tut at such slovenly negligence). The damp air has shrunk the sisal and pulled the rope tight, and one of the circus people is walking on it, or playing on it. He knows they have started to come back to town as they come every winter and camp out on the open ground to the west of the High Street. He has heard talk about it in his pharmacy over the last week and he is glad. Secretly he likes the circus folk – their colourful foreign voices and raffish cheer of which he ought to disapprove, but never quite can. He loves the skill and swagger of them; the outrageous unrespectability which contrasts with his own steady demeanour. So now he clasps his hands behind his back and stands, his heels together and toes turned out as his mother taught him half a century ago and watches with deep pleasure.

The aerialist senses an audience, shifts from exercise to performance, pirouettes fast, holds an elegant arabesque perfectly still for a poised moment and then suddenly completes a running sequence of handsprings along the rope, flipping off over the iron wheel that twists the sisal into strong strands, and landing on the ground not one yard away from him, hands clasped behind the back and toes turned out just like his. They both laugh. He sees it is a young woman, very dark, very slender and shockingly under-clothed. But he goes on laughing. She curtseys, sweeping low and, still moved by his angel vision, he reaches out, takes her hand and kisses it with an almost successful assumption of style. She laughs again, runs off down the High Street and disappears into the mist.

Nearly three weeks later she reappears in his shop. The young man who serves behind the counter comes back into the laboratory and says, 'There is a young person outside who seems to want to see you.' He says 'young person' with a sneer, and in a reflex of horror John Walker sees the young man has learned that tone from him and he is ashamed.

He does not want to leave his experiment. For some years now he has been wanting to find a way of making fire simply, quickly, on the spot – with no need to wait for sunshine and a curved glass, no need to carry a flint and tinderbox, or keep a dangerous slow fuse burning: such a simple, useful thing, but elusive, magical, mysterious. It appeals to him and he pursues it doggedly. He knows it can be done. A few years earlier a friend from his student days in York had sent him a book, translated on the wave of the Chinese fashion: *Records of the Unworldly and the Strange* by Tao Gu, written 1,000 years ago. The friend knew him well, it is his sort of book and it tells him:

'An ingenious man devised the system of impregnating little sticks of pinewood with sulphur and storing them ready for use. One gets a little flame like an ear of corn. This marvellous thing was called a "light-bringing slave".'

He thinks he too could be an ingenious man. So now, as in many other spare moments, he is dabbling little splinters of stick with sulphur in various compounds – with antimony and chlorate of potash and gum. These burn all right, but what is the point of a stick which burns when you touch it to a fire that is already burning – just a quick flare and a strange smell. Nothing more. Now he is laying a line of sticks out on his hearth stone, each with a chalk number corresponding to the details of the mixture neatly recorded in his notebook – the kind of fussy precision that makes people laugh at him. He does not want to see any young person, but the mirror of his sneer has shamed him and he forces a smile.

'Well, show them in,' he says.

'Her,' says his young man.

'Show her in.'

And it is his aerialist, his dancing angel.

She is smaller than he had realised, little and lithe. Pretty. Today she is wearing more clothes than that morning; in fact she is tidily though simply dressed. Her eyes slope up above her sulphur-coloured cheek bones and they have smooth, flattened lids: strange and lovely to him. Perhaps like Tao Gu she is from China, but she is with the circus and all the Chinese he has ever encountered are seamen, they come up on the tide not down from the hills. His curiosity – always near the surface – bobs up with his pleasure and he smiles a welcome to her.

They cannot really speak to each other because she seems to speak no English, nor respond to his clumsy French. He tries a little Latin and catches himself wondering if Greek would be easier because it too has funny letters like Chinese, if she is Chinese.

She mimes, gesticulates, shapes a comprehensible world with her mobile fingers and suddenly he knows what she wants, what she has come for and he is very sad.

'No,' he says, 'not me.'

She understands the 'no' at least and the tears spring up in the corners of her sloping eyes. He cannot bear it. He reaches for a bit of paper and writes the name and address of the old woman who will, who does, who says 'yes.'

For one moment she lowers her head and looks so terribly sad that he wants to explain to her that for him it is not a moral issue, he just cannot bear to be so close to injured bodies, to cut into them, to touch so intimately and to hurt; that is why he gave up his training as a surgeon and became a more humble pharmacist instead. But then her mood changes, like the moment she changed from poised stillness to the glorious springing head-over-heels of that morning in the Ropery – and she picks up three little mortars from his table and starts to juggle with them, so clearly displaying and performing her gratitude that no words are needed. The rounded mortars skip and fly through the air like she had done; she reaches out for another and turning round he opens the cupboard so that she can see a full row of the pots. She circles the table without missing a beat and starts adding to her act: five, six, eight little clay bowls whizzing around his usually sober laboratory, catching the light, a waterfall, a rising tide of movement and joy. When she reaches out for yet another, it becomes harder; he feels her tense a little, step backwards, watching not her own hands but the very highest point of her cascade.

As she settles the new flow of them she steps backwards and her heel catches one of his tipped shards of pine wood, grinding it against the rough hearth-stone and it sparks into life. She is startled, but unfazed... she glances down swiftly then holds out her skirt and the pots fall into her lap. But he is not watching this; he is on his knees, his wig askew, looking at the bright little flame like an ear of corn.

Punctiliously, he notes the chalk number then picks up the stick next to the flaming one and pulls it across the stone – and it too sparks, shimmers into unexpected light. Instant fire. He tries some more – some of them do not burn but with one there is a tiny explosion and the burning head darts across the room and lands smouldering on the rug; but with the pots still in her skirts and a transfixed look on her face she stamps it out, while he notes that number too. At least half the little sticks give birth to fire, fire from friction.

Very solemnly he stands up, bows to her as she had curtsied to him before and says,

'We have invented the friction match; we have bought instant light and fire to humanity.'

Her laughter and delight peel round the room. She unloads the pots on the floor, returns his obeisance with a deep sweep and claps her hands in applause. He gives her a little stick and in her turn she strikes it against the stone and laughs again as the flame spurts out.

He goes to the table, picks up a quill and writes the date and the chalk number in his notebook. Then he writes *vici* – 'I conquered' and signs it, 'John Walker.' He smiles. After a moment he crosses out *vici* and writes *vicimus* instead – 'we conquered.' He offers her the quill and points to the space below his name. She hesitates and then scrawls an X.

'John Walker,' he says and points at himself. Then he points at her and she smiles shyly and says, 'Vesta.'

It is only as he writes it down beside her X that he remembers that Vesta is the goddess of fire in the hearth, the domestic flame. Slowly, he goes to the cupboard again and takes out his cash box and opens it. He reaches careful fingers into the pocket of her skirt and takes out the little scrap of paper he had given her earlier, offering her the open box and an interrogative expression. She smiles a deep solemn smile, quite different from the merry smiles of before; she takes the paper back from him, picks up one more little stick from the hearth, strikes it and sets fire to the scrap, letting the ashes fall slowly to the ground. Then she goes to the box and takes a couple of coins, leaving the rest undisturbed.

A few days later she comes into the chemist's shop again.

She gives him a tiny packet and watches as he unwraps it. It is a small piece of card folded in half and when he opens it he can see that it is sandpaper. He looks at it, baffled; she laughs again, goes through into the laboratory, picks up a new fire-stick, slips it between the fold of the card and pulls sharply: the tip of the stick ignites with a little hiss and burns steadily. She takes another stick and the little striking paper and tucks it into his breast pocket. It is his turn to laugh.

Now whenever she visits he leaves the cash box open on the table and she takes what she needs, never very much and he never counts. Sometimes she juggles for him. Always they smile, often they laugh and all winter he is happy. Just as the catkins are swelling on the hazel bushes, a tall man knocks on his front door in the earliest grey hour of a morning. He goes down in his nightcap and the man says, 'She says to ask you to come.'

He gets dressed, pulls his wig on, washes his hands and goes out, along the Ropery – stepping carefully over the piles of sisal and coils – to the shanty village on the west side of the town. There, overcoming his aversion to bodily procedures and striking light from the small sticks he always carries in his pocket to the stunned amazement of the women who are gathered with her, he helps her deliver her baby son.

The child spends its first days in the laboratory, as she pops in and out from her rehearsals.

'Is that child yours?' asks his sister sternly.

'No,' he says indignantly. But afterwards he wishes he had been bold enough to say, 'Yes. Sort of.'

Three weeks later she comes to say good bye, standing up on tip-toe to kiss his cheek. She laughs and he cries a little.

'Will you come back?'

She nods, takes the child and is gone.

It is a good summer. The fire-sticks catch on – he sells them in boxes of 50 and each box comes with a little folded piece of sandpaper, so they can be lit even in the rain. His neighbours are impressed and no longer think of him as a fussy little man, but as a scientist and inventor. The great Michael Faraday comes all the way from London to discuss experimental chemistry and advise him, most sincerely, to patent his invention. He cannot do that of course, because it is not just his, but he does not explain this. He just nods and shrugs. Even his sister is civil after that visit.

When the autumn mists return and the fret rolls in from the sea again, he makes his preparations. He decides to enlist poor boys from the town to help him soak long strands of thin rope in pitch and carefully mixed chemicals and then drape them from the roof tops, over the Shambles and the Town Hall, high above the market and the broad roadway − a complex spider's web of fine cords. He keeps an ear to the ground and hears when the circus folk are approaching. So when she comes dancing down the Ropery with the child in her arms, he blows sharply on a whistle and each lad runs to his place and lights his rope with a fire-stick. Suddenly all the High Street is a sparkling, exploding, dancing fire show of noise and light, and flames and sparks − red, orange, yellow, green, blue, purple, gold and silver.

And she lifts the baby high to see the show and she laughs and laughs and laughs.

Every year when the circus folk come down the valley along the restless river he makes a new show to welcome them. And when the lad gets big enough, he and his friends reciprocate; they explode out of the Ropery, tumbling, juggling, stilt-walking, clowning, drumming, singing, fire eating, performing.

Each year more people come to enjoy it. The show grows and flourishes until the citizens of the small town where the down-rushing river meets the up-coming tide forget why they are lighting fireworks and putting on shows and welcoming strangers. They just do it and enjoy it. They barely notice the old man in the old-fashioned wig and the middle-aged woman with the strangely sloping eyes who stand outside the Chemist's shop on the High Street, watching the show, holding hands and laughing.

Afterword:

The Unpatented Spark

Gemma Lewis

SARA MAITLAND SETS the scene of Stockton as a restless hive of activity on the north bank of the river Tees, evolving and changing as the tide ebbed and flowed. At the time of John Walker's teenage years (the 1790s), it was just that. Stockton began to develop and expand rapidly, using and adapting the rich natural resources that the landscape had to offer. Even the water course it sat upon, the Tees itself, was moulded and manipulated to suit the needs of the town: a cut was put in between Portrack and Stockton which not only dispensed with the need for 'trackers' – men who hauled brigs around the holmes and sand shoals where the silt continually built up into the sand banks, making navigation difficult – but also provided additional farmland to feed the increasing population. The town prospered, building on the wealth of its exports – iron ore from the Eston Hills, clay from the banks of the river, and agricultural products from the surrounding area, not to mention its own manufacture, including brick, sail and rope making (the latter two being mentioned in Sara's story of course). As the town prospered, so did its residents.

John Walker was born on May 29th, 1781, to John Walker and Mary Peacock. Walker senior would have been at the centre of Stockton's commercial and political world, as a grocer, wine merchant and burgess of the town.

We know little of Walker's childhood, but he is believed to have attended the Grammar School, established in 1785, which was situated just behind the family shop.[1] This was the start of his education, but he would have had access to other resources to further any interests, with the founding, in 1776, of a literary society and, in 1795, the opening of a subscription library.

At about the age of fifteen, John was apprenticed to Mr. Watson Alcock who was the principle surgeon of the town and, either at the end of, or during his apprenticeship, he spent a number of years in London. As to what, exactly, he studied in London we cannot be certain, but it is believed that it was here that he nurtured and developed his fascination for botany. At the end of this period he returned to Stockton to become Mr Alcock's assistant, during which time he began to show his scientific proclivities. Walker was constantly making chemical experiments and attained a considerable reputation in the locality as a botanist, and later on as a mineralogist.

At the end of his apprenticeship, Walker was a qualified surgeon. However, he never practised as he was horrified by surgical operations, which during the early nineteenth century were still relatively bloody and brutal. Walker was never able to overcome this horror. He abandoned the profession and spent some years in Durham and York acquiring commercial experience in the employment of wholesale druggists. Eventually at the age of 38 he returned to his native town, where he established himself in business as a chemists and druggist at No. 59 High Street. Walker joined his mother and younger sister in a house at the Quayside, where they would have seen the hustle and bustle of the town as a port.

As to the type of man John Walker was, we know very little. His great niece Annie Maria Wilson was just five when he died, however she recorded in 1925: 'He was a very clever man, and he was just as good as he was clever [...] My great uncle was a very learned man, in fact, he was affectionately known all over as the "Stockton Encyclopaedia". He was very strict that when we visited him at his little shop we must not address him as anything but "Mr Walker"; his reason for this was that the shop was a centre where people would meet, especially the members of the big country families for the outlying area.'[2] This connection with the families in the outlying areas and even some of the larger homes is backed up with evidence from his day book, which includes the likes of Marshall Fowler the owner of Preston Hall and the game keeper of the Pennyman's, from Ormesby Hall in Middlesbrough.

It was during this time as a chemist and druggist on the High Street, that Walker would invent the 'Friction Light'. The Friction Light – which was the term used by John Walker rather than the 'friction match' – may not strike you as the most revolutionary invention, however, it revolutionised domestic life and helped the progress of the industrial revolution, simply by enabling the effective lighting of boilers needed to power machines. This need for effective fire lighting would have been very evident to Walker throughout his time in London, Durham and York, perhaps also for the lighting of the gas lights which were added to Stockton in 1822 and would have greatly aided Walker on his journey to and from work each day, or perhaps it was the arrival of another great local development.

In 1825 the Stockton and Darlington Railway – the world's first public railway – was launched. Perhaps this, more than anything, underlined the need for a quick and effective way to create fire. On the trial run of 'Locomotion Number 1', in 1825, at Aycliffe Level, the boiler was full and the coal piled for firing, but no one had a light. A messenger was dispatched for a lantern, but a navvy stepped forward with a burning glass; this piece of apparatus was similar to a magnifying glass and could concentrate the sun's rays to start a fire. All this meant that the trial run was delayed, and raises the question: without the invention of a convenient way to create an instant flame, would the Steam Age have fired into action like it did?

What this story also shows is how complex it still was to make instant fire. The skills, techniques and tools to make and sustain fire hadn't changed in millennia. Fire was either made through friction, tools which created sparks, or techniques using chemicals. It was one of these latter techniques that Walker exploited.

The most common technique used to make a fire in the late eighteenth century was the tinder box. This consisted of a box to keep its contents dry, charred-rag tinder, a flint and a steel. This flint method had been used, relatively unchanged, for thousands of years. But there had been some progress in the seventeenth century, when people began to use amadou, a fungus that grows on decaying trees, and which, when mixed with salpetre (potassium nitrate), helped combat the problems of wind and damp tinder, and reduced the physical effort required. Another addition came in the form of sulphur matches; these were non-striking matches that could be easily lit from smoldering tinder but were extremely unpleasant.

Despite these small developments, there still remained no single, cheap and instantaneous way to create a flame. The wealthy could afford elaborate and expensive solutions to the fire-starting problem, such as the 'tinder pistol' (aka the 'flintlock tinder pistol' – effectively a musket but with a candle poised to light from the firing mechanism, rather than a barrel) or the 'Instantaneous Light Box' patented by Henry Berry in 1824. This latter worked by using a system of pulleys and stoppers to firmly open and close a bottle of vitriol. When the box was opened a measured amount of the flammable solution was administered to the match head, which in turn would burst into flames, when struck.[3] John Walker, as a surgeon, chemist and botanist, would have been experimenting with not only tried-and-tested remedies but with new materials and chemicals, as many others were. We know from John Walker's day book that in 1825 he was experimenting with explosive mixtures, mainly for percussion caps and weapons, which was most likely to aid country families in hunting and shooting. This is an extract from his day book:

Die Saturni Nov. 19th...1825
Mr. Walkton, Junr. Norton
Ry Potassa Chlorat 3j Ant. Sul. Nigr 3j
Muc.g..l Aqua qs   1 6
Fiat pasta
N.B. Excellent

What this means is that he was using potassium chlorate (an oxidising agent), black sulphur of antimony (which has a low kindling temperature) and mucilage (which could have been a starch).[4] These are the basic ingredients of the friction light he was working with.

How and when the eureka moment came we will never know. In Sara's story, it is a Chinese girl who catches her heel on the hearth and a stick mixed with the right ingredients – a moment of chance, as many inventions are. In a newspaper article of 1852, another fortuitous accident is suggested: that Walker was preparing some lighting mixture for his own use, when a match, after being dipped in the preparation took fire by accidental friction on the hearth.[5] Walker however, never divulged the exact formula of his matches and this story could have been spread as a jest or in modesty. Walker's day book also lists the first reference to the match on 7th April 1827.

Die Saturni April 7th 1827
No. 30: Mr. Hixon
Sulphurata Hyperoxygenata Frict. 100
               Tin Case 2d   1...........5

The term Hyperoxygenata Frict was the initial name Walker gave his lights until the term 'Friction Light' was applied. They were made of thin splints of wood, 7.6cms long, one-sixth of an inch broad, and one-twentieth thick, tipped with a secret composition of equal parts: antimony sulphide and potassium chlorate. They were sold by Walker at 100 for a shilling, in a cylindrical tin case, for which he charged an extra two pence. Included with the matches was glass paper to ignite the matches.

The matches needed to be pinched at the end and dragged through the paper, the match would then ignite with a sharp fizzling crack. However, by today's standards they still weren't the easiest of things to use. They gave off a strong sulphurous smell and the tips were apt to break off under the pressure of the sandpaper. Still it meant fire could be cheaply and instantly created rather than taking three to five minutes usually needed for a tinder to produce a light.

Walker only sold the matches for a few years, in 1827 he sold 23 boxes, in 1828 72 and in 1829 72, although there would have no doubt been wholesale orders as well.

News of technological progress travelled much slower back then, of course, and Walker's invention would have been seen as one of the special proprietary lines that many chemists cultivated on a regular basis. Walker never made any attempt to create a large business out of the general sale of Friction Lights, and generally concentrated on meeting local demand. However, in 1829 notice of Lights appeared in the *Quarterly Journal of Science, Literature and Art*, under the title of '*Instantaneous Light Apparatus*'[6] and fame was further spread when Professor Michael Faraday exhibited some of the matches at a lecture at the Royal Institute in London. It is thought that Faraday had visited Walker and encouraged him, like others around Walker, to patent and mass produce the Friction Light. Walker didn't take his advice; he didn't believe that his matches would benefit the wider public, and felt that he had sufficient finances for himself.

The last record for Friction Lights is in the year John Walker stopped making them (1829). Others however, had started, including Samuel Jones of London, who in 1828 produced the 'Promeathan Match'. These had a single drop of vitriol enclosed in a tiny glass bead; they were wrapped in slips of paper, to which a mixture of chlorate of potash, finely pounded sugar, and gum arabic had been applied. To light a match, the tip was nipped with a small pair of pliers; the vitriol would then react to create a flame. These proved quite successful but after the announcement of Walker's Friction Light, Samuel Jones began to produce direct imitations which he called 'Lucifer's'. Jones soon had competition himself, and the match evolved rapidly from this point on, ever improving. In 1830 Charles Sauria substituted antimony with white phosphorus, the Friction Light could not compete with these. In England, these phosphorus matches were termed 'Congreves', and gradually different parts of the matches were improved, from fireproofing the split, to the development of the safety match.

As for John Walker, after ceasing to sell the match, he continued as a successful chemist. He never married but achieved enough success in business to be able to move, with his sisters, to a relatively desirable house in the town's square. Described in local literature as a man of wit and with a cheery disposition, Walker was clearly respected. He retired in 1858 and died a year later in May 1859. His decision not to patent the match meant that Walker was all but lost from the annals of nineteenth century invention. Indeed the fact that we know him at all is thanks, largely, to a local artist and antiquarian, one Joseph Parrot. It was Parrot who discovered John Walker's day book lying on a pile of rubbish at the back of the shop many decades later, and who subsequently argued for Walker's invention to be properly credited. Perhaps Sara Maitland's story will also go some way to help write him back into history.

Jacob's Sheep

ALL NIGHT JACOB wrestled with the stranger.[7]

    It was a vicious, unrelenting fight. At first, when the stranger leapt out from behind the rock, he had thought it was only a robber and cursed his own foolishness and fear trying to hide instead of camping out on the wadi floor like any wise desert traveller should. But before they had fought for very long, Jacob knew this was no ordinary bandit or criminal – the stranger was too silent, too determined and too calm.

    In later years, Jacob would tell the story differently; re-shaping it to match his self-image and to preserve his secrets. Although he could not hide the limp where the stranger had dislocated his hip, he still managed to make himself out a victor in the struggle. But the truth was that, just as the sky was first tinged with pale light and the stars were fading one by one, the stranger finally forced him to give up his gift, the treasure his God had given him over twenty years before.

Jacob was a smooth man.

    He was smooth in the physical sense, unlike his brother Esau who was as hairy as a goat, but more he was a smooth operator. Laban knew he was being cheated somehow, but he could not work out how.

    Laban himself was no slouch when it came to manipulation, manoeuvring, and outwitting the opposition. For more than twenty years the two of them – uncle and nephew; husband and father-in-law; partners and rivals – had circled each other in endless unrelenting competition. But now Jacob had won – his herd filled the wide plain below the encampment; his camels wandered through the scrubby grass picking and pulling; his eleven sons – all spoiled, pesky boys – shouted and yelled in a swarming gaggle around the tents; his four wives were, for the present at least, on reasonably good terms; he was as rich as a priest in Ur; and now he was leaving Haran and Laban's company, going south towards Bethel, depriving Laban of any chance to get his own back. And lovely, clever Rachel, his beautiful daughter and the best lamb-midwife a sheep lord could hope for, was leaving with him – taking both his joy and his future with her, smiling all dewy-eyed at her slimy-smooth husband.

Jacob was a smooth man, but his sheep were not: tup, yow, or wean, they were all spotted, blotched, striped, raggedy, some even polycerate.

Laban, who was no fool and had a lifetime's experience of sheep, as well as of trickery, deceit and the pursuit of raw profit, knew he was being cheated. Left to themselves the sheep bred predominantly white and single-horned: about one in twenty, apparently regardless of the colour of ram or ewe, would be blotched, spotted or striped; a smaller proportion would have four horns and occasionally even six. One in twenty seemed a proper wage for a good shepherd, and Jacob was undeniably hard-working and competent. Plus he had Rachel. One sheep in twenty for seven years shepherding was a fair enough wage and Laban had further tipped the odds in his own favour by removing all the spotted tups before the contract started, just in case that made a difference: one in 25 or so, even possibly just one spotted lamb in 30 white ones. He had felt pleased with himself.

It was not until the fourth of the seven years that Laban began to get suspicious. The first year the lambs ran about par, perhaps a few more spotted ones than he would have liked, but some of the ewes were probably in lamb before they started the contract. The second year was disastrous for everyone: it was very dry through the winter, almost a drought; it was a cold spring and all the herds lost a lot of lambs at birth. It was surprising perhaps that Jacob did not do better than average, rather than markedly worse, but there was always an element of luck and Rachel had still been nursing Joseph – at last – and, like so many once barren women, was obsessed by the baby and stayed in the tents longer than most husbands would have allowed. The third year was a good lambing and there were plenty of pure white lambs to keep Laban happy and smug. There were a surprising number of spotted ones too, but he was pleased about Rachel's baby and doing well enough himself to feel generous and glad for the couple's luck.

Come the fourth spring, though all the other herds, even the ones with the extra spotted tups, produced patterned and blotched lambs at the expected rate of about one in twenty, in Jacob's herd it was one in ten, even one in eight with the late lambs. For the first time Laban remembered that he had offered Jacob a deal in year one that had been generous enough in all conscience – and Jacob had turned it down for the unusual 'all the spotted ones' contract. Laban's heart sank. By year five Jacob was bringing in more than half his new season lambs spotted, striped and blotched. Laban knew that was not natural. He moved some of his own white rams from his herd and drove them in with Jacob's sheep and he sent out spies to see what was going on. The spies came in with ridiculous stories: that Jacob brought the rams to the ewes in the dappled shade of bark-stripped poplar twigs, fresh white sap blotching and striping the darker bark, to give them a powerful suggestion; or that Rachel took the lambs into a cave and sang spells over them to change their colours. Laban knew that had to be nonsense.

And it made no difference. The following year Joseph came to the autumn sheep gathering with a herd in which barely one sheep in 50 was plain coloured. Their mothers made all the boys little coats of un-dyed wool, patched and spotted, black and white, and Laban knew they were laughing at him. Of course Jacob was up to some trickery but he could never work out what.

He knew that Rachel knew – there was, within her beauty, a new knowingness, a serene certainty and self-satisfaction. He had even thought she might be pregnant again so full of inner calm was her demeanour, but seeing her with Jacob he realised that whatever he was up to, they were up to it together. Before Joseph was born, when she was living through all the torments of her infertility, consumed by barren-ness and jealousy of her sister Leah with her six sons, he might have been able to suborn her, bribe or bully her into telling him, but since she had a son of her own she had moved on, cleaved to Jacob in that self-interest which is both a sort of love and stronger than love.

Rachel did indeed know. In fact you could almost say it was Rachel's scheme, although Jacob claimed it and made it work.

Some years before all this, quite soon after they were finally married, Rachel was looking for something in Jacob's tent, working tidily through his storage sacks, when she came upon the little twisted golden column – two spiral threads wound round each other and linked by little cross-rods, a pretty toy at first sight.

'Nice,' she said, spinning it between her fingers. 'Can I have it?'

'No,' said Jacob, 'El Shaddai gave it to me. You do not give away his gifts.'

'El Shaddai? And who's he when he's at home?'

'God,' said Jacob, 'and do not talk about him like that. He is my God and the God of my father and my grandfather. He is the God who laughs, the God who travels with us. The God who has blessed me and promised me and my descendents all the land between here and Egypt as an inheritance forever.'

'Jolly good,' said Rachel laughing, 'my descendents too.' This was before she had stopped joking about babies, when she was still planning to have as many sons as her sister Leah. 'Why did he give it to you?'

She was mocking him and he knew it and was stung;

otherwise he would probably not have told her. He kept fairly quiet about such things. Hard to explain about his mad grandfather and his shadowed father and how he had tricked his twin brother out of his inheritance and stolen his blessing by an extremely underhand trick and had been forced to flee in fear of his life. But even Rachel, who looked so like his mother, her aunt, that he could refuse her nothing – even Rachel was not allowed to laugh at his God. So he told her, starting a bit jokily, off-hand, pretend casual.

'My mother can't stand those Hittite women,' he said, 'and who shall blame her? Esau my brother had two for wives and your aunt could not bear the thought of any more of them in the camp so she sent me off up here to get a decent woman from her own people. You at least can't say I wasn't a good son...'

He had been heart sick, weary, guilty, alone. Esau wanted him dead and it was hard to blame him. His father was furious. His father preferred Esau. Even his bold and adoring mother was anxious. She packed him off under cover of darkness, promising only to send for him when things were better. He trekked north, fearful of his brother's anger and angry at his own fear. Then after a long day of forced march, he was caught out by nightfall, miles from any encampment, any well, far from his mother and his own people. He had slept out, under the burning stars, and the huge silence of the desert reverberated around him and he had been shaken, shaken with the terror of the empty places and spaces. He had fallen asleep with fear and bravado competing in his heart and missing his mother like a child.

He had dreamed that night.

There was a procession of angels, brighter than light and winged and rising and falling. Up and down the great spiral staircase, between earth and heaven they came. Angels coming and going, descending and ascending and singing and singing:

Allele... allele... alleluia.
At first it had been hard to follow them with his eyes, to see what they were doing, how they were coming down and going up in their great solemn joyfulness and singing:
Allele... allele... alleluia.

Then it grew clear; it was a double staircase, the angels came down on one flight of tightly coiled steps and went up on the other and the two were twisted together; two spirals, double, lovely, orderly, twinned and glorious. The angels came and went as continuous as their singing, down from heaven and up again, a movement so graceful, once he had understood it, that it reminded him of his mother and now of Rachel. And El Shaddai, standing at the top of the staircase had spoken to him, reassured him, soothed him, promised him the world, and heaven too, and he believed it.

Allele... allele... alleluia.

In the morning, as the sun leaped up from behind the rocks and pounced upon him in glory, he had found the little golden model of the double spiral lying beside the stone he had rested his head on and he had not been frightened any more.

Now, after all the years, he told Rachel his dream. He started shy and self-mocking, but he could not suppress the glory and beauty of the moment. And almost to his surprise, she did not laugh at him, but smiled a smile of deep sweetness and took his smooth face between her lovely rosy hands and kissed him tenderly. After that she would often sit, her legs crossed under her in his tent and spin the double spiral ladder between her fingers, attentive, silent, thoughtful.

Telling her the dream made it alive again for him. He felt full of courage and hope. He began to think about going home. But he needed to go home rich – no slinking back for him. He already had his father's blessing, his brother's inheritance and his God's promise. Now he needed only wealth. He would, he told his wives, enter into one more contract with Laban – another seven years and then they would go back to his own land and his father's people. He and Laban opened negotiations.

'I know what it is for,' whispered Rachel in the night, 'I know why El Shaddai gave it to you.'

'To remind me of his promise?' said Jacob. 'Don't worry.'

'And to make my son very rich,' said Rachel, smiling.

She showed him. Deep inside the coil of the spiral there were two tiny – so small he had never noticed them – two tiny shadow marks on the gold model.

'That is what makes the sheep blotchy-coloured. It's a model from inside a sheep. With that mark in their double spirals they would all be spotted and striped. I think it may have to do with the extra horns too, although I am not sure. The spotted sheep have a different mark from the plain sheep. The plain colour is stronger – plain tup, spotty ewe; plain ewe, spotty ram; plain both – you get plain lambs. You need this bit, this little bit here, in both the tup and the ewe and then you get spotted ones, and striped and blotched.'

It took him a while to understand. He was not sure he ever did understand really. But she did.

'How do we get it into the ewes?'

'We don't. We get it into the lamb. Before it's born. I think we have to get the ewe egg and the ram punk together outside their bodies; then we take out the plain colour marker from each lamb foetus, when they are just beginning to grow, and put the spotty bit in and then it should flow all through them, blotched all over, all through.'

'How?' he asked.

'I'm not sure; perhaps we could shock the foetus with heat, or the getting-drunk bit in wine, or a little salt, or prick them in with a fine needle. Then...' she hesitated, fearing he might be cross, '...I've been trying it out; in a cave up in the hills. You can put them back into the ewes. I've lost quite a lot. But I think it can work. Once we get it started, each year more and more of the ewes will have the spotted marker. It only needs to work sometimes. We only need to tip the odds a little.'

'Nothing wrong with tipping them a lot. If we can.'

'It's cheating,' she said, with a sly and sexy grin.

'So?' he said. 'Laban would do it if he could.'

But later he thought of something better: 'El Shaddai would not have given the spiral to me for nothing; for no reason. It is part of the promise. I have a religious and moral obligation to try it out.'

It was a risk, but a risk he had to take. There was no time to experiment or test it. He had to come to a deal with Laban immediately. El Shaddai's promise made him bold; Rachel's sly smile gave him confidence.

It took another ten days to hammer down the details – Laban could not really understand what he was after, but was too cunning himself to suppose that Jacob was innocent or generous. He just could not imagine any way Jacob could shift that one in twenty. And he wanted Jacob signed up and working for him and not wandering off southwards with both his daughters and all his grandsons. He thought he could probably refine the small print later on if he had to, and if it all went seriously awry he would simply not hand over the remaining portions of the girls' dowries which he had retained on the fairly specious grounds that they were still resident in his camp. Jacob won the argument and retired to the caves with Rachel and an unprecedented new contract. He would work one of Laban's herds for seven years and at the end of it would take all the parti-coloured sheep for his wage.

The first year they experimented, it was technically difficult to do and they were not entirely certain; but where they managed to change the foeti and get them re-established in the ewes, they could see that it was working. The second year was disastrous: they were greedy, worked too fast perhaps, and some infection got into the main batch of artificially inseminated lambs; where they did not die and where Rachel managed to re-insert them, they cross-infected their dams, many of whom died too. They wondered if they ought to abort the project, but it was too late now; they had put their hand to the contract and could not turn back. Jacob sat in his tent fidgeting and twiddling the gold spiral.

Then, suddenly, unexpectedly, Rachel was pregnant. After all those years. Jacob reckoned it had to be a sign: El Shaddai was keeping his promises; all would be well.

The third year they were more cautious, and Rachel slower because she was still feeding Joseph and made that her priority. They reduced the number of ewes they tried it with and were content with figures only slightly over the odds. By the fourth year, although it was still difficult and demanding, and the results were still modest, they knew that they were onto a winner.

'How did you know?' he asked Rachel, once.

' I...' there was a long pause, 'I thought about it a lot, because of being barren. I could see it was a family thing. Each generation your oldest sons have come up to Haran and marry one of the family women: Sara, Rebecca, me – we're all barren. It had to be something, something we were passing on.'

'But not Leah,' he said. He was afraid she might sulk if he compared them, but he wanted to know.

'Like the sheep. It isn't every sheep. Leah is a blotchy one!'

They sniggered. Then, horrified, he said, 'Did you... did you do Joseph like we do the lambs?'

'That's women's business,' she said. 'You'll never know.' But she could see he was appalled, frightened even – happy to get rich that way but he wanted his favourite son, the child of his favourite wife, to owe his life to his father's sexiness not his mother's cunning. It made her laugh, but the laughter made her kindly. 'Use your brains, Jacob, of course I didn't.

You have to do it to the lamb not the mother – and the problem was no lambs, not ones the wrong pattern.'

She knew he would never be certain, never perfectly assured again. It gave her power.

After a bit she said, 'When the time comes I think we should send Joseph down to Egypt, instead of up here to Haran, and get some new mother lines in.'

The final three years of the contract were a triumph. In the seventh, the final year, they even allowed some of the sheep to breed pure white, just to prove to themselves that they could control it all, and out of some scoffing pity for poor old baffled Laban.

Then, as soon as the shearing was over, they collected all Joseph's rich property together and set out south, towards Canaan. Unable to re-claim their own independent wealth, Rachel and Leah stole their father's household gods in substitution – the little jewelled statues that he put such store by. Since, quite apart from the breeding programme, Jacob was hard-working and competent and Rachel was a wonderful lamb midwife and Leah's, Bilhah's and Zilpah's boys were big enough to work now, they had done very well: Jacob, who had come to Haran poor, alone and frightened, left with vast herds of sheep and cattle; with asses and camels and servants; with four wives and eleven sons and all his lovely daughters.

Jacob was a smooth man; sleek and subtle and rich and immensely powerful.

But in the desert dawn, on the very boundary of his home territory in Canaan, before the sun rose, after a fight that had lasted all night, the stranger forced him to give up the gold spirals that had made him rich.

'Why?' Jacob asked sulkily.

'Because you used it to get too rich and you kept it secret to yourself.'

Jacob was outraged. 'El Shaddai gave it to me. Why else would he have given it to me?'

'Because it is beautiful,' the stranger replied calmly, 'and the source and truth of life.'

In the silence that followed, the first spears of golden light from the sun poured over the rim of the world, suddenly warming the air.

'Who are you?' asked Jacob.

'Wouldn't you like to know,' replied the stranger, and twirling the double spiral between his fingers he walked off into the desert, singing softly, almost to himself.

Allele... allele... alleluia.

Afterword:

Genetic Profiling, 21st Century Style

Dr. Neil Roberts

SARA'S STORY OFFERS an alternative explanation for how the biblical characters Jacob and his wife Rachel win a flock of sheep and goats from her father Laban. Under the agreement Jacob reaches with Laban they are allowed to take all the non-white sheep in his flock, and during the next seven years the flock produces unprecedented numbers of speckled, spotted and dark-coloured lambs, allowing them to become rich. Sara's idea is that unlike the biblical parable, which may suggest some form of direct spiritual or divine intervention, the couple combine God-given knowledge of the genomic basis of sheep coat colourings with impressive fertilization techniques that Rachel has been working up. So it seems like an interesting exercise to explore further how Sara's explanation might have been achieved.

First, though, a word on the role of genetics in sheep colouring. Two of the most important loci – the specific location of a gene on a chromosome – found to determine sheep coat colour are the spotted locus 'S', that produces *micropthalmia-associated transcription factor (MITF)* and determines the uniformity of coat colour, and the Agouti locus that produces the *Agouti signalling protein* gene (*ASIP*). In both cases only if both alleles (alternate forms of the same gene – there are two copies per genome, one on the chromosome from the mother and one from the father) are recessive copies of the gene will the coats be non-uniform and non-white. *ASIP* is a particularly interesting gene due to its role in the development of modern genetics over the last century, through studies of the Agouti mouse. Where the Agouti gene is expressed (becomes RNA then a protein) a switch from dark pigment to lighter pigment results, and consequently over-expression of *ASIP* in most mammals results in a lighter coat colour. The Agouti mouse was therefore very valuable as it made it very easy to identify which alleles were present in an animal.

Back to the sheep. Wild sheep are mottled, with brown and tan coats (presumably for camouflage) while modern domestic sheep are usually uniformly white. So how is it that Laban's ancient flock was also primarily white? A recent study that investigated the genetics of modern sheep coat colour offers some clues. In domesticated sheep a duplication on chromosome 13 was identified that is not present in wild (and non-white) populations of sheep. This duplication included the *ASIP* locus and adjacent genes, and resulted in a second copy of *ASIP* that is regulated by the promoter region of a close, but different, gene. The result is that expression of *ASIP* is deregulated (i.e. inappropriately over-expressed), causing the classic white coat colour (Norris and Whan 2008)[8], and means that an allele with this mutation is dominant over the tightly regulated wild-type allele. It is likely that the ancestral mutation arose in an ancestor of all modern domestic sheep, and it is possible that the allele arose many sheep generations before Jacob's time. From the 'founder', this mutatuion was either deliberately or unconsciously selected by shepherds, including those in the Levant – where and when the original white sheep lived is unknown.

Thus Jacob, by preferring the non-white sheep, was re-selecting the ancient recessive wild-type alleles for his flock. Even with the non-white sheep removed from the flock there would have been a significant proportion of recessive colour alleles within the sheep population. For example, in modern Australian Merino flocks, and after many generations of industrial-scale selective pressure for white coats, the rate of recessive non-white *ASIP* has been calculated at 0.03 (Hayman et al. 1965).

Using this knowledge, a clever breeding program by Jacob and Rachel over the seven years would have increased their sheep considerably. But how could they have grown the flock to biblical proportions – how could they tip the odds beyond a classical breeding program? The details given by Rachel to Jacob, and therefore us, are limited (maybe she wanted to keep control of the technical aspects by not sharing too much with Jacob, a man not necessarily famed for his trustworthiness) so we can only guess at the exact protocol. However, using their advanced knowledge, one route would have been to create a library of mutations. By exposing embryos removed from the sheep to gene-changing chemicals such as alcohol and salt, or to UV from the sun, random genomic mutations would be introduced. Inducing these embryos to divide, taking and storing single cells, and then re-implanting the embryos would allow them to determine which embryos had desirable (i.e. colour coat) mutations. Using this information they could take the relevant embryonic stem cell from storage, grow and divide it then re-implant the cells in multiple sheep. Easy? No, but they had God's grace on their side. Assuming their mastery of the technical aspects they would be able to alter the proportions of colours in the flock however they wished.

A final question is why Jacob may have requested the non-white, and presumably less valuable, mottled sheep at all? Maybe he knew more about genetics than we are led to believe – either by Sara or by the Bible. There is a large body of evidence that shows deleterious effects on, amongst other things, fecundity and metabolism in mammals (mice in particular) which over-express the Agouti gene. Jacob knew enough about breeding, as shown in the biblical passage, to try to select the strongest sheep for his breeding scheme, so perhaps he was trying to improve the health of his flock as well as increase its size.

Lighting the
Standard Candles

Magellanic Cloud (Great) so bright. It always makes me think of poor Henrietta. How she loved the 'Clouds'... Very, very, sad.
— Annie Cannon, unpublished diary, 1923.

Miss Leavitt inherited, in a somewhat chastened form, the stern virtues of her Puritan ancestors. She took life seriously. Her sense of duty, justice and loyalty was strong. For light amusements she appeared to care little. She was a devoted member of her intimate family circle, unselfishly considerate in her friendships, steadfastly loyal to her principles, and deeply conscientious and sincere in her attachment to her religion and church. She had the happy faculty of appreciating all that was worthy and lovable in others, and was possessed of a nature so full of sunshine that, to her, all of life became beautiful and full of meaning.
— Solon Bailey. Obituary notice. *Popular Astronomy, 1922.*

SHE TRIES TO focus on the pain. Even for her this is difficult.

Once upon a time a little girl – *how old had she been? About ten perhaps, still small enough to have to reach upwards to hold her father's hand...* Once upon a time a little girl was walking home from evening service holding her father's hand. It was early evening but already winter-dark and the snow piled on the street sides sparkled in the moonlight. She had a brand new pair of button boots and a little rabbit-skin muff of which she was inordinately proud, and inordinately anxious that her parents should not notice the pride or they might take the muff away. To set against these delights were the horrible mittens, lumpy and two different sizes. She had knitted them on her mother's instruction for her little brother's Christmas present, but her knitting was so bad and clumsy that her mother made her wear them herself. When she thought about her pride or the mittens she briefly felt both aggrieved and guilty. But she did not think about them much because there were all the other nicer things to think about: the muff and the boots and Christmas coming only next week and how large and warm her father's hand was and how firmly but kindly he was holding hers, despite the ugly lumpy mittens and what a good mood he was in and how the tune of 'While Shepherds Watched their Flocks by Night', which they had been singing in Chapel, danced in her head and seemed to hold all the other bits and pieces into one happiness.

And then, suddenly, there was an extra, bonus happiness. She looked up and there, above the Boston street, was a sharp streak of light, and then another, as though someone had suddenly scratched the sky with a sharp knife. And a couple of moments later, another.

'Papa,' she said, 'is it angels?'

'What?'

'Look. Oh, do look up, Papa.'

He looked up. They both stood still for a moment and then another vivid streak rushed overhead.

'No,' he said smiling, 'it's not angels. It's shooting stars. But it might almost be angels, because they always appear just before Christmas. Another work of Our Good Lord, and just as praiseworthy. They are called the Geminids.'

Her father knew everything – or nearly everything. He didn't know about her pride in her muff. At least she hoped not. She liked it when he told her things, especially if they were things her mother did not know, which covered more or less everything interesting. She wanted to keep his attention.

'What makes them, Papa?'

'God makes them.'

She draws in her breath, and is careful now, 'Yes of course, Papa, but *how* does God manifest his glory in them?'

She had got it right; he gave a bark of genuine laughter and said, 'Oh Ettie,' very affectionately. 'I understand they are little bits of dust and rock burning up out there in space.'

'How far away?'

'We don't know. We can't tell. We can't measure out there; we don't know how to.'

'Why not?'

'Well,' he paused. 'Think about it. See that big bright star up there, the one in the line of three. Now can you see there is a little one just beside it, not bright at all? How can we tell if it is smaller and less bright or further away? We can't. So we can't measure how far away anything out there is.'

'Is it God's secret? Or would He like us to be able to?'

'Ettie,' he says solemnly as she knew he would, 'God likes us to know things. Whatever anyone tells you, never forget that God always likes us to know and understand more about His mighty works and deeds. He wants us to have knowledge so that we may have wisdom. Everything we know is to His glory, so the more we know, the more we can give Him glory. He is a great force of intelligence, especially in his creation. We must never be afraid to learn and to know.'

She knows her mother doesn't think that and is gratified by his trust in telling her.

'Well,' she says, as still more Geminids shoot away overhead, 'I think that's what I'll do when I'm big; I'll glorify God by finding a way to measure up to the stars.'

'That would be excellent, Ettie; but you will have to learn to pay better attention. Once there was an astronomer, a star man, called Mr. Herschel. He made his own telescope and looked and looked and he wrote down all the new things he saw. And other astronomers did not believe him and said to him, in angry letters, "We do not see what you see." But he was ready with an answer, "Perhaps you do not take the care in your observations that I do." He took great care; he would leave his telescope out in the cold for hours so it would be the right temperature; sometimes he even stood out in the cold himself so his warmth wouldn't get in the way, and that's how he was able to learn so much. If you want to glorify God through learning about the stars you'll have to learn to concentrate. Your mamma tells me, I am sorry to say, Ettie, that you don't always pay good attention, or take enough pains.'

'I'll try to learn,' she muttered.

'Good. Mr. Herschel had a sister who was his assistant; perhaps you too could be an assistant to an astronomer. I believe that would please God very much.'

So she had learned to pay attention, to concentrate, to focus.

Now, nearly half a century later, she tries to focus on her pain; to angle the mirror of her mind so as to cast the clearest possible light on the black spots of pain, sharp against the smooth white surface of her belly. It is her job to calculate their brightness and record their relationship to each other and to herself. If she could still sit up and write she would, in her tiny immaculate handwriting, list them one by one, their position, their colour and their magnitude, in numbers and with annotation.

This is what she had done for her North Polar Sequence, the 96 stars which she had recorded with such authority that the magnitude of every other star in the sky was graded by her standard. Her very high standard. When, for just a few moments, she can leave the careful study of her pain, she occasionally thinks of her North Polar Sequence with some modest pride, but not often. The pain is her data now and she has always found it difficult to break her intense concentration on the data, which is why she was good at her job. Whatever they may say, she knows it was the concentration that made her deaf, not deafness that made her concentrate. Compared to the distant silence of the stars there is nothing else much worth listening to, not since her father died. But even when she takes a little time off from measuring the pain, she does not really care very much about the North Polar Sequence. She prefers to think about the Magellanic Clouds – *Nubecula Major* and *Nubecula Minor* – those beautiful drifts of shining sidereal smoke that had guided Magellan round the world, once he had sailed too far south to see the Pole Star; and about the 1,777 Cepheid Variables within the clouds, which she discovered, and which will guide the astronomers to the size of the universe once they have sailed too far out for parallax, and for which she will always be remembered. Her pride here is less modest.

If she could find the energy, she could push away the pillows, lie flat on her back, stretch her arms out and use parallax to measure the distance to the pain. From fingertip to fingertip her physical span is 64 inches. If she can then measure the angle from her fingertips to the points of pain, she can triangulate and work out how far away the pain really is; because it is the pleasing nature of a triangle that it can be fully drawn on the information provided by the length of one side and two angles, or the lengths of two sides and one angle. That is why they know how far away the Moon is, and Venus measured when it transited the Sun. Then they had widened the length of the baseline, doing the sums at either end of the year – a base line of 186 million miles. This is easier for her to think about than it is for some of them because she still believes that God is glorified in measurements, and that 186 million miles is not that much in relation to the infinite glory. They had pinned down Alpha Centauri, and Vega and 61 Cygni. Nearly 100 stars have been measured now, but most of them, like the points of her pain, are too far away, the shift is too small and parallax fails. It is huge out there, she knows that, as huge as the pain.

Then, gradually, after paying perfect attention through drawn-out, pain-filled nights and wearisome pain-filled days, she perceives that the points of pain pulse, variable and rhythmic. The intensity of blackness deepens and expands; then slowly it greys out a little, narrowing and paling on the white background of her belly. It gives her a strange joy that her pains should be periodic, should wax and wane on a steady beat, on a rhythm. Like her stars. For Henrietta Leavitt, head of Stellar Photometry at the Harvard Observatory, stars come black on white, dark on light. Occasionally, Edward Pickering, the Observatory Director and her boss, had led her off to the telescope itself and let her look at flaming white stars on the deep black sky. She had never really cared for it – there was too much mess, of weather and technology; it kept her up late and her doctor had warned her that the cold night air would hurt her ears. She prefers her stars as neat columns of numbers, black on white paper or as tiny marks, black on the white photometric plates. She prefers them at her own desk and in her own time. She likes to be able to compare yesterday's stars with how they were last month, or last year, or today. She likes to feel intimate with them and in control. The photographic plates were her own black stars. Certainly now the black pains are her own pains. And they pulse.

She can still laugh at herself. She knows that her pains are not the stars at all; that the pain is here, contained neatly within her tired body and that when she dies, which will be soon, they will die with her. Meanwhile, the stars will burn on. Her finely observed and immaculately measured Cepheid Variables will continue to pulse in a preordained and constant rhythm; the period of their pulsations will always be a measure of their intrinsic brightness. If any two Cepheid Variables pulsate at the same speed they will have the same intrinsic brightness. If one of the two seems to be dimmer then it *is* further away. You can tell how much further away using an elegantly simple, completely reliable aspect of light itself: light spreads and diminishes according to the Inverse Square Law: so if one of the two variable stars is four times dimmer than the other but has the same pulse rate then it is twice as far away. If it is nine times dimmer it is three times as far away. She found 1,777 Cepheid Variables in the Magellanic Clouds where no one had ever seen any before.

She smiles. They had laughed at her. 'What a variable-star fiend Miss Leavitt is – one can't keep up with the roll of new discoveries,' wrote a colleague to Edward Pickering. Even the *Washington Post* had commented flippantly 'Henrietta S. Leavitt has discovered 25 new variable stars. Her record almost equals Frohman's [the famous theatrical agent].' It was admiring laughter, teasing like her brothers; she knew that and liked it. But her mother had been embarrassed – being in the papers was not ladylike.

'Mother,' she had said gently, 'it is astronomer-like.'

'I don't care about that,' her mother had said pettishly.

That is how it is. Always. She had not even been able to go and hear Pickering presenting her paper, because single ladies ought to go home for Christmas. Their widowed mothers are more important than measuring the stars.

She always takes very great care in her observations, measures very precisely, and writes very clearly so that people can see what she has seen. She had tabulated 25 of the new variables on a graph on axes of periodicity and brightness. There is undeniably, as she wrote, 'a remarkable relationship.' So now they can measure the distances and darling – though she has never met him – darling Ejnar Hertzsprung, a European astronomer has proved it. He has made a 'very pretty use' of her discovery and begun to calculate the size of the Universe. It is the first time anyone has been able to measure space, to begin to calculate how big it all might be. She, Henrietta Swan Leavitt, computer at the Harvard Observatory, has found a way to measure the vast distances out beyond the reach of parallax. She has lit the first 'standard candle' to the glory of the Lord. It will never be put out. Once upon a time she told her father she would and she has.

And if she had been given time perhaps she would have been able to calibrate her Cepheid yardstick and turn the theory into actual numbers, real distances. Someone will do it anyway now she has given them the tools; already the debate about the size of the Universe is hotting up. This fills the spaces in between the pains with white joy. It did not really matter who, though she likes to think she could have contributed; it would have been good fun and God would have been glorified again.

She has never been given the time. Pickering and her pain have had other agenda and she is the servant of both. Once upon a time her father had told her that she could be an assistant to an astronomer. He had been right. Her mother is still winning. She is not a real astronomer; she is one of Pickering's computers, one of his girls, cheaper than men, than graduates, than real astronomers. She is employed, at rock-bottom wages, to measure and record the precise brightness of each star in the North Polar Sequence, or anywhere else in the sky that Pickering is minded to attend to. He was kind, he was respectful, he was knowledgeable and he was her boss. She represses the thought that as slave owners go he was a good slave owner, but that slavery had been abolished elsewhere. All his girls had laughed and chafed to an equal degree under his benevolent despotism.

She had liked him because he was a meticulous observer. She chafed because that was all he believed in; he never asked what they were observing so carefully *for*. He never encouraged theorising, convinced that the job of the Harvard Observatory was purely to accumulate facts. And... *she does not know, she still does not know and it is better not to think about it, especially now the pain may warp her charity*... from the day he read out her paper, her beautiful, groundbreaking paper on the *Nebecula Minor* and its Cepheid Variables, he never found time to set her to work on that again, even though she knew, because the other computers told her, that other astronomers all over the world wrote to him begging for more. Even after she completed the immaculate North Polar Sequence he had thought of other projects for her. So 'she had hardly begun work on her extensive program of photographic measurements of variable stars.'

Finally Pickering died, after over forty years as Director. They have appointed Harlow Shapley to succeed him. She may have doubts about the carefulness of his observations, but none about his willingness to theorise. And none about the admiration in which he holds her work. He was one of those who had asked Pickering for more:

> *Her discovery of the relation of period to brightness is destined to be one of the most significant results of stellar astronomy, I believe. I am quite anxious to have her opinion.*

He had arrived in the spring and was treating her like a colleague. But it is too late now; the pain has become her new slave owner. She is laid out like a nebula on the sea of pain focused on the slow rhythmic pulsing. Everyone knows. When Shapley, as the new director of the Harvard Observatory, as her new boss if she still needs a boss, comes to visit her, he brings her flowers, not anxiety for her opinion. She will never have time or opportunity to measure any more stars, their pulse rates and their intrinsic brightness.

It really does not matter very much. All the Cepheid Variables in the lovely Magellanic Clouds will go on pulsing, in their subtle elegant way, go on revealing what they have to reveal of the glory of God and the knowledge of his ways. Shapley's flowers are beautiful too. Everything seems beautiful now. Perhaps death will be beautiful and will certainly bring new knowledge so that she may get wisdom, new wisdom. Now it is a different hymn that dances in her mind:

> Out beyond the shining of the furthest star
> God is ever spreading, infinitely far.

So she is smiling when she dies. She sees the glory of God coming like a shooting star to greet her. God judges gently, questioning her humility.

'Who has marked off the waters in the hollow of a hand?'

'Only you, Lord.'

'Who has weighed the mountains in scales and hills in a balance?'

'Only you, Lord.

'Who has measured the heavens with a span and called each star by its name?'

'You have, Lord.'

'And who else?'

'I have.'

'Well done thou good and faithful servant. Come enter into the joy of your Father.'

Her last moments are filled with modest pride, which turns out to be very acceptable.

She is buried on the 14th December. It is a grim day, bitterly cold. Because of the dark clouds, the biting wind and the general desire to get inside as quickly as possible, no one even remembers that this is the day of the Geminid shower.

Afterword:

Henrietta Leavitt and the Period-Luminosity Relation

Prof. Tim O'Brien

YEARS OF CAREFUL measurement of photographic images of the sky led Henrietta Leavitt to a discovery that is fundamental to how astronomers measure the scale of the Universe.

Distances in space are so vast that we don't write them down in kilometres, there'd be too many zeros. We use units called parsecs or sometimes light years. Light travels at 300,000 kilometres per second. At this speed, it takes eight minutes to reach us from the Sun (a distance of about 150 million km or 93 million miles). This same light, passing by the Earth, would take a further 4.2 years to reach the nearest other star, 40,000,000,000,000 km away. We call this distance 4.2 light years. Our galaxy, the Milky Way, contains several hundred billion stars and is about 100,000 light years across. Light from the most distant galaxies we can see has taken billions of years to reach us.

Since we can't just take out an extremely long tape measure, we have had to adopt some ingenious ways of measuring their distances.

The most accurate and direct way is called parallax. It relies on measuring the apparent change in position of a star as seen from different points on the Earth's orbit around the Sun. The closer the star the more its position appears to move relative to stars in the background. However, the change in position is tiny. So, although fundamental, its use is limited to relatively nearby regions of space. It is used however as the first rung on a 'distance ladder', calibrating other techniques that work at greater distances.

One of the most common methods of estimating much greater distances in the Universe is the use of 'standard candles'. Imagine two identical candles which shine with equal brightness. If one is placed farther from an observer than the other, then it would appear fainter. In fact the brightness follows an inverse square law: so for example if it appeared 100 times fainter this means it is 10 times farther away (10 squared $=$ 100). In practice, of course, the candles are replaced by stars or other objects which are thought to be of the same intrinsic brightness. The technique then allows their relative distances to be estimated. If the distance to the nearer one is known by some other method, say parallax, then the actual distance to the farther one can be calculated.

At the time that Henrietta Leavitt was working at the Harvard Observatory, we did not know the scale of the Universe. Indeed in 1920 there was a 'Great Debate' on the subject between astronomers Harlow Shapley (who later replaced Pickering as Director of Harvard Observatory as described in Sara's story) and Heber Curtis. Curtis argued that the 'spiral nebulae', the most famous of which was the Great Nebula in Andromeda, were galaxies in their own right, lying outside our own Milky Way galaxy. Shapley however thought that the Milky Way was itself huge and that the Universe was essentially one large galaxy. Objects like the Andromeda Nebula were simply clouds of gas inside the Milky Way. Leavitt's work proved crucial to resolving this debate.

Leavitt worked as a 'computer' at the Observatory. Before iPads and PCs, a computer was a human being who carried out calculations by hand or with the aid of mechanical devices. Commonly the computers were educated women who found it one of the few ways into a scientific career. Observatories and other organisations would often employ teams of computers at rather low salaries. Problems would be organized so that they could be fed into the 'computer' room, worked on by a team of people and the answer fed out at the other end. Beginning with astronomical calculations of the orbit of Halley's comet in the 1700's, this practice continued through to applications such as atomic weapons development during World War II.

Leavitt's work focused on the detailed analysis of photographs of the sky taken with Harvard's 24-inch Bruce Telescope in Arequipa, Peru. Large glass plates covered in photographic emulsion were used to record the images. These were then returned to Harvard. Her job was to take each plate, mount it on a device which illuminated it from behind and, with the aid of a magnifying eyepiece, carefully measure the sizes of the black dots representing each star on the negative image. The larger the dot, the brighter the star. Each plate would contain many thousands of stars. This was a painstaking task, requiring patience, attention to detail, accuracy and stamina.

Sara's story makes clear how the Observatory Director, Edward Pickering instructed her to work on the North Polar Sequence and other important tasks in calibrating the brightness of stars. However, her major contribution and lasting legacy was her work on the Cepheid variable stars in the Small Magellanic Cloud.

Many stars change in brightness. Some because of flares or explosions, others because of eclipses by an orbiting companion star. The Cepheid variables repeatedly brighten and then fade with periods ranging from a few days to a few months. They are named after the prototypical example, delta Cephei. Although the cause was not clear when Leavitt was studying them, we now know that this variability is because the stars pulsate. The combination of changing size and temperature causes the variation in brightness.

The Large and Small Magellanic Clouds were of particular interest. Looking like small clouds in the night sky, we now know that these are actually two dwarf galaxies close to our Milky Way. Most easily viewed from the southern hemisphere, they are named after Magellan, the famous explorer who sailed the southern oceans.

Plates of the Small Magellanic Cloud were sent from Peru back to Harvard for analysis. Leavitt carefully measured the brightnesses of stars on repeated photographs over months and years. Since the stars in the 'Cloud' were grouped together, they were all approximately the same distance from us, and so there was no confusion caused by one star appearing fainter because it was much farther away. Like many of her colleagues, Leavitt was not simply a human calculator – she improved her measurement techniques, thought carefully about the data she collected and what it meant. In particular, she noticed that the brightest Cepheids rose and fell in brightness more slowly than the fainter ones. This has become known as the Period–Luminosity Relation. Pickering published Leavitt's statement of her results on 25 of these stars in a Harvard Circular of 1912.

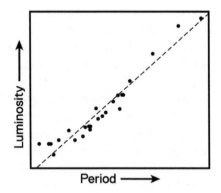

Leavitt's 25 Cepheid variables showing the Period–Luminosity Relation

By simply measuring the period with which the brightness of a Cepheid rises and falls, the relation can be used to determine its luminosity, the intrinsic brightness of the star. A comparison with its apparent brightness then allows the use of the 'standard candle' technique to determine its distance.

Leavitt's discovery has proved crucial to measurements of distances in astronomy.

In the mid-1920's Edwin Hubble found Cepheid Variable stars in the Andromeda Nebula and was able to use Leavitt's relation (as calibrated by Shapley) to measure the distance to the Nebula. This showed that it lay at much greater distances than previously thought, outside our Milky Way. It was therefore a galaxy in its own right, contrary to Shapley's earlier views in the Great Debate on the scale of the Universe.

Working with Milton Humason, Hubble went on to use Cepheids and other indicators to gauge distances to other galaxies. They found that the distant galaxies were all moving away from us, the most distant moving the fastest. This is now a cornerstone of our understanding of the expanding Universe and its origin in the Big Bang.

Even today, Cepheid variables remain a major rung on the cosmic distance ladder. However, developments in technology mean that modern equivalents of Leavitt's painstaking measurements have been massively expanded. For example, OGLE (the Optical Gravitational Lensing Experiment) uses a robotic telescope in Chile to study the Magellanic Clouds and the centre of our Milky Way. Each clear night, about 100 images are automatically taken with CCDs (similar to those in domestic digital cameras, albeit of better quality). These are processed through pipeline software (the modern equivalent of the old 'human computer' room) resulting in huge databases of the changes in brightnesses of hundreds of millions of stars.

The OGLE survey is used to study stellar variability including Cepheids as well as variability caused by the warping of space-time as predicted by Einstein. Other similar automated surveys are used to find planets orbiting other stars or study the explosions of stars which map the expansion of the Universe.

Modern astronomy and our understanding of the

Universe owes a great debt to Henrietta Leavitt and her dedication to the measurement of variable stars in the Magellanic Clouds.

The Metamorphosis of Mnemosyne

WHEN THEY DECIDED to close the Library, the Librarian brought a case for constructive discharge and wrongful dismissal.

Such a suit was unprecedented in the courts of Olympus. There, individual gods tend to hold their posts for eternity or at least until no mortal requires their services any longer. This latter is sad obviously, but such retirement is seen as honourable, like a no fault divorce. There had been, of course, the long drawn-out departmental squabble between Apollo and Dionysius; but by now they had more or less resolved it, melding their responsibilities and dividing their duties and remunerations more by geography than divinity. Though, even after all this time, Apollo was occasionally heard describing his colleague as a bi-polar nutcase as well as an old lush, and − when drunk − Dionysius not only called his golden rival an upstart but also a pederast. Since all these charges were, broadly speaking, true, the other gods have learned to live with it.

This was a different matter. This was serious. Not just for Mnemosyne. For them all. For what becomes of ancient gods in a fading heaven if memory is not set in stone, and the past becomes a personal confabulation inscribed and re-inscribed in the present, at the moment of need?

So, despite the problems of protocol, the Olympians knew it was a case they had to hear, and Zeus did his best to round them all up, calm them all down, sort them all out and get them all to pay attention. He felt tired. He had enough problems managing himself without having to manage the whole unruly bunch. He sat on his high throne and fidgeted with the tassel on his quiver of thunder bolts. He tried not to look at Mnemosyne because her classical drapes hinted, to the precise degree that he found most alluring, at the depth and softness of her cleavage. He wished that he did not wish to tell her to take off her prim librarian spectacles so that he could, once again, drown in the sweet dark depths of her brown eyes. He was after all the father of her nine daughters and, for better or for worse, he knew what he was missing. Her hair looked dryer and somehow wispier than he remembered it. It was escaping from the severe knot into which she had rather inefficiently tried to confine it. He knew it would do no good at all to re-call how it used to ripple down her back in the green woods where they had played together. He felt old and very tired.

There was a hubbub in heaven – the usual greetings and gossip of the gods. But finally Zeus drew a deep breath, rang the great bell and called them to order. Eventually they were all seated, and he looked round for a moment with pleasure and pride: so much glory and power; so much knowledge and wisdom and beauty. Surely they would all be safe.

He opened the formal proceedings and called upon Mnemosyne herself to explain her situation, to remind them all of what she did and why she had been dismissed, and to make a formal claim for reinstatement or whatever it was that she wanted.

She got to her feet, laid her glasses carefully on the bench beside her, smiled slightly long-sightedly at them all and began to speak. She was a mistress of rhetoric, deeply imbued with tradition and learning, and with a lovely, well-stocked mind. The agitation in the hall died away as she spoke. The gods listened attentively, carefully, admiringly.

She was, she said, the Librarian. Since the beginning of time, since the mortals were first formed from the dust, from before Olympus was established on its mountain, she was the Librarian. The Goddess of Memory. Her duties were hard – and grew harder as the world grew older and the mortals increased in number and the files in her system grew ever more extensive and complicated. She had never minded the hard work – because it was her work.

Each evening, as Phoebus brought the horses of the sun chariot into their stables, she would take delivery of all the events of all the mortals' day. They would arrive in great disorderly batches and she would spend all night sorting through them and filing them, each neatly in its place in the individual carrel of each individual mortal. Millions and millions of moments, stacking up in the reception area. Not just words, but sounds and smells and tastes and touch. The weather. Emotions. Bodily functions. Each breath taken. Each heartbeat. And they had to be filed while their owners slept.

'She's not a librarian,' muttered Hera, spiteful always to her husband's floozies, while forgiving him over and over and over again. 'She's just a filing clerk.'

'Be quiet,' said Zeus, while vaguely remembering how sexy Mnemosyne was when she got angry.

But the Librarian just smiled at Hera, a smile serenely triumphant.

'No,' she said, 'no, it is not a filing clerk job. It is administrative and pastoral. If they cannot access and trust their memories they cannot know who they are; they couldn't be themselves. They wouldn't be selves. Just blurry, wispy things, like smoke, like tears.'

'Do we care?' Apollo called out.

'Oh for Olympus' sake,' said Mnemosyne, irritated by the heckling, 'you are such a heartless bastard.' Zeus sighed with pleasure, but she regained her composure. 'I care. I like them. But think about it, golden boy – no solid memories, no gratitude. No gratitude, no worship. They won't be trekking off to Delphi with adoration and precious gifts for you then.'

Apollo had the grace to look a bit abashed.

'It is not a simple filing task,' Mnemosyne said, 'though they do all have to be filed. First, I have to guess what each mortal might need, which means pressing memories into the future. Then I have to discard large quantities of stuff – because it is useless, like each breath they took; they do not need their allocated library space used up with that. They would get overloaded. So I edit out all the excess unnecessary events, and sometimes events that would make them too frightened or too unstable. Then I have to work out where to file each little film, or sound, or incident – they need a set of references, and indices so they can shuffle through and find the bit they need. I make an album of each life for them, each different. Human brains don't use a fixed-address system, and memories tend to overlap, combine, and even disappear, get lost. But that always distresses them; I try to make it as easy as possible. But it is very hard work, it requires both decisiveness and tenderness as well as knowledge, and it has anti-social hours. It all has to be stored and completed each night before they wake up. Each little memory carrel tidied and ordered. There is a lot of pressure.'

'Well, you're not very competent.' There is a mean tone of triumph in Hera's voice. 'You often get it wrong.'

'Not often,' said Mnemosyne defensively, 'and then it does not usually matter much. In fact it is good – that's how they can have strange dreams and bright imaginations. Other people's memories mis-stored, wrongly filed I admit, but it has interesting repercussions. They can share ideas that way. If you remember,' she laid a subtle rhetorical emphasis on the word, 'that is why we decided to give them sleep in the first place. Not just to give me time to do the filing, but so that they could process it, manage it, make the connections, and then dream it all into beauty and usefulness. A little misfiling is a positive advantage.'

She went back to her prepared speech. 'In addition, though obviously of great importance, the poets come daily to consult with me. I am, as you all know, the mother of the muses. Without my careful work, without these little solid chunks of pure memory, retrieved from the depths of the psyche, there can be no art. I keep, as it were, the engagement diaries of all my daughters, I assign the hours and places where the poets can meet with them and draw their sweetness into themselves. Surely, we do not want to live in a world where there can be no poetry, no drama, no visual art, no music, because there will be no certain shared images, grounded in the knowledge of a shared past, shored up by what has gone before?'

She left a long and eloquent silence after that telling point and then continued.

'I used also,' she said, 'to do a considerable amount of Youth Work, educational sessions and such like. The mortals used to believe that it trained the young mind, ordered it, prepared the memory for its more significant tasks later on. I handled irregular Latin verbs, spelling, the dates of the Kings and Queens of England, elementary poetry and lovely, lovely, rhythmical, elegant times-tables. This also gave them solid matters to think about and protected them from the arrogance of adolescence – that withdrawal from the adult world that they are endlessly tempted towards.'

She gave Aphrodite a sideways glance; they were full sisters, daughters of the Titan Lord, and often shared the feeling that the whole present pantheon, their nieces and nephews, were both callow and arrogant. But it was nonetheless the case that while she tried to bend young mortals towards tradition and knowledge and the disciplines of arts, Aphrodite seduced them with sexual longings and deflected them from these more worthwhile studies.

'Sadly,' she continued, 'there is a mistaken view now that the young should be spared such labours; that forgetting the answer to 9 x 7 might lower their self-esteem – which you might suppose would be a good thing, but alas memorising has quite gone out of fashion.'

There was a murmur of sympathy. Gods of the Olympian type tend, for obvious reasons, to be conservative in matters of education and child-rearing.

'But that is beside the point. We are speaking here of narrative, of autobiographical, memory and the great Library that I have been given to manage, so that they can search and find the truth and act in the light of it; and know who they are. How will they know who they are if they do not have a whole and reliable story of their own?'

Her bosom quivered between tears and outrage, and Zeus had to reach for his quill pen, look fixedly at his sheet of papyrus and pretend to scribble notes.

'They've gone for relativity,' she continued, 'so nothing can be very true. They've been making a silly fuss about memory for a while, but now there's a crisis. They've made a machine that lets them see inside their own heads and they've been seduced, bewitched, by the little blinking lights. Now they say they can prove there is no Library, there are no true memories. People just make them up, they're like stories, little fabulations – they say that is how it works. They don't want a filing system anymore. They don't want a Librarian.'

'What do they want?' someone called out.

Mnemosyne looked up, paused and then said, 'I'm coming to that. It is always difficult to know what they do want, because they never quite know themselves. When I first started to hear about this I thought they just wanted to modernise – to replace the Library with a Computer, with what they call a "data-base". I was content with that, though I do love books and physical objects, but all librarians have had to learn to live with Information Technology, as they call it, and I was perfectly willing to take that on board. They changed how they remembered, how they organised the memories, when they learned to read and write after all, and it did not change anything important.

'But no, now they want to tear down the Library and build a theatre. Not a proper, formal dramatic theatre, where memory of course plays a central role, but some sort of studio theatre. For improvisation. They say their brain machine shows them there is a space in their heads where little individual fragments of this and that come together to work out a narrative spontaneously, different every time, new and fresh and, as far as I can see, pointless. They say they cannot trust their own stories; that they make them up anew every moment; that what they think they remember is just a mish-mash of what they want it to be and what they thought it was last time and all the ways they have told it and thought it and used it. They just reconstruct, rebuild the past each and every time. No Library, no filing system, nothing solid or real or true. No job for me. No job for any of us in the long run.'

She drew herself up for her summary. She raised her eyes and looked straight at Zeus on his throne.

'Your Majesty, I appeal to this high court of heaven, not just for my own sake, but for yours, for all of us. If memory is allowed to turn slippery, unreliable, invented, there will be no place for the gods. There will be no trustworthy witness and so no justice; there will be no narratives, no art, no beauty; there will be no sense of place, no childhood, no natural piety, no continuity of the ego.

'I appeal to you all. Demand my instatement. Force them to abandon this folly, for their own sake and for ours. We cannot exist in a world where Odysseus will not need to go home to Ithaca.'

It is a finely judged conclusion. Something these gods can understand, because they are all gods of place really, of shrine and grove and cave and fountain and little city state – titular deities. They exist in the love and longing that mortals have for the homes and hills of their childhood that they have believed they can remember in clear and actual detail. It is either generous or cunning of Mnemosyne, for she is the goddess of memory and of an older, darker inheritance than these childlike divinities.

She sat down and, her performance over, made some

futile attempts to pin her hair back up.

After a short pause Zeus picked up the white linen scarf from the table in front of him and blindfolded himself. This is ritual only, that he should hear the arguments without prejudice, unswayed by personal knowledge of the speakers. Of course he knew them all from their voices, but from time immemorial this is the protocol and he must abide by it. He asked for comments, arguments and advice.

Mars was on his feet quickly, his red hair flaming. 'May I speak first? I have to rush off. I've got a nice little rumble building up in Syria. Again. I'm frantically busy all round just at the moment. But I want to say that this idiocy has got to be stopped right now. Not just for Mnemosyne's sake, but for mine. If the mortals once start doubting that they remember the whole of the past completely accurately and truthfully, then they won't be able to believe that the other side are liars and we won't have proper deep rooted hatreds and before you know it I will be out of a job too, and teaching Taekwondo in some damn village hall in the provinces.' He laughed at his own wit, scooped up his helmet and charged off back to his duties.

Once quiet was restored, after his crashing exit, the gods gave their opinions in a reasonably orderly way. The arguments broke down fairly evenly.

Artemis, goddess of the wild places, of hunting and purity of heart, supported Mnemosyne, deeply moved by the thought that mortals might lose their capacity to treasure their roots in the wild, in their childhood and their innocence. Against all the odds, she continued to believe in innocence and believed that it was grounded in truthful memories of solitude and joy.

Poseidon supported her, arguing that since the mortals had originally come out of the oceans those half-drowned memories were part of the reason why he was held in such honour. What, he asked Mnemosyne, were they planning to do about body-memories, truths embedded deep in the blood and the tissues? She did not know the answer, but, with impressive honesty tried again to describe the constructive space the mortals claimed to have found. She suspected that they would decide these reflexes of mortality were constructions of the imagination. Poseidon humphed a bit, but calmed down when he heard that the mortals were calling their new playful space 'the Hippocampus' after his great sea-horse monster.

To considerable surprise, Aphrodite was also opposed to the new idea. Given the general chaos that followed so closely on sexual arousal, even in the courts of Olympus, never mind among the unstable mortals, they had anticipated that she would be enchanted by the chance of further detaching desire from the rigorous control of incontestable experience. But she thought differently, she thought that being able to create new individual memories would make them all more self-sufficient, less needy and longing, less likely to seek comfort in bodily contact.

Apollo, on the other hand, thought it was a really good idea. Unlike most of the Olympians, he loved innovation. The new excited him. It held such bright promise. He tried not to regard his colleagues as faintly fuddy-duddy and conservative, but even as he listened his deep ambition stirred. He was playing a long game, but one day he would oust his father, as golden sons always do, and fragmenting memory and replacing it with story-telling fitted well into his schemes. The new sort of memories, as Mnemosyne was describing them, would work forwards, would give people creative ideas about the future as well as the past. He thought they could burn the Library and build a new and glorious stadium for his – and others' – original, unique, individual performances. Naturally enough, he did not say all this; he said he thought these new sort of memories would increase their freedom and expand their options.

Zeus sighed. The last thing he needed was more options. He was in enough domestic trouble as it was. He glanced nervously at Hera. She was looking disapproving.

Apollo was supported enthusiastically by Vulcan, who was fascinated by the technology. He wanted a brain scanner himself, more to see how it worked than to use it. He tried to interrogate Mnemosyne, and was disappointed by her obvious ignorance of the detail. He also thought it could prove both useful and amusing to be able to know what others were thinking at any given moment.

Hermes also favoured the new model. Laughing, he reminded them that he was the god of liars, con artists, tricksters and advertising. He thought that memories like quick-silver, flowing, dividing, rejoining sounded like a great deal of fun. Mnemosyne should lighten up and get a life.

Pluto said he had no opinion. The dead drank the waters of Lethe and their memories were wiped out. How they acquired them in the first place was no business of his.

Hera had a great number of opinions, but they were so clearly vindictive, personal and spiteful that the whole court ignored them.

The discussion went on for hours, and at times became quite heated, but eventually they all fell silent. After a long pause, Zeus suddenly snatched his blindfold off and scanned the great hall, until his eye fell on Athena. He smiled tenderly and almost humbly, as fathers often smile at favourite daughters.

'There you are,' he exclaimed. 'I wondered if you were here. We haven't heard from you, even though you are the goddess of wisdom. We need your opinion. What do you think?'

She stood up slowly, gracefully and looked round her.

'I think you are all asking the wrong question.'

'Go on,' said Zeus.

'You are all asking do we like it? Is it in our interests? Does it feel good? But the real question is, "Is it true?"'

There was no response.

'Because if it isn't true, there is no problem – we can just ignore it. They get things wrong all the time. But if it is true then... we are the gods, we cannot and we may not, just write it off. If it is true we have to accept that it is true and learn how to adapt ourselves to the truth.'

After a pause, she turned and spoke to Mnemosyne directly, but very gently. 'I'm sorry, Mnemosyne, I can see why it hurts. I am sorry that it hurts. But I think it is true.'

In the shattered silence that followed, tears welled in Mnemosyne's brown eyes, hovering on the long lashes, but she kept her head up and looked back at Athena with dignity.

And then...

And then outside there was a sound of clear laughter, like water breaking out of ice when the spring time comes and everything melts into green; and a ripple of music, of pipes and lyres and a soft playful drum beat. And singing and giggling and suddenly there are nine lovely women, dancing into the court room and encircling Mnemosyne. They are her daughters, the nine muses: Clio; Enterpe; Thalia; Melpomene; Terpsichore; Erato; Urania; Polyhymnia; Calliope. Their very names are harmony and freedom and inspiration and hope. They sing as they dance, and they laugh as they sing.

They surround their mother and in the middle of the circle of love Mnemosyne begins to change; she grows young and prettier. Her hair springs out of its bindings and flows down her back like the waves of the sea, like the tendrils of honeysuckle. Her worries and her glasses drop to the floor.

'Metamorphosis,' shouts Apollo in high and holy glee. Zeus can scarcely contain his delighted amazement, and even Hera has to smile at so much loveliness.

And the girls turn and draw all the gods into their circle of joy, into their ecstatic dance; and Mnemosyne stands there, a child, a girl on the very cusp of womanhood, all potential and sweet promise and joy. And all Olympus is alight with merriment

'Look,' sing the girls, 'look at what we have made. Look.

We have set imagination free. We are putting creativity and art and beauty at the very centre of the world. We are making all things new. From now on the muses are the mother of memory.'

Afterword:

Memory was the Mother of the Muses

Dr. Charles Fernyhough

IT IS FITTING that this story sets its squabble over the true nature of memory on the slopes of Mount Olympus. If anyone has known what it is like to be reconstructed at the whim of the rememberer, it is Zeus and his entourage, with their many divergent and colourful myths of creation.

'The Metamorphosis of Mnemosyne' dramatises a profound change in our view of memory, or at least that aspect of memory that relates to our remembering of events from our own lives. Deeply rooted in our folk psychology is the idea that 'autobiographical memory' is a recording device, like a video camera, storing representations of past events for later playback. In a couple of recent surveys, the psychologists Daniel J. Simons and Christopher Chabris have shown that roughly half of US respondents endorse the view that memory works like a video camera. We often talk about our memories as though they were fixed, unchanging possessions, and fictions such as the sci-fi movie *Total Recall* like to imagine them as discrete objects that might (with some future technological wizardry) be moved from one brain to another.

That's a quite different picture of memory from that emerging from scientific work on autobiographical memory, and indeed from the insights of the many writers and artists who have reflected on memory over the centuries. There is now a commanding consensus within the scientific community that memory is reconstructive rather than reproductive. That is, when we generate an autobiographical memory, we do not do it by pressing PLAY on some mental DVD of the event, but by integrating information from several different sources into a reconstruction of what happened. Because a memory is an active, dynamic collage of different kinds of information, assembled in the present moment, it is prone to many varieties of distortion. Memory scientists study these distinctive memory errors to work out how this complex machine breaks down, and thus to get insights into how it ordinarily operates.

The cognitive neuroscientist Daniel L. Schacter has described what he calls the 'seven sins' of memory. To give one example, Schacter shows how the memories we generate are affected by our own personal biases. To a certain extent, we remember what we want to remember. The US magazine *Slate* recently ran an online study in which photographs of real political events were interspersed with doctored photographs showing events that had never actually happened (such as President Obama shaking hands with Iranian president Ahmadinejad). Around half of the respondents claimed to 'remember' the fictional events. What's more, their likelihood of falsely remembering was influenced by their political biases. Conservatives were more likely than liberals to claim a false memory of the Ahmadinejad handshake, for example, suggesting that their own leanings were shaping what they remembered.

Mnemosyne is right to point out that the rise of neuroimaging has provided powerful confirmation of the reconstructive view. A remembering brain shows activity in many different areas: in the association–building powerhouse of the hippocampus, for sure, but also in the prefrontal cortex (important for strategic retrieval and self-understanding, among other things) and several other cortical and subcortical regions. But the reconstructive view of memory dates back to psychological research conducted long before the era of functional neuroimaging. Groundbreaking work by Elizabeth

Loftus and others, from the 1970s onwards, showed that many experimental participants are prone to the 'implanting' of false memories. In a typical study, subjects are asked to watch a video of an event and are then exposed to information that contradicts the original narrative. Many participants in this situation go on to incorporate the misinformation into their subsequent retellings, effectively creating a false memory.

The gods' resistance to the new view of memory is telling about human needs as well. Our selves are to some extent rooted in our recollections, and early childhood memories have a particular power in this respect, arguably functioning as the human equivalents of the gods' myths of creation. It is no wonder that we cling to the idea that memory works like a video camera, tirelessly and faithfully recording the past for later playback. The Olympians' worry is understandable, but I think it is misplaced. The reconstructive view does not have to lead to the erosion of personal identity or the doubting of the self. Rather, it requires that we change our relationship to our memories, by better understanding how it is that they come into our heads. It certainly doesn't mean that we will lose art, creativity and beauty – quite the opposite. Memory and imagination share common psychological resources; it may be that we remember the way we do because we imagine the way we do. The muses and Mnemosyne share an ancestry, and we should celebrate, not fear, that fact.

Anaka's Factors

'HEY, SHINY,' SHE called from the kitchen, 'what have you been up to?'

'Hang on a moment.' There was a short pause and then Anaka appeared in the doorway. 'What is it?'

Sally noticed suddenly how much she had grown recently, from charming chubby child into something wilder, more colt-like, all legs and eyes and eagerness.

'I have here,' she said, picking up the sheet of paper 'recovered from the depths of your lunch box, a note from Mr. MacLean asking Fumiko and me to make an appointment to see him. Urgently.'

There was another short pause. Sally tried to look stern, although Anaka was, to be honest, pretty good at school and such a summons was unusual.

'So I asked you what you had been up to.'

Sally looked up and realised immediately that Anaka was genuinely baffled. 'I haven't any idea,' she said. 'Perhaps he wants to tell you how brilliant I am.'

'He did that at parents' evening last month.' Sally smiled, 'OK, Shiny, I'd better make the appointment and find out. Pity Fumiko's away for another fortnight. He does say it's urgent.'

'Well you're always better at that stuff than Fumiko – she never pays attention to school things.'

There was no umbrage in her voice, which was lucky because in many ways what she said was true.

So, three days later she sat down in Mr. MacLean's tidy office and tried to look like an attentive, concerned and serious-minded parent.

'What seems to be the problem, headmaster?'

He said, 'I'm sorry Dr. Kobayashi couldn't be here.'

'She's in the States, at a conference. She doesn't go away more than she needs to, you know. And you did say "urgent".'

'Yes, I know. I apologise.' He shifted a pen from one side of the desk to the other.

Abruptly she realised the man was embarrassed. She was surprised; he had always seemed tolerant, unperturbed, more than capable. It was one reason why they had wanted Anaka in his primary school. There was never any point looking for trouble. She waited.

'Yes, I know,' he repeated. 'We're not really used to internationally distinguished parents. I tend to forget how eminent she is.'

She went on waiting.

'Look,' he sounded aggressive, but she realised it was more that he felt awkward and forbade herself to respond in kind. 'Look... obviously it is your own business, but Anaka and her whole class are getting bigger now, and I can't... I mean, I'm not sure it's a good idea to... perhaps you will only confuse her... she's so bright... and I... well, you know what I mean.'

'To be frank, Mr. MacLean I haven't a clue what you mean. When I got your note I asked Anaka what she had been doing and she hadn't a clue either.'

'No. Good. Well. Ms. Favell was very careful, of course; she thought it better to bring it straight to me. Which I agree with.'

It sounded odd. She was confused now, but smiled calmly. Her friends would have been amazed and impressed by her patience. She was amazed and impressed herself. Perhaps it was mother-love or something. She copied her daughter's management technique and let the pause go on. Eventually, he drew a deep breath.

'When you first came to see me, before Anaka started here, you explained, I was pleased at your openness; it makes things so much easier, doesn't it? I mean, you explained about you and Dr. Kobayashi...' He really did not want to have to say the word 'lesbian' which was making things difficult for him, poor thing '... that you and Dr. Kobayashi were... were a couple, in a partnership, and really, as I well know, that is quite common nowadays and has never been a problem for us at St. James's and... There's a tendency to assume with Church Schools that we'll be judgemental, prejudiced, but... well, I don't think so... I hope not. But anyway, on Monday Anaka's class were talking about parents and how everyone, and every mammal indeed, had a mother and a father and Anaka suddenly announced that you were her father, her − Ms. Favell said she actually used the expression − that you were her 'biological father'. And I felt we needed to sort this out. I can't feel she should be allowed to believe that, or to confuse the other children.'

'Thank you. But you see, the thing is, I am.'

What followed was not a pause. It was definitely a silence. He looked at her, almost squinting. She guessed what he was thinking.

'No, I am not a post-operative transsexual. I am not a transvestite either. We − Fumiko and I − we conceived Anaka *in vitro* by making one of my stem-cells... perhaps 'persuading' is a better word... by persuading one of my stem cells into becoming a spermatozoon. My cells, therefore my genes and therefore I, me, am, in point of fact and for what it's worth, Anaka's biological father. I'm delighted to be sure that she understands that.'

She felt some sympathy for him. When Fumiko had first raised the idea with her she had been a bit dumbstruck herself. And it was always worse for men; she could understand that, though frequently in a somewhat smirking sort of way which she tried valiantly but not always successfully to suppress.

'You can't, surely, expect us to lie to her, or ask her to lie to other people?'

'No. No, of course not.' He moved his pen again. It rolled over as he released it and his hand shot out and banged down on it hard. 'No. But...'

'Do you think,' she had to be careful, she had to be clear, 'do you think it might help if I explained it to you, I mean the science?'

'I am not very good at science.' He sounded almost sulky, like one of his Year Four boys. She tried not to smile.

'Nor am I unfortunately, but it is quite a lovely story – and I know people can find it helpful.'

He looked more nervous than ever. He picked up the pen and this time, rolled it between his fingers and appeared to inspect it extremely carefully. She ignored this.

'You are a bit younger than me, Mr. MacLean, and perhaps you grew up in a very different environment, but I was born in the late 1960s and so I was quite a small girl when my mother got heavily involved in the early Women's Liberation Movement. Looking back, it was quite strange for a child because it made her terribly happy and excited and fun – but at the same time she lost her full focus on me. My father picked up a lot of the slack – and I adored him. You must understand that he was deeply sympathetic, not just to me but to her too. Until he died a couple of years ago, I would say they had one of the strongest relationships I have ever known. My mother still finds things terribly difficult without him. But – and this is hard to describe in these more PC days – he was a terrible tease and extremely funny. And one of his jokes was... there was this slogan in the early women's movement: Biology is not Destiny. And whenever it, or anything related to it, came up he would turn his toes out and waddle round the house, flapping his arms and saying "quack-quack". When anyone asked him what he was up to, he'd say he was a duck and if challenged in any way he'd announce, "If I choose to be a duck, I am a duck: biology is not destiny." And when I told him and my mother about Anaka, there was a long silence and then he said, "Oh dear, I really am a duck." And we all laughed a lot.

'So you see the idea that biology is somehow 'natural' and everything else is 'fake' never had much root in me. Fumiko is rather the same, though for different reasons: like a lot of Japanese people, she really does not have that Frankenstein horror thing. For Japanese children most forms of technology, like say robots, are positive, playful and helpful. So perhaps it was easier for the two of us than for other people.

'So although of course we know Daddy's-seed-in-Mummy's-tummy is a pretty good story, a true and useful story, it is not the only story. You know that. There are rubbish stories, like the storks and cabbage patches ones, which really we would both agree children should not be told any more. But there are more stories which are true and useful but differently from the common biological one: Adam and Eve, Leda and the Swan, cosmic eggs, saintly miracles... so you can see ours like that. We think it is a deeply true story and one that will become more popular because it is completely child-centred; it sort of is not about Mummies and Daddies at all, but about the child herself.

'In our story something beautiful and unique happens at the moment of conception; the sperm and the egg each bring their 23 genomes into a moment of fusion, where the two become one, a mystical marriage if you like. This is the moment that Augustine saw as the source of Original Sin, because of the parents' sexual pleasure, but we see it quite differently – as the moment of Original Grace, solidarity, community, what I would shamelessly call love. Suddenly, miraculously and delightfully, there is a new life form – a brand new organism. I see that moment as the source of the desire that drives us through life, the desire for unitive love, and it is good for even very small children to know it.

'That glory is very brief. Just a day or so, that's all, and then – and this is what I think of as Original Sin if you need that concept – there is a terrible wrenching, a splitting. That lovely unitary cell pulls apart, becomes two. I think this is the first, the core binary. Our desire to divide everything into twos – female, male; good, bad; black, white; dark, light; whatever – they're all secondary to and imaginatively grow out of that first division.

'And once it has started it goes on and on – 2, 4, 8, 16, 32. But – and this is the bit that matters – these new cells are totipotent. That means they have the power and the capacity to become anything, any kind of human cell at all; after about five days they move on from being totipotent, and after a week they decide what sort of cells they will be. First they choose one of three (not two, three – it is very theological, Trinitarian, you see, almost a proof of God) different kinds of cells to be, which will go on to make guts and lungs, the nervous system and skin, and thirdly muscle, bone and blood. And then these go on to produce ever more specialised cells and clump together into organs. They give up unity in exchange for complexity and diversity. And within the groups there are always stem cells which are pluripotent – they can't become *anything* but they can become lots of things, for doing repairs and so on.

'OK so far? Then, in what I am told is one of the most elegant pieces of research, a doctor called Shinya Yamanaka – after whom Anaka is named of course, though most people think it is after Fumiko's anarchist youth – discovered exactly which genes get switched on in order to make these changes: there are about four key genes – all with rather silly names like $Sox2$ – which can seduce, say, a skin cell into reverting, and then lure it into being something else. Once you know exactly what is going on, you can replicate in the lab what happens in the body. If you see what I mean. You bathe these cells in precision quantities of the necessary ingredients. It is extremely delicate and tricky and no one is very good at it yet. You have to treat the cells very tenderly; you lay them on a bed of human proteins, wash them in a bath of hormones and so on – just like caring for a tiny baby really. But it can be done and we did it: we took some of my cells and lured them back into pluripotency and then redirected them and after about a fortnight they became mature spermatozoa and Fumiko got pregnant and that is Anaka's story. She has two parents who both have XX chromosomes, but one of them is her father. Biology is not destiny – except of course that we always knew she was going to be a girl.'

It has to be said that Mr. MacLean did not look reassured. He looked appalled. He put the pen down, picked it up again, focussed his attention on it and said, 'It sounds terribly risky. How do you know she will be all right?'

'We don't. There are risks – cancer perhaps. In the early laboratory stages too many of the mice got cancer, though they say they've sorted that out. And Dolly the Sheep aged too fast – her chromosomes were too short for her real age, and she got arthritis and stuff – so possibly, perhaps, these cells have some sort of memory of their own past, know they are not freshly minted, that they were something else before they were sperm. We don't know. But we do know that everyone said this sort of "risky", "dangerous", "unnatural" stuff when Louise Brown was born in 1978 and now you yourself have just told me that IVF babies are perfectly ordinary nowadays, even for lesbians. And we – Fumiko and I – had the opportunity for proper informed consent, at least we believe so, which is more than Lesley, Louise's mother, did. I'm not going to say it isn't risky, or that I don't care that it is risky. I am going to say that she is ten now and there have been no problems so far – and we watch her like hawks, seeking out grey hairs and wrinkles – so the sense of risk diminishes year by year. I am going to say that someone has to be first: Fanny

Longfellow, Louise Brown, Anaka Kobayashi–Morton. I am going to say that from the day she was born, from the day she was conceived, I have never thought the risk too great. I have never regretted it for a single moment.

'You know, it is all so risky, every pregnancy is risky, every life is terribly, terribly risky. You just have to catch the joy as it flies. Anaka is a very pure joy to us, Mr. MacLean. Our sunrise. The risk is part of the joy.'

The two of them sat there for a moment. She could see that though he understood he was not consoled. He did not like it. She did not know him well him enough to guess whether his distress was moral or the terrified reaction of too many men who saw terminal redundancy on their horizon whenever she or Fumiko tried to explain. She could understand, sort of, but there was nothing she could offer them. It was his problem.

He transferred his pen to his other hand and then back again. And again. It looked like fidgeting to Sally. Finally he said, 'What are we going to do about this?'

'Sorry?' she said startled.

'Well, we can't have her muddling up the other children, upsetting them. Babbling on about it.' He sounded cross.

'She hardly babbles on about it. She's been here for five years. She's known about it all that time. And this is the first time it has come up.'

'You know perfectly well what I mean. I don't need to remind you this is a school with a strong Christian ethos; that is why parents choose it.'

'No you don't; that is why we chose it. Tolerance, love, truthfulness, high standards. You said at the start of this that you appreciated our 'openness.' And we appreciated yours. What's changed?'

He dithered a little. Then muttered that it must be against the law, criminal.

She laughed. 'Actually it isn't. Not like cloning. It

probably would be but no one has caught up with us yet. You only make laws against things you know people are doing. Like Cannabis in 1928. You don't have to worry about that. Though to be honest it's why it was never announced. Anaka was first, but she's not the only one – we did not want to rob other couples of that. It was pretty generous of Fumiko's colleagues really. I mean they published on 'viable sperm', but never actually said 'live birth from': so the media never really picked it up. Soon they'll go public, which is an extra reason why Anaka needs to know.'

He mumbled some more. She wanted to say, 'Oh, get a grip,' but she also did not want Anaka to have to change school. He started on something about the Church and traditional morality. She began to feel exasperated.

'For heaven's sake, headmaster! Every year this school lays on a charming little play, in which Anaka along with all your other pupils participate with delight and the parents love it. It's called the Nativity and it celebrates a God who does Virgin Births. I very much doubt, theologically speaking, that he is going to have much of a problem with Anaka.'

She got up and left. She was determined neither to laugh nor to cry.

Over tea, Anaka asked, 'What did Mr. MacLean want you for?'

She was caught out. Tolerance, truthfulness, high standards. Love. She told her daughter, 'He wanted me to tell him about the Yamanaka factors and how Fumiko and I came by you.'

'I thought Miss Favell didn't believe me. I did try to explain.'

'You shouldn't have to now. I think Mr. MacLean will explain it to her. He and I had an interesting chat about whether or not biology was destiny.'

'Did he go "quack" like Granddad?'

'No.' But she laughed suddenly and happily.

'Fumiko gets home tomorrow, doesn't she? It's lucky she was away. She never enjoys those things like you do.'

'Oh Shiny, I did not enjoy it.'

'Bet you did really.'

Afterword:

Yamanaka: Factors to Consider

Dr. Melissa Baxter

WE ALL START life as the ultimate stem cell. The fertilised egg; a single stem cell that goes on to form all the different, specialised cells of a body. This single stem cell divides into two stem cells, both identical to the first. These two both divide into more stem cells which keep dividing and dividing. Each has the potential to become any type of cell in the body, only hasn't decided which one yet. They have all the potential, but remain unspecialised. After four days decisions start to be made in the tiny embryo (which is now about as big as this dot: ·). Stem cells sense where they are, what environment they are in and how many other cells they are next to. All these different clues form instructions that change the cell's identity from a stem cell into a cell destined to become fully specialised like a liver cell, a bone cell or a skin cell. Once a stem cell receives instructions that 'program' it to form a particular type of cell the decision is final and won't be reversed. That's why the different instructions that program these decisions must be so neat and precise.

In 1998 scientists discovered a way of growing the stem cells from four-day-old human embryos in the lab. Human embryonic stem cells are grown in very specific conditions: submerged in a sugary soup of nutrients and proteins. These precise conditions keep the stem cells in an artificial state of limbo. Where normally they would start deciding what they will become, in the lab the cells continue to divide but remain identical. In fact their ability to divide but remain identical – to self-renew – is unlimited. Each one, like cells of the early four-day-old embryo, still has the potential to become any cell of the human body. This is why we describe them as 'pluripotent' stem cells meaning 'many powers'.

The difficulty scientists face is to recreate the complexity of the developing embryo that instructs the stem cells to change into a specialised type of cell. While this may take months in the body, it takes only weeks in the lab so conditions must be very precise. It is even more difficult to create the correct series of instructions to direct a stem cell only into a particular type of cell that you might be interested in. And there are lots to choose from. So far scientists, including myself, have managed to turn stem cells into liver cells, nerve cells, retina cells, cartilage cells, pancreas cells, bone cells and blood cells to name a few. The potential application in medicine is vast and should not be underestimated.

One of the most promising advances scientists have recently made has been to turn human embryonic stem cells into retina cells. There is good evidence that transplantation of these cells might improve vision in patients suffering macular degeneration – the leading cause of blindness in the developed world. Already these cells are being used to treat human patients and early results are promising. Similar advances have been made in instructing stem cells to become nerve cells that have the potential to repair spinal injuries; pancreas cells that can make insulin and when transplanted could cure diabetes, cartilage cells that could be used to repair damaged joints. Or liver cells that can be used to safety-test newly developed drugs and reduce animal testing.

Let us pause now for a moment, because you can not write about embryonic stem cells without referring to the ethical issues involved. I want to be completely transparent here; human embryonic stem cells are isolated only from embryos from IVF clinics that would otherwise be incinerated. Not any embryos that would be used for implantation and pregnancy. Also, embryos are only used for stem cells after fully informed consent from the human donors. However, with the derivation of embryonic stem cells the embryo itself is destroyed. This is why some people find embryonic stem cell research hard to accept.

But what if pluripotent stem cells could be made from specialised adult cells like skin cells instead of embryos? This is exactly what was done by Yamanaka and colleagues in 2007. Any cell in our body (including skin cells) contains the same DNA that the original stem cells did in the developing embryo. But the difference between a skin cell and a pluripotent stem cell is that they have different genes switched on and off. So skin cells still contain stem cell genes, only they are switched off. Yamanaka and co. discovered that if you switch on four 'stemness' genes in a skin cell, it can be 'reprogrammed' in a week or so into a pluripotent stem cell. These four particular genes (SOX2, OCT4, cMYC and KLF4) are now known as 'Yamanaka factors'. It has since been shown that these Yamanaka factors can reprogram not only skin cells, but other cells including liver cells, blood cells and nerve cells into pluripotent stem cells. Like embryonic stem cells these reprogrammed stem cells can remain in limbo, dividing indefinitely until they are instructed to turn into any specialised cell of the body. It has already been shown that these reprogrammed stem cells, like the embryonic ones can make specialised cells including pancreas cells, liver cells, nerve cells and retinal cells. Experiments have shown that reprogrammed stem cells have the potential to treat Sickle Cell Anaemia. They have also been made from skin biopsies of patients with diseases such as Parkinson's and diabetes and been used to generate cells that display the symptoms of the disease. This technology is already being used to model diseases in-a-dish and help develop new therapies.

Last month it was even reported that stem cells made from skin cells can turn into immature sperm cells. So patients that have been made infertile as a side effect of cancer therapy might one day be able to have sperm cells made from their own skin. The fact that they are only primitive sperm cells highlights one of the main hurdles; how to make stem cells turn into cells that are mature. Most often the liver cells, pancreas cells and nerve cells that are made from pluripotent stem cells are immature, like they are in the foetus. The myriad signals and instructions that occur during normal development are very complex. So complex that reflecting the right conditions to generate a mature type of cell is (and believe me I know this!) …very difficult, to put it mildly.

Since 1998, when scientists first discovered human embryonic stem cells, the field has expanded enormously. It is still early days and to make stem cell therapies ready for the clinic will take time, but advances have been rapid. In just fourteen years we have learnt how to grow stem cells, turn normal cells into stem cells, keep them dividing and instruct them to become useful cells for therapy. Anaka's Factors is an extremely specific example of a wide range of possible applications of stem cell research. However, for me, this intriguing and surprising story emphasises how equally exciting the next fourteen years of stem cell research could be.

The Beautiful Equation

IT HAD BEEN a long day and he was tired. He came into the house and was faintly relieved to realise that Derek was still at work. He went into the kitchen to make a cup of coffee. As he waited for the water to boil, he noticed there was a black smear just above the power point that the kettle was plugged into. He reached out for a kitchen sponge to clean it off ('I'm getting as anal as Derek,' he thought) but just before he wiped it away he saw that it was not in any usual sense a 'smear': it was tiny writing done with a slightly smudgy felt-tipped pen. It said,

$$i\gamma^{\mu}\delta_{\mu}\Psi = m\Psi$$

He wondered, a little wearily, what Derek was up to now.

David McIntyre had moved back home when his mother died, and spent the next months grieving and learning with appalling clarity how much energy and love she had devoted to protecting him from his twin brother. The process was painful. It required him to rewrite the whole narrative of his life. He had come to believe, he had let himself believe, he had perhaps even encouraged himself to believe, in a way that began now to feel petulant and immature, that Derek was his mother's favourite and that he himself had never been properly loved. Worse, he had blamed her for all the difficulties he had ever encountered, emotional, professional and social. He had invented a story which exonerated him from all responsibility – and it was founded on a fundamental self-deception. The revelation of her lifelong tactful care nearly broke his heart. In the clear space that often opens up when one dispenses with an old and clogging lie, he also knew that he had not come

155

home in noble self-sacrifice to look after Derek as she would have wanted, but because it was a bloody nice house, nicer than anything he would be able to afford for years. He would, in exchange have watered her beloved houseplants and cleaned her green kitchen but Derek already did those things to a densely complex, highly precise timetable that it would be insane to interfere with. So in fact all he could do was 'look after Derek'. One problem with looking after Derek was that it was nearly impossible to pin down why Derek needed looking after, though he did, or what the looking after should involve. His mother had looked after Derek. Now David learned that what that meant was loving Derek and he found that nearly impossible.

Being identical twins did not help. It was more frightening than touching to see just how very alike they were. Looking at Derek he realised just how warped one's idea of one's own face was because of seeing it only in a mirror, only flipped around, reversed. Derek looked more like him than his own mirror image did. David was two hours and nine minutes older than Derek, slightly less than an inch taller and about 5lbs heavier. That was it. Since he had moved back into the house of his childhood Derek had even taken to wearing the same clothes as David wore.

'But we won't know what's whose,' he had said with heavy patience when Derek had come home with three more shirts, identical to his favourite ones.

'Yes we will,' Derek said.

'How?'

'I can smell you on yours.' After a pause he added, 'And me on mine.'

And, God knows, he probably could.

Over the next few days he started to find it all over the house in unexpected places.

$$i\gamma^\mu\delta_\mu\Psi = m\Psi \quad i\gamma^\mu\delta_\mu\Psi = m\Psi \quad i\gamma^\mu\delta_\mu\Psi = m\Psi$$

He kept coming across it, bumping into it. One evening he went to look for the number of the Chinese take-away in the Yellow Pages and discovered that Derek had written it, as neatly as ever, across the top of many of the pages; he could not decide if the pages were random or if there was some Derek type logic at work; probably the latter. But then he noticed that he too had doodled on the Yellow Pages, presumably while waiting for calls, and his doodles, though more untidy, made no more sense than Derek's.

But he did not doodle on the inside of the bathroom cabinet door; nor neatly around the tops of tins of tomatoes. Nor meticulously along the edges of the stair carpet – once for each tread; and he remembered his mother painting them years and years ago and was irritated and then irritated that he should feel irritated.

The light bulb in his bedroom failed one night and he got up crossly and went to the store cupboard to get a replacement – and found that every little box had been opened and $i\gamma^\mu\delta_\mu\Psi = m\Psi$ inscribed black on each pearl-coloured glass dome.

It became like a game of hunt-the-thimble. They had played a lot of hunt-the-thimble when they were small because Derek loved the game and was astonishingly quick. David on the other hand had been less keen; it was one of the few games in which Derek was the consistent winner – hunt-the-thimble and Pelmanism. Middle class games he had thought with contempt as a teenager and his mother allowing and encouraging them because she loved Derek best. But he caught himself looking for the $i\gamma^\mu\delta_\mu\Psi = m\Psi$ and found he experienced a childlike thrill of triumph each time he discovered a new one.

Except they began to get bigger:

$$i\gamma^\mu\delta_\mu\Psi = m\Psi$$
$$\iota\gamma^\mu\delta_\mu\Psi = \mu\Psi$$
$$\iota\gamma^\mu\delta_\mu\Psi = \mu\Psi$$

One day he found it written 23 times in a rigorously straight column on the back of his mother's photograph that they kept on the sitting room mantelpiece. He wondered suddenly if it had something to do with Derek grieving, then shook himself sternly: Derek did not do grief; that was one of his problems.

And anyway grief could have nothing to do with writing $i\gamma^{\mu}\delta_{\mu}\Psi = m\Psi$ in highlighter pen right across the hall mirror – not even a cunning hiding place. Except that he then had a swift passing image of his mother who never left the house without pausing to peer at herself and check that her hair was tidy.

He decided he would not mention it, he would ignore it. Perhaps, he thought, Derek had always written $i\gamma^{\mu}\delta_{\mu}\Psi = m\Psi$ on washable surfaces all over the house and his mother had just wiped them away. He would just wipe them away. Derek never mentioned them either. David just wiped them away.

But once he went into Derek's bedroom. He never went into Derek's room, and Derek never came into his. They had been given separate rooms when they were about six and this privacy rule had been imposed firmly and absolutely. Now he realised that this must have been about the time that Derek had been diagnosed. And about the time his father had left. He had never put these things together before. Now he went into Derek's room with a sort of sly curiosity and some vague moral justification about 'duty of care' while knowing at some other more honest level that it was sheer nosiness that drove him.

In size and shape their rooms were identical. They had exactly the same decor and furniture. This he knew was no imitation or oddity of Derek's. Their mother had chosen the furniture and she had given each of them precisely the same things. He thought he had been allowed to choose his own colour schemes, changing as his growing tastes had changed, but either Derek had chosen the same or their mother had imposed it. Neither room had been redecorated since he left home. But the similarity stopped with her actions. The two of them inhabited their own space quite differently. David did not think of himself as particularly messy or slovenly, but compared to Derek he certainly was. The room was immaculate – each pen on the desk was straight; there were no clothes on the floor, nor even on the chair and Derek had made his bed before he had gone to work. Did anyone make their bed anymore? Derek did, and he had laid a white cover over the duvet with its ends tucked in, its surface unruffled. Before leaving home David had tacked adolescent posters to his blue walls and since coming back he had taken them down, leaving the darker shadows of unfaded paint behind them and he had hung three more adult paintings. Derek's walls were pristine. Except that, immediately over his bed, about a metre above his pillows, in huge black letters, was

$$i\gamma^\mu \delta_\mu \Psi = m\Psi$$

David stood just inside the door and looked. He realised that he had no way of knowing whether Derek had written them up with obvious care and attention recently in the last few weeks or if they had been there for years.

He gritted his teeth and said nothing even when, a few days later, he found the mysterious message written on the bottom of every single plate in the cupboard. He washed them clean carefully and put them away in the tidily aligned stacks he knew Derek preferred to maintain.

And then finally he came in from jogging one Sunday afternoon, sweaty and tired, and found

$$i\gamma^\mu \delta_\mu \Psi = m\Psi$$

gouged into the lovely pale wood of the kitchen table, each symbol at least eight inches high and irremovably deep, right across the smooth scrubbed surface which had been the centre of his mother's life. He found himself weeping. When his twin came in he could not be silent.

'Derek, what is this?'

'Call me DerAk. I've told you.'

'Oh, come on.'

'I won't talk to you if you don't call me Derak.'

'Don't be silly.' Then after a long pause, 'OK, Derak – WHAT IS THIS? Why are you writing it everywhere?'

'Because it is beautiful.'

'It is? It's not beautiful to ruin Mum's table.'

'Yes. It is so beautiful that we know it is true.'

'What?'

'Beauty is truth. Truth beauty. That is all you know on Earth or need to know.'

'Derek!' There is no answer. 'OK, OK, Derak then. But what is it? Why are you doing this? I don't understand.'

'No you wouldn't.'

'Look at me.' And Derek did indeed raise his head and look straight into his brother's eyes with a benign and open gaze. But it didn't... it didn't work somehow. David knew it did not mean what it was meant to mean, what all his instincts told him it meant or should mean. Derek had done all that CBT; they had taught him to look at people when they spoke to you; to let them catch and hold your eyes; that other people liked that even if you did not, and you should do it to please them. But David knew it was an act, an empty gesture, there was nothing, no meaning in it.

He felt weary and sweaty; he wanted to take a shower and lie down. He did not want to take Derek on.

'Please Derak, please don't. Just don't scratch this... this whatever it is. Just don't do it anymore. Please.'

'OK,' said Derek, apparently completely unfazed.

'And don't draw on the walls. If you want to hang a picture up you put it on a nail. You don't write on walls. You know that.'

'OK,' said Derek again, exactly as though he had received some well-meant instructions for some activity he had no particular interest in. Then his eyes drifted away, downwards, inwards and David was alone. He went up to take his shower. Derek had written $i\gamma^\mu\delta_\mu\Psi = m\Psi$ along the ceramic rim of the shower stall. David wiped it off without any thrill whatsoever and stood trying to breathe calmly under the vigorous flow of hot water.

But it seemed to have worked. David found no more graffiti over the following weeks and Derek seemed calm and busy. He felt no qualms about going off on a long-planned week's holiday with some of his own friends walking in the Highlands, an annual and relaxed event. He knew his mother had happily and safely left Derek for occasional weekends on his own once he was grown up – and he felt he had earned a break. Just as his mother had, he let a friendly neighbour know Derek was on his own in case anything complicated happened and gave her a phone number where he could be reached.

They had a wonderful five days in the harsh hills and loneliness of Wester Ross, walking high and hard during the day and drinking, eating and laughing through cheerful evenings. He did occasionally notice, internally, that the other four were now two couples, and speculated as to how he might be able to make that work for him with his responsibility for Derek. Once he wondered if that was why his mother had never found, or even seemed to look for or want, a new partner. But it did not feel as though it mattered very much: he was content within his own body and within this old and easy companionship.

He arrived home in the early evening. As he walked down the street, the neighbour waved from her house and threw up her window. He crossed the road towards her,

'No, no,' she said, 'you get on home. Everything has been fine. He came in from work about an hour ago. He's been no trouble at all.' She smiled sweetly, shut the window and went on with her life. Something in him that he had not known was taut, relaxed. He went up his garden path with real pleasure, a sense of security and home coming.

Every inch of every wall – in the hallway, the sitting room, and the spacious green kitchen – was covered with column after column of black symbols

$$i\gamma^{\mu}\delta_{\mu}\Psi = m\Psi$$
$$i\gamma^{\mu}\delta_{\mu}\Psi = m\Psi$$
$$i\gamma^{\mu}\delta_{\mu}\Psi = m\Psi$$
$$i\gamma^{\mu}\delta_{\mu}\Psi = m\Psi$$
$$i\gamma^{\mu}\delta_{\mu}\Psi = m\Psi$$

There must have been over a thousand of them. And, neatly and precisely in the little space between the two lines of the equals symbol, every single equation was punctuated by picture nail with a little bronze coloured head, hammered in with an elegant efficiency.

'Derek!'

There was no answer. He swung off his knapsack, sank onto the sofa and started to unlace his boots. All the weariness of the week leapt upon him in a single pounce, a wolf at his throat.

After a long pause he called again, 'DerAK.' Almost immediately he heard his twin come out of his bedroom and down the stairs and into the sitting room. He sat down in an armchair, looked at David and said, 'Oh, hello, it's you. Did you have a good time?'

'Yes,' David said, so thrown for a moment that he had to look at the walls again and check he had not dreamed it. He hadn't.

'Yes,' he said, 'yes, I had a very good time until just now. What the fuck have you been doing?'

'I put the nails in,' said Derek.

'I said, "No writing on the walls."'

'I had to,' said Derek. 'I had to. It is so beautiful and it proves me. So I know I am real.'

'What is it Derek? What does it mean? What are you talking about?'

'Look at it, stupid, look at it.'

'Don't call me stupid.'

'Well don't be stupid then. You can see, it proves me, it proves I exist. It's obvious.'

'It's not obvious to me.' David suddenly heard his mother explaining to him, when he was about ten, that if you let Derek spin his story in his own way he often said interesting things. So he took a deep breath, 'Explain it to me, Derak. What is that... that maths-thing you keep writing?'

'It's not a maths thing. It's a physics thing.'

'What's the difference?'

'It's for something... .if it is for something it's physics; if it isn't for something real, something that is really there, it's just mathematics. Just metaphors. I don't do metaphors, you know that.'

'OK. And what is this one for?'

'It is Paul Dirac's equation. It's a relativistic equation of motion for the wavefunction of the electron. The theory described the structure of the atom. He made it in 1932 and said that it was too beautiful to be false; that it was more important to have beauty in one's equations than to have them fit experiments.'

No one should say such bizarre things in such an uninflected monotone. David did not know how to respond. 'I see,' he said.

'No, you don't,' said Derek flatly.

'No?'

'No. Look. Look at it. You can see, I just fall out of the bottom of the equation.'

'Derek... Derak...'

'Can't you see? He predicted me. You are the electron. Everyone knows about you. I'm the positron. He predicted me and Carl Anderson found me. And they gave me to Mum.'

Then he said, 'I am your anti-particle.' After a pause he added quite casually, 'Paul Dirac had Aspergers too, you know.'

David sat and looked at the ruined walls of his mother's lovely house. He felt an infinite resigned exhaustion. But Derek was on a roll now.

'We're exactly the same, we're exactly the same but I'm different. I spin the other way. "All efforts to express the fundamental laws of Nature in mathematical form should strive mainly for mathematical beauty. You should take simplicity into consideration in a subordinate way to beauty. It often happens that the requirements of simplicity and beauty are the same, but where they clash, the latter must take precedence." And I think it would be more beautiful if there was the same muchness of both of us. But there isn't.'

He was too tired to answer, too tired to care.

'Why isn't there, brother? Why is there more of you than of me? Why? Nobody knows why. It isn't fair. Why is there more of you than there is of me?' Derek was beginning to get het up; David knew he should soothe him, talk him down, try and engage him. He was too tired.

'Why is there more of you than of me?'

'Half an inch. And if you ate more you could be the fatter one.' He knew it was not the right answer, but he could not find the energy.

'Don't laugh at me. Don't laugh at me. Just because there is more of you, you think you're better don't you? You think you are normal and I'm just anti, just wrong and unnecessary. But, you know what? I'm better than you. I have a positive charge. You have a negative one. That is why Mum loved me best.'

Something snapped.

After 31 years of self-control he was the one who lost it, not Derek, not how it ought to be, not right. The weariness fell away and with it, the responsibility. Furious, he hurled himself across the room, charging at Derek, like an eight-year-old, a child having a tantrum, but stronger, angrier, more dangerous. And Derek rose out of the chair to meet the charge, suddenly as angry, as engaged, as involved.

'Normal,' thought David, triumphant. I've made him normal. They smashed into each other on the rug in front of the fireplace and...

... and...

'MYSTERIOUS DISAPPEARANCE OF IDENITCAL TWINS' said the local paper the following week. It seemed to have all the right ingredients for a great story. (Our community is too small and tight-knit to want too much of a sexual angle.) But from the very start it was all unsatisfactory and stuttering because there was not a single clue as to what had happened. A neighbour, who knew them well and had been an old friend of their mother's, had seen them both go into the house in the early evening. Poor Derek first: he came home from work at his usual time; his routines were very important to Derek, poor boy, he always came past at the same time. That's how she knew it was him. And dear David about an hour later. Back from some holiday, which he surely needed. What a good boy he was giving up his lovely flat and coming home to look after poor Derek when their mother died. Devoted to each other, those boys were. David had spoken to her, just briefly, just to check up on everything, as he went past. Very nicely spoken he was. Like his dear mother. Not a day went by when she did not miss their mother; such a good friend she had been, and such a good mother. She had seen them both go into the house, definitely. No, she had not seen either of them come out. Yes, she was sure she would have noticed if one of them had – though she might well not have been able to tell us which. As alike as two halves they were.

But that did not take us very far. They had gone into the house, both of them; neither of them had come out. The house was neat and clean, no sign of any trouble. Oh yes, there were some strange drawings on the walls, quite artistic really. Someone said it had something to do with maths. Or it looked like a game they had been playing, odd but harmless. And one of them had laid out all the food and stuff for supper in the kitchen. There was not a single clue about what had happened. They had vanished.

Actually, there was a clue. A small boy was walking up the road with his dog, rather late in the evening. And, suddenly he had seen strange rays of light streaming out of the house, like fireworks, but faster, brighter; straight up through the roof. And then gone. But he was not supposed to be out at that hour and had no wish to explain himself to his grown-ups so he never told anyone.

Afterword:

The Ultimate Other

Dr. Tara Shears

$$i\gamma^\mu \delta_\mu \Psi = m\Psi$$

SARA'S STORY RECOUNTS the fate of David and Derek, identical twins whose lives are best kept apart. Their destiny is hidden in the 'beautiful' equation that gives the story its name. This is Dirac's equation, a simple far-reaching collection of symbols that led to the prediction of antimatter. It is fundamental, succinct, and so beautiful that, like Dirac, Derek was convinced that it just had to be true.

The equation arose from Dirac's attempts to describe how an electron moves in the most general way possible. Electrons are subatomic particles and require quantum theory to describe their behaviour with any degree of success. This theory governs behaviour up to the small distance scales corresponding to atoms, and is notoriously unintuitive. Quantum physics was a young theory when Dirac embarked on the problem, and he was by no means the only person trying to use it to find an answer. The other factor complicating the mathematics is that electrons can also travel extremely fast, reaching speeds close to the speed of light. If Dirac's theory was going to be useful it needed to be able to describe this situation too, and that meant using Einstein's theory of special relativity.

Dirac's equation unites both of these theories in one short phrase. The information contained within it is condensed and needs teasing out before the underlying sense appears.

167

Quantum theory enters in Ψ, the particle wavefunction, the quantum physical object that describes the electron and its behaviour. Special relativity enters in the symbols γ^{μ} and δ_{μ}. These are the equations of electron motion and describe high velocity behaviour as well as everyday speeds. The other elements are m, the electron mass, and i, a numerical constant. Dirac realised that these five symbols encapsulate everything needed to describe the behaviour of an electron. That gives these symbols a great significance and power; they work for electrons and other subatomic particles too.

This equation proved to work amazingly well. It could be used to explain the subtle details of light emitted from hydrogen atoms when atomic electrons switch energy levels, which no other theory had managed. There was just one catch, which was that the equation had twice as many solutions as you'd expect. It gave a solution that described the electron, but one other solution too. This corresponded to an almost identical twin of the electron, a subatomic particle identical in every way, apart from having the opposite electric charge.

Other particle theoretical physicists found this extra solution hard to stomach. With no grounding in reality it was hard for many to regard Dirac's approach to solving the problem as anything more than a convenient mathematical tool. Dirac disagreed. He was guided by notions of symmetry and order, by the idea that the universe could be made forever simpler if deep interconnections in its structure could be revealed. This simplicity was beauty. His equation was so beautiful in that regard, that it simply had to be true. Derek's inability to countenance any other interpretation, and obsession with the equation, mirror Dirac's. His behaviour may also mirror Dirac's in other ways – a recent biography (*The Strangest Man*, G. Farmeloe) hints that Dirac may have exhibited behaviour we would now identify as characteristic of Asperger's Syndrome. Derek's lack of empathy and social polish coincide with that idea.

The extra solution was real to Dirac. It was christened 'antimatter'. Amazingly, experimental evidence for the 'positron' was found some four years later by Carl Anderson, who was investigating the composition of cosmic rays. These particles from outer space contained electrons, and also electrons with positive charge – the positron (anti-electron) predicted by Dirac's equation.

I love this prediction. It comes from nowhere, and literally falls out of an equation constructed with the most rigorous and general of arguments. It is an idea born of logic, not human prejudice. For it to be true reaches another level of beauty altogether, a humbling level that this beauty is remotely within our reach to experience. It makes you think that perhaps the universe is simple too; despite its size, no matter how complex it appears, underneath everything there is a very simple structure.

Nowadays, we think that antimatter is everywhere, or at least used to be at the time of the Big Bang. Half the universe was made of it at the beginning but, due to the tiniest of differences in the nature of matter and antimatter, matter ultimately prevailed and evolved into the universe we know today. In Sara's story, David and Derek embody this similarity and subtle difference. They are identical twins who even take to wearing similar clothes. All that separates them is a slight difference in outlook and nature – a rigid adherence to rules for Derek, less so for David. A hallmark of antimatter is that when it touches its matter equivalent, both annhilate. No trace is left of the originals save the energy released in their collision; a flash of light, a burst of energy. Little do David and Derek realise that they are destined to share that same fate.

It is a mystery why such a difference exists. Dirac's beautiful equation leaves us with no clue as to why there should be so little antimatter or what this imperfection in its otherwise identical nature is. Why this should be is one of the biggest questions in physics. I work on a particle physics experiment at CERN, the European centre for particle physics, which is designed to investigate this, and it's by no means the only one. Dirac's beautiful equation has left us struggling to comprehend the consequences.

The Mathematics
of Magic Carpets

AT THE END of each working day he walked along the green bank between the yellow river and the yellow city, from the House of Wisdom to the House of Happiness. The wide marble steps that linked the city and the river and the well-tended gardens made it a peaceful, quiet place, even when there were many other people also walking there in the cooler air of evening. When the Caliph founded his city he had named it 'Madinat al-Salaam', the City of Peace, and although, like everyone else, al-Khwārizmī usually called it 'Baghdad', every evening as he walked home he would recall this name and smile peacefully to himself. Here in this brief time of solitude he could rest, be blank and empty and open: he has left his busy brain in the House of Wisdom and has not yet taken up his sweet heart-break in the House of Happiness.

The walk took barely half an hour and then he turned his back on the river, strolled up a narrow alley and came to the small door in the huge wall. He slipped through it and into the dark passage-way within. He never liked to have the doorkeeper open his front door for him as though he were a visitor; a man, he thought, should come in and out of his own house freely. He passed along the thickness of the street wall and broke abruptly into the brightness of his courtyard garden. As he so often did, he stood for a moment taken up into his own delight at its beauty and peace and order. The ponds were arranged according to subtle and playful games

171

with Euclids's geometrical proofs, but like all good mathematics the physical forms were simple and harmonious; the various sizes of rectangle contrasted pleasingly with the ogee arches of the shaded colonnade that ran around all four sides of the garden, elaborately incised with lettering; and the air was soft and rich with the perfume of roses and myrtles. Just inside the entrance, there was a small brazier burning brightly on a plinth. He had come originally from the Eastern Mountains, and for all he was a man of science and a valued member of the House of Wisdom, inside his own home, he still kept the rituals of his childhood, more for their comfort than for their God.

As he stood there he could hear lute music and soft laughter coming from the harem, but he did not even raise his eyes to the balconies above. Because at the far end of the garden there was a pair of pomegranate trees, and in their shade, on a pile of elaborately embroidered cushions, his heart's delight was sleeping.

He walked softly up the garden following the elaborately tiled path until he stood looking down at her in the shade of the trees. There was a sheen of sweat on her face and he sat down beside her, rung out the cloth that was soaking in a bowl of rose-water, cool in the evening shade and began to wipe her forehead, very gently. None of the doctors could explain the sweating. None of the doctors could explain anything much about her. He thought she was from the magic lands, a child of the djinn, so delicate that her bones snapped and her golden skin bruised from a touch of the wind apparently and yet her heart and her soul were so tough and joyful and enduring.

She woke up, opening her strange eyes, blue-grey where other people's were white, and smiled dreamily at him.

'Good evening, little apricot bud,' he said.

'Good evening, thief of the Indian numbers.'

'Not thief,' he said, grinning. 'You cannot steal numbers because they do not belong to anyone. And you should not so disrespect your father. You should call me, "Master of the Place Marker", "Improver of Ptolemy", "Cartographer of the Cities and the Stars".'

'Hmm,' she said looking wicked. Like many children who have lived in pain all their lives she had a curious dignity and a way of speaking that was often unlike a twelve-year-old. And every evening her father, one of the most creative and wide ranging scholars and thinkers in the employ of the Caliph al-Ma'mūn came and talked with her, ambling through his day in the House of Wisdom, settling himself in her love and need, so she heard a great number of things that twelve-year-olds do not normally know about. 'And how was it today, in the House of Wisdom?'

'It was good. In the morning al-Kindī and I had another discussion about the Qur'an and his beloved Aristotle. He is, he truly is, a man of extraordinary ability and goodness too, but for him all learning is about approaching God and becoming virtuous – and for your unworthy father it is about getting things done, understanding how they work and finding our way through the world. So we are fortunate to have each other – we spread the spirit of reason more wisely. And we make sparks for each other to light our own work.

'And also al-Jahith dropped in.'

'Are his eyes really goggly? In the harem they say the Caliph's children found him so scary that he had to be sacked from being their tutor.'

He laughed. 'That is what they say everywhere. And they are very fierce and staring. But he would be a good tutor I think, because he writes wonderful stories as well as reading Aristotle and arguing with al-Kindī. But today he was talking about something you would like. He believes that animals change to be comfortable in different places – so if you think of foxes and wolves and dogs they are so alike that they must have had the same great, great, great grandmother – only lots more 'greats' – back a long, long time and then they changed, wolves for the mountains, foxes for the woods and dogs for the garden or for hunting. Al-Kindī thinks not, because his Aristotle says that all the animals are the same from the beginning. I listened to them and thought about you and whether we should get a baby lion and see if we could it turn it into a pussy cat. I like al-Jahith because he makes all his ideas out of what he can really see. He believes in what he calls "a spirit of rational inquiry". And that is what will make us all great, little myrtle bush. Do you have a spirit of rational inquiry?'

'Yes, I think so.'

'I think so too.' In as much as she could, he thought sadly. 'Anyway, it was a very talkative morning. I enjoyed that. We were all gathered because the Caliph came to visit us towards noon. He asked me to present you with his salaams, little figling, and says he has been sent a huge emerald from the lands of the sunset, and he will give it to you if you will leave me and be his Calipha.' They both smiled. 'He was, as always, full of new plans; he has set poor al-Hajjaj to make another new translation of Euclid; it makes me glad I know no Greek.'

'The Greeks are silly.'

'No. No, my rose without a thorn. You must never say that; you must not even think that. They were so wise and clever. But... but perhaps they get in the way now, if we honour them too much. You see, they did geometry and philosophy; and the Indians did numbers and sums. And we... we are adding on – we are doing those things, doing them better, perhaps, because our Caliph al-Ma'mūn... I have never heard, in all the history of the world, of a Caliph, a great King, an Emperor who loves knowledge so much and loves and supports his scientists, his men of knowledge. But we haven't made anything new – anything that is ours... so all this translating and translating... But without the translating we would not know enough things to make a new thing. So... Your revered father, my peach blossom, is very greedy.

'But I think he will give us our observatory, he was

speaking today about a site at al-Shammasiyya. Perhaps when the weather is cooler I will have you carried there on a litter so that you can see it.' Even as he said this he was struck afresh by his sadness that she could no longer walk. He drew a small breath, so quietly he hoped she would not hear, and after only a tiny pause, went on, smoothly, 'And, in the House of Happiness, little pearl drop – has it been a good day here?'

'Quite. The new slave from the cold north played *shataranj* with me, and unlike the illustrious scholar of the House of Wisdom, he was able to beat me, which makes me suspect, oh Father of my heart, that you have been reverse cheating, because he is not really quite so very clever as you are.'

He blushed a little. 'Would you like to play now, with me? There will be no cheating anymore.'

'I would rather play on the Magic Carpet, please.'

'I'll go and fetch it,' he said, getting up, smiling. He walked away under the portico into his own quarters. A slave jumped up from his waiting squat and al-Khwārizmī saw that it was the new slave with his flat northern face.

'You played *shataranj* with the little one today?'

'Yes, Master.'

'You won?'

'Yes, Master.'

'Do you know that I have never won against her?'

'That is a father's privilege,' said the young man politely. And then after a pause added, 'I was not wrong to do so? My master is not displeased?'

'No, not displeased at all, a little ashamed of myself perhaps. She accused me of "reverse cheating".'

'She is...' he searched for a word.

'Yes, she is,' said al-Khwārizmī. The two of them exchanged slightly self-conscious grins. His daughter had made another new conquest; another man to have his heart broken.

'My master desires something?'

'No, no. I am fetching another game for the child.' He picked up a small filigree carved chest and a little rolled rug. As he was leaving the room he said, 'You should always try to win if you play with her. It will be good for her. The day that she wins against me properly, by herself, with me trying, I will give you a reward.'

He went back into the garden and joined her in the shade. He opened the box, lifted out a book, carefully unwrapped the silk cloth from around it, and laid it beside her.

'Choose the cities,' he said and then, leaving her to it, he turned and unrolled the frayed rug, splotched with stains and worn through to the warp thread in places. He smoothed it out on the tiled ground, still under the shade of the pomegranate trees. In the old stories a flying carpet was always shabby and battered; ignorant or arrogant characters were always tossing their magical gifts aside; only the wise could detect the mysterious power.

'Today,' she said, assuming an imperious tone, which was part of the ritual of the game, 'we will go to Cordoba and then to Medina by way of Athens. The improver – the perfecter – of Ptolemy will prepare a map.'

'I think that is too long a journey for one evening, Sultana. Why don't we alight in Athens on our way home, so that you can see for yourself how wondrously wise the Greeks were.'

'Good. Convey me to my carpet.' She stretched up her thin arms to him.

When he picked her up as gently as he could, he felt how light she was becoming, like a little bird. He settled them both onto the carpet, held her safe between his crossed legs, the back of her head secure against his chest and the book balanced on his knees. With his arms round her he started to turn the pages through the long list of co-ordinates that pin point the location by latitude and longitude of every city of the world. Ptolemy the Alexandrian had made such a list 700 years before and he had corrected and improved and added to it, and, in sets of neat and careful instructions, shown any reader how to use it to make their own map. The Caliph was setting scholars and artists to the task of creating a new map of the whole world, based on his figures.

'So,' he said, 'we are all ready. We have made our map and are all set to go. Hold tight.'

And together they chanted their summons:

Come, you Djinn, whom Solomon tamed;

Come, you Houri, from paradise;

Come powers of air and movements of the sun;

The Queen of Sheba calls you

To make her carpet fly to...

Cordoba.

She closed her eyes and leaned against his chest and they flew together in their minds, free and without pain over the desert and the middle sea and the ruins of Rome towards Cordoba.

Once the carpet was steady in the imaginary air they were free to chat, although occasionally he would rock her suddenly or would peer over the side of the carpet and indicate particular glories that might be passing beneath them. They both knew it was a game and they delighted in it.

Somewhere over Crete she said suddenly, 'Father, the other day, in the Harem, the wives' – her own mother had died in childbirth; she was free to load the word 'wives' with a subtle scorn – 'the wives were wondering why you did not make maps for people who wanted to go travelling. They said we would be very rich if you did.'

'But, almond flower, we are very rich.'

'Richer.'

'Well, you may tell them in the Harem that their Caliph, the ever-to-be-honoured Abū Ja'far Abdullāh al-Ma'mūn ibn Harūn, would be mortified if one of his scholars were to set up a market stall; and that mortifying a Caliph of his infinite grandeur and dignity is never a good idea. And it would be true.

'But there is a truer reason: if you have Ptolemy's lists, especially improved, if not perfected by your unworthy father, and you follow the stage-by-stage instructions this same unworthy scholar gives you in his book, you can make your own map, you can go anywhere. You do not need to know and measure and calculate – you just need to follow the pattern of the instruction. Then you are free. My map would give you one good way to go perhaps, but I want people to choose their own journey; I want people to know how to do the thing themselves. The journey is the unknown thing, the thing to be discovered. My way you make the journey into a thing itself.'

A thing itself. The *shay*. And a method, a working method, an effective, finite list of well-defined instructions and he could set people free. No. Not just set people free – set the *shay* itself free, detach it from numbers, even elegant Indian decimal numerals – the *shay* could a be a free thing, ready to be applied – like the co-ordinates were ready to be applied to any map. It was, it was his new thing. A new strong thing – where the energy of the Arabs and the subtlety of the Persians would come together. Useful, enormous. He could... he would...

'Has the Master of the Place Mark, the Thief of the Indian Numbers, fallen asleep?'

'Certainly not, impertinent child; were you to glance down to your right now you would see a column of smoke and dust rising into the air. It is an exploding mountain which throws up flames and rocks, and once upon a time it vomited up so much burning rock that two whole cities were buried and have never been found again.'

But she was not fooled. 'If you haven't dozed off then a science idea has swallowed you up. Is it a big idea or a small idea?'

'I think it may be a big idea.'

'Can I understand it?'

'I hope so. That is part of the idea.' He held her, rocking gently, carefully. 'Suppose I said to you that we each have a bowl of pomegranates, but we do not know how many. We do know that if you give me one of yours we will both have the same number, and if I give you one of mine you will have twice as many as me. How could you tell how many we each had?'

She thought about it. 'Well the first bit is easy... I have two more than you in my bowl.'

'And then?'

'Well I could get lots of pomegranates and try it out, but...'

'But I could give you a list of things to do, in the right order, which would set you free to find the answer yourself even if pomegranates were out of season.'

'That does not sound like a big idea to me.'

'Well, my little pomegranate, it isn't. It is just an example – but it would be very useful for inheritance and measuring fields and building things and solving problems and measuring stars and... and everything. And it works for every possible number... and whether it was pomegranates or stars or taxes or... anything, the list of things to do, the instructions would be the same. There are things called "equations" – two things that equal each other: we have lots of examples, doing the maths with different numbers; worked-out solved little mysteries, but no general rule. And it will stretch our heads out until we count all the stars. The Greeks did it by geometry, lots of squares, but I will do it by order and reason. In my idea the rules will not apply to the numbers, they apply to the thing itself. The thing to be discovered. The shay. The x.'

They rocked in the garden while the sun sank and the shadows lengthened.

She knew he was thinking, even as he was also loving her. She was safe. Eventually she said, 'The Queen of Sheba

SARA MAITLAND

is a little tired. We will not go to Athens today. If the man who counts the stars has had a big idea, we will not need the Greeks anymore.'

He tutted at her dismissal of the Greeks. But he wanted to follow his thoughts now, so they steered the magic carpet towards home. Just before they landed he said,

'I will write a book for you. We will call it *al-Kitāb al-mukhtaṣar fī hisāb al-jebr wa'l-muqābala*. The Compendium on Calculation by...'

'*Al-Jebra*,' she interrupted. 'But that means setting broken bones, fixing them.' She knew altogether too much about that.

'Yes,' he said smiling down at the top of her head. 'That will be our little secret joke, so that you will know it is your book. *Jebra* means 'restoring' or completing something – you can do it to bones, but you can do it to equations too. You take a negative something, move it over from one side of your equation – your two parts that are equal to each other – to the other and then it is "restored" to positive. *The Compendium on Calculation by Restoration and Balancing.* It will be a very big idea. Forever in the future, school children throughout the world will learn about you. But they will not know it. You will be the *Shay*, the thing to be discovered.'

'Will it make me well?'

He wanted to say yes, yes it would. But unlike losing at *shataranj* that was not a father's privilege. There would be no more reverse cheating. He would not so dishonour her. After a long silent moment, she looked at him out of her strange blue eyes and said,

'Never mind.'

'I do mind,' he said.

She died that winter, in excruciating pain, in his arms, before he could finish her book. He wanted to scratch out the title and call it something different, but he did not. He followed the custom and began the book with 'In the name

180

of God the most Gracious and Compassionate' but in the copy he kept in his house he added in his own hand:

For my Calipha, blossom of the spring, sweet kernel of my heart, whose loss nothing can restore or balance.

Afterword:

The Algorithm Man

Prof. Ian Stewart

ABŪ ʿABDALLĀH MUḤAMMAD ibn Mūsā al-Khwārizmī is not exactly a household word today, but he thoroughly deserves to be. Every day, in thousands of different ways, billions of people across the globe unwittingly use a very important idea that is named after him, as they browse the Internet, phone a friend, get cash from an ATM, use satnav to cruise the motorways...

Or, for that matter, switch on the dishwasher.

It is a rare person indeed who, when taking advantage of any of these now-familiar gadgets, finds their thoughts turning to the third Islamic Caliphate of ancient Persia, ruled by the Abbasid Dynasty, or to the House of Wisdom in Baghdad founded by the fifth Abbasid Caliph, Harun al-Rashid. Yet the historical link is very clear, and very strong. For it was in the House of Wisdom that al-Khwārizmī worked, helping to keep alive the knowledge that Europe was fast losing. He translated key Greek and Sanskrit manuscripts; he made his own advances in science, mathematics, astronomy, and geography; and he wrote a series of books that we would now describe as scientific bestsellers. Among them was *On Calculation With Hindu Numerals*, written around AD 825. It made his name a household word among the educated in Europe and the Middle East. And it led, in the fullness of time, to cash machines, web browsers, mobile phones, and touch-sensitive buttons on dishwashers.

Here is how it came about.

Between the first century BC and the fourth century AD a new and remarkable symbolic representation of numbers came into being. It probably started in China, and then spread westwards through India to Arabia. This innovation was the system of Hindu-Arabic numerals, now the basis of our decimal number notation. Its cleverest feature: the same symbol can denote different numbers according to its position. The symbol '7' might mean seven, seventy, seven hundred, seven thousand... seven quadrillion, for that matter. It's one of those ideas that in retrospect looks so simple that it's hard to see why so many people missed it for so many centuries. Yet it's now so deeply embedded in our educational system that the very word 'number' immediately has us thinking of a row of decimal digits.

One advantage of Hindu-Arabic numerals is that once you have learned how to do arithmetic with a mere ten symbols, 0-9, it takes only a few short steps to do the same with arbitrary numbers, however big and complicated. Long multiplication using pencil and paper may seem cumbersome when we first meet it, but compared to what went before, it's simplicity itself. Practical arithmetic has progressed through three main stages. In ancient times it was done using an abacus, moving stones along grooves in sand, or beads along wires. Then it was done on paper with pen and ink, using Hindu-Arabic numerals (although the abacus never went out of use in many cultures). Now, we have gone full circle and use electronic calculators; the only numbers we write down are the problem and the answer. Just as people did when they used an abacus.

The Hindu-Arabic numerals were invented in India; the reference to Arabia stems almost entirely from the success of al-Khwārizmī's book on Hindu arithmetic, which led many to assume that the idea originated with him – even though he explicitly stated the opposite. The book was translated into Latin as *Algoritmi de Numero Indorum*, and it almost singlehandedly spread the news of this amazing new way to do arithmetic to Mediaeval Europe. The first European book with that specific intention was the *Liber Abbaci* of Leonardo of Pisa, written nearly 400 years later. Along the way, 'Algoritmi' became 'Algorismi', and methods for calculating with these numerals were called algorisms. In the 18th century, the word changed to algorithm, possibly because in classical Arabic the pronunciation is al-Khwarithmi. (Or did a hint of that very similar anagram 'logarithm', firmly associated with mathematics and calculation, creep in somehow?)

Even towards the end of the 20th century, an algorithm – a word so obscure that few dictionaries included it – was still just a computational procedure in elementary arithmetic. Not any more. With the advent of electronic computers, a key feature of al-Khwārizmī's methods became indispensable, and every dictionary now contains the word 'algorithm', with a much broader meaning.

The everyday miracles that we now take so much for granted rest on two key techniques. One is the manufacture of extremely small electronic circuits, able to store and carry out complex instructions with breathtaking speed. The other, often forgotten, is the list of instructions that these devices obey. It doesn't matter how fast you are if you don't know what to do. More subtly, unless the instructions are compiled in a sufficiently clever manner, even the fastest microprocessor in the world would take so long doing anything that it would be effectively useless.

Computers must be able to do arithmetic, but the requirements are far broader. They have to be able to search a file for a misspelt word, flip a digital image left-right, make contact with an Internet Service Provider, or make a noise to tell you that someone is trying to contact you on Skype. Every task of this kind breaks down into a complex series of simpler tasks, and the whole process is organised using algorithms. Which today means lists of systematic, precise instructions, guaranteed to carry out specific tasks.

The modern world's electronic marvels would not work without gigantic numbers of algorithms. Algorithms read keyboards, touch screens, and dishwasher controls. They display symbols and images. They convert our voices into streams of zeros and ones, break those streams into packages, transmit them across networks, and reassemble them at their destination. They compare our PIN with what's on the cash card before disgorging the money. They analyse how long it takes signals to get from GPS satellites to our car, do the necessary trigonometry to work out where the car is, and even compensate for the relativistic effects of gravity and the high speeds of the satellites.

In our global society, the Algorithm Man's fingerprints are everywhere. You just have to know how to look.

But algorithms are not the only thing that al-Khwārizmī gave us. In the dictionary, a few words before 'algorithm', we find another of his hugely important inventions: algebra. The 'al' correctly suggests an Arabic derivation, this time from part of the title of his 830 AD book *al-Kitāb al-mukhtaṣar fī hisāb al-jebr wa'l-muqābala*. The literal English translation is 'The Compendious Book on Calculation by Completion and Balancing'. The Latin translation by Robert of Chester retained two of the Arabic words: *Liber Algebrae et Almucabola*.

Algebra, of course, now refers to the use of symbols such as x and y for unknown quantities, and methods for finding those unknowns by solving equations, which provide some information about how the unknowns relate to known numbers. The idea is fundamental to mathematics and science. So it comes as a bit of a shock to find that although al-Khwārizmī is considered to be one of the key figures in the development of algebra, he did not use symbolic notation. That goes back to the ancient Greek mathematician Diophantus of Alexandria, who used symbolic notation in a text written around AD 250, confusingly titled *Arithmetica*.

Actually, it is about the solution of various types of equation, in either whole numbers or fractions.

Although Diophantus used symbols, they were mainly employed to state the problem. When he came to explain how to solve it, he used specific examples. So where we would tell students that the solution of $x+a = b$ is $x = b-a$, Diophantus would take a more specific tack, along these lines. 'Suppose that $x+2 = 5$. Subtract 2 from 5 to get 3; this is the value of x.' He didn't use x, of course. Or 5, 3, and 2, for that matter. He used Greek letters and abbreviations. More importantly, students had to infer for themselves that the numbers 2 and 5 could be changed to whatever they wished, without affecting the underlying method: subtract the first number from the second.

So although al-Khwārizmī explained his methods using words (one step backwards), he dealt in generalities (two steps forward). He would write something like this: 'Suppose the unknown plus some number is equal to a second number. Then the unknown is equal to the second number minus the first.' He explained the solution of algebraic problems in terms of generic *processes*.

Algorithms, indeed.

This, at least, is what most historians of mathematics think, but I caution you that this claim is slightly controversial, because al-Khwārizmī also gave specific examples to illustrate his methods. Mathematical textbooks do the same today. The examples may come before the general technique, as motivation, or after it, as illustration, or both. Despite the presence of examples, the general process is the pivot on which all else rests. It is definitely so today, and it looks like it was also the case for al-Khwārizmī.

If this claim is correct, and I think it is, then he took the first, key step towards turning algebra into an abstract technique in which a symbolic expression like $x+a$ takes on a life of its own. If we subtract another expression such as a from it, we get a third expression, $x+a-a$. But now, in the world of *expressions* (not specific numbers) we can explain to students that *x+a-a* is the same as *x*. Therefore, since *x+a* is the same as *b*, it follows that *x* is the same as *b-a*. Notice how we make this deduction *without* assigning specific numbers to any of the symbols. Algebra then becomes a way to calculate with symbols – which are of course designed to *model* the behaviour of numbers, but are not numbers as such. It's a subtle distinction, but without it we don't even get school algebra in today's sense, let alone the far more abstract algebraic systems that research mathematicians have developed.

Al-Khwārizmī, then, made vital contributions to arithmetic and to algebra. That statement is not controversial: the scholarly arguments are about the precise nature of those contributions. Those alone would have cemented his reputation for millennia, but he did much more. His *Astronomical Tables of Sind and Hind*, dating from slightly earlier, around AD 820, includes more than 100 astronomical tables, mainly derived from Indian sources. Among them are tables of how the Sun, Moon, and the five then-known planets move across the sky. There are also tables of trigonometric functions, and it is thought that he wrote on spherical trigonometry, important in navigation.

Later, in AD 833, he produced yet another major work: *Book on the Appearance of the Earth*. As its starting-point, he took Ptolemy's *Geography*, an ingenious do-it-yourself map kit which lists the coordinates (in effect, longitude and latitude, except that the prime meridian didn't pass through Greenwich) of over 2400 cities and geographic features, together with a variety of grids on to which those coordinates can be transferred. al-Khwārizmī corrected and extended Ptolemy's list. It may be significant that while Ptolemy showed the Atlantic and Indian oceans as seas surrounded by land, al-Khwārizmī left them unbounded.

Historians know quite a lot about the rich and exotic culture in which al-Khwārizmī flourished. They also know a little about al-Khwārizmī himself, but much is obscure. His name suggests that he was born in or near Khwarizm (Chorasmia) in central Asia, south of the Aral Sea, and the bibliographer and biographer Ibn al-Nadim stated as much. But another part of al-Khwārizmī's full name – more precisely, what some scholars think is his full name, but others believe refers to two separate people – suggests that he might instead have come from Qutrubbull, near Baghdad in the fertile zone between the Tigris and Euphrates rivers.

Al-Khwārizmī was born around the time that Harun al-Rashid was ruling a huge empire reaching as far as India in the east and much of the Mediterranean in the west. Al-Rashid founded the House of Wisdom, a library in which writings from other cultures could be translated. His younger son and successor al-Mamun completed its construction, and also built several astronomical observatories. Al-Khwārizmī did his main work under al-Mamun, to whom two books – those on algebra and astronomy – are dedicated. Practical issues were clearly important to al-Khwārizmī as well; indeed, al-Kitab devotes a relatively small amount of space to algebra, and spent the rest discussing such topics as inheritance, lawsuits, trade, land measurement, and the digging of canals. In ancient Persia, mathematics was revered both for its inner beauty and for its utility in everyday life.

Until fairly recently, and with several important exceptions, the bulk of scholarly work on the history of mathematics and science, aside from ancient Babylon and Egypt, concentrated on western Europe and the legacy of the Greeks. Al-Khwārizmī's works are a vital part of the evidence for a different message: that, at a time when western Europe had become scientifically backward, it was the intellectual giants of the Far and Middle East that kept the torch of learning alight and carried it forward.

Two centuries after al-Khwārizmī, another Persian added to our understanding of equations, from a complementary point of view. This was Omar Khayyam: not only a great poet, but an outstanding mathematician. Khayyam went one step beyond al-Khwārizmī's algebra by using methods from Greek geometry, especially conic sections, to solve cubic equations. Only during the Renaissance did European mathematics catch up, and then make major progress beyond the work of the Greek and Arabian scholars, with the discovery of purely algebraic methods for solving cubic and quartic equations. By then, the ideas that al-Khwārizmī had so presciently introduced had acquired escape velocity, and mathematics would never look back.

Sara Maitland's charming story brings the Algorithm Man to life, shows him as a sympathetic and intelligent human being, weaves in references to many of his major discoveries, and takes only very slight liberties (justified by the needs of narrative) with technical aspects of the history. I hope it will help more of us to appreciate how much this remarkable Islamic mathematician achieved, and how great his influence remains today.

Moss Witch

PERHAPS THERE ARE no more Moss Witches; the times are cast against them. But you can never be certain. In that sense they are like their mosses; they vanish from sites they are known to have flourished in, they are even declared extinct – and then they are there again, there or somewhere else, small, delicate, but triumphant – alive. Moss Witches, like mosses, do not compete; they retreat.

If you do want to look for a Moss Witch, go first to www.geoview.org. Download the map that shows ancient woodland and print it off. Then find the map that shows the mean number of wet days per year. Be careful to get the right map – you do not want the average rainfall map; quantity is not frequency. A wet day is any day in which just one millimetre of rain falls; you can have a high rainfall with fewer wet days; and one millimetre a day is not a high rainfall. Print this map too, ideally on tracing paper. Lay it over the first map. The only known habitations of Moss Witches are in those places where ancient woodland is caressed by at least two hundred wet days a year. You will see at once that these are not common co-ordinates; there are only a few tiny pockets running down the west coasts of Scotland and Ireland. Like most other witches, Moss Witches have always inhabited very specific ecological niches. So far as we know, and there has been little contemporary research, Moss Witches prefer oak woods and particularly those where over 20,000 ago the great grinding glaciers pushed large chunks of rock into apparently casual heaps and small bright streams leap through the trees. It is, of course, not coincidental that

these are also the conditions that suit many types of moss –
but Moss Witches are more private, and perhaps more
sensitive, than the mosses they are associated with. Mosses can
be blatant: great swathes of sphagnum on open moors; little
frolicsome tufts on old slate roofs and walls, surprising
mounds flourishing on corrugated asbestos, low lying velvet
on little used tarmac roads, and weary, bullied, raked and
poisoned carpets fighting for their lives on damp lawns. But
Moss Witches lurk in the green shade, hide on the north side
of trees and make their homes in the dark crevasses of the
terminal moraine. If you hope to find a Moss Witch this is
where you must go. You must go silently and slowly, waiting
on chance and accident. You must pretend you are not
searching and you must be patient.

But be very careful. You go at your own peril. The last
known encounter with a Moss Witch was very unfortunate.

The bryologist was, in fact, a very lovely young man, although
his foxy-red hair and beard might have suggested otherwise.
He was lean and fit and sturdy and he delighted in his own
company and in solitary wild places. Like many botanists his
passion had come upon him early, in the long free rambles of
an unhappy rural childhood and it never bothered him at all
that his peers thought botany was a girly subject and that real
men preferred hard things; rocks if you must, stars if you were
clever enough and dinosaurs if you had imagination. After
taking his degree he had joined an expedition investigating
epiphytes in the Peruvian rainforest for a year and had come
back filled with a burning ecological fervour and a deep
enthusiasm for fieldwork. He was, at this time, employed, to
his considerable gratification and satisfaction, by a major
European funded academic research project trying to assess
the relative damage to Western European littoral habitats of
pollution and global warming. His role was mainly to survey
and record Scottish ancient woodlands and to compare the

biodiversity of SSSIs with less protected environments. He specialised in mosses and genuinely loved his subject.

So he came that March morning after a dawn start and a long and lovely hill walk down into a little valley, with a wide shallow river, a flat flood plain and steep sides: glacier carved. Here, hanging on the hillside, trapped between a swathe of ubiquitous Sitka spruce plantation, the haggy, reedy bog of the valley floor and the open moor was a tiny triangle of ancient oak wood with a subsidiary arm of hazel scrub running north. It was a lambent morning; the mist had lifted with sunrise and now shimmered softly in the distance; out on the hill he had heard the returning curlews bubbling on the wing and had prodded freshly laid frogspawn; he had seen his first hill lambs of the year – tiny twins, certainly born that night, their tails wagging their wiry bodies as they burrowed into their mother's udders. He had seen neither human being nor habitation since he had left the pub in the village now seven miles away. He surveyed the valley from above, checked his map and came down from the open hill, skirting the gorse and then a couple of gnarled hawthorns, clambering over the memory of a stone wall, with real pleasure and anticipation. Under the still naked trees the light was green; on the floor, on the trees themselves, on rotted branches; and on the randomly piled and strewn rocks – some as big as cottages, some so small he could have lifted them – there were mosses, mosses of a prolific abundance, a lapidary brightness, a soft density such as he had never seen before.

He was warm from his walking; he was tired from his early rising; and he was enchanted by this secret place. Smiling, contented, he lay down on a flat dry rock in the sheltered sunlight and fell asleep.

The Moss Witch did not see him. His hair was the colour of winterkilled bracken; his clothes were a modest khaki green; the sunlight flickered in a light breeze. She did not see him. She came wandering along between rocks and trees and sat down very close to where he slept, crossed her legs, straightened her back and began to sing the spells of her calling, as every Moss Witch must do each day. He woke to that low, strange murmur of language and music; he opened his eyes in disbelief but without shock. She was quite small and obviously very old; her face was carved with long wrinkles running up and down her forehead and cheeks; she was dressed raggedly, in a loose canvas skirt and with thick, uneven woollen socks and sandals obviously made from old silage bags. Her woollen jumper was hand-knitted, and not very well. She wore green mittens, which looked somehow damp. He was still sleepy, but when he moved a little and the Moss Witch turned sharply what she saw was a smiling foxy face and, without thinking, she smiled back.

Tinker? he wondered. Walker like himself though not so well equipped? Gipsy? Mad woman, though a long way from anywhere? He felt some concern and said a tentative 'Hello.'

Even as she did not do so, the Moss Witch knew she should not answer; she should dissolve into the wood and keep her silence. But she was lonely. It had been a very long time. Long, long ago there had been meeting and greetings and gossip among the Moss Witches, quite a jolly social life indeed with gatherings for wild Sabbats in the stone circles on the hills. There had been more wildwood and more witches then. She could not count the turnings of the world since she had last spoken to anyone and his smile was very sweet. She said 'Hello' back.

He sat up, held out his right hand and said, 'I'm Robert.'

She did not reply but offered her own, still in its mitten. It was knitted in a close-textured stitch and, effortlessly, he had a clear memory of his mother's swift fingers working endlessly on shame-inducing homemade garments for himself and his sister, and recalled that the pattern was called 'moss stitch' and this made him suddenly and fiercely happy. When he shook her hand, small in his large one, he realised that she had only one finger.

There was a silence although they both went on looking at each other. Finally he said, 'Where do you come from?' Suddenly he remembered the rules in Peru about not trying to interact with people you encountered deep in the jungle. Uncontacted tribes should remain uncontacted, for their own safety, cultural and physical; they had no immunities and were always vulnerable. He shrugged off the thought, smiling again, this time at his own fantasy. There were, after all, no uncontacted tribes in Britain.

'Gondwana we think; perhaps we drifted northwards,' she said vaguely. 'No one is quite sure about before the ice times; that was the alternate generation, though not of course haploid. But here, really. I've lived here for a very long time.'

He was startled, but she looked so mild and sweet in the dappled green wood that he could not bring himself to admit that she said what he thought she said. Instead he turned his sudden movement into a stretch for his knapsack and after rummaging for a moment produced his flask. He unscrewed the top and held it out to her. 'Would you like some water?'

She stretched out her left hand and took the flask from him. Clamping it between her knees she pulled up her right sleeve and then poured a little water onto her wrist. He stared.

After a pause she said, 'Urgh. Yuck. It's horrible,' and shook her arm vigorously, then bent forward and wiped the splashes delicately from the moss where they had fallen. 'I'm sorry,' she said, 'that was rude, but there is something in it, some chemical thing and I'm rather sensitive... we all are.'

She was mad, he realised, and with it felt a great tenderness – a mad old woman miles from anywhere and in need of looking after. He dreaded the slow totter back to the village, but pushed his irritation away manfully. The effort banished the last of his sleepiness and he got to his feet, pulled out his notebook and pen and began to look around him. Within moments he realised that he had never seen mosses like this; in variety, in luxuriance and somehow in joy. These were joyful mosses and in uniquely healthy condition.

There were, before his immediate eyes, most of the species he was expecting and several he knew instantly were on the Vulnerable or Critically Endangered lists from the Red Data Book and then some things he did not recognise. He felt a deep excitement and came back to his knapsack. She was still sitting there quite still and seemed ancient and patient. He pulled out his checklist and *taxa*.

'What are you doing?' she asked him.

'I'm seeing what's here – making a list.'

'I can tell you,' she said, 'I know them all.'

He smiled at her. 'I'm a scientist,' he said, 'I'm afraid I need their proper names.'

'Of course,' she said, 'sit down. I've got one hundred and fifty-four species here, not counting the liverworts and the hornworts, of course. I can give you those too. I think I'm up to date although you keep changing your minds about what to call them, don't you? My names may be a bit old-fashioned.'

She chanted the long Latin names, unfaltering.

Leucobryum glaucum. Campylopus pyriformis. Mnium hornum. Atrichum undulatum. Dicranella heteromalla. Bazzania trilobata. Lepidozia cupressina. Colura calyptrifolia. Ulota crispa...

More names than he could have thought of, and some he did not even know. He sat on the rock with his list on his knee ticking them off as they rolled out of her mouth; there seemed no taxonomic order in her listing, moving from genera to genera along some different system of her own, but her tongue was elegant and nimble around the Latin names. He was both bemused and amused.

Once he stopped her. *Orthodontium gracile* she sang, and paused smiling. He looked up and she was glancing at him quizzically. 'The slender thread moss.' She looked sly.

'No,' he said. 'No, you can't have that here. It grows in the Weald, on the sandstone scarps.'

She laughed. 'Well done,' she said, 'that was a sort of test. But I do have it. Come and see.'

She stood up and beckoned to him; he followed her round a massive granite boulder and up the slope. There, behind a hazel thicket and free of the oak trees, was a little and obviously artificial heap of sandstone, placed carefully in strata to replicate the scarps of Cheshire and the Weald. And there were two small cushions of *Orthodontium gracile.*

'I like it very much,' she said. 'I like it because it is a bit like me – most people don't know how to see it. It is not as rare as you think. So I invited it in.'

'You mustn't do that,' he said shocked, 'it's protected. You mustn't gather or collect it.'

'No of course not,' she said. 'I didn't. I invited it.' She smiled at him shyly and went on, 'I think perhaps you and your people are more like *Orthodontium lineare*, more successful but not native.'

Then she sat down and sang the rest of her list.

After that she took his hand in her maimed one and led him down beside the stream which gurgled and sang in small falls and cast a fine mist of spray on the banks where rare mosses and common ferns flourished. He knew then that something strange was happening to him, there in the oak wood, although he did not know what. It was a magical space. It said a lot for his true devotion to bryophytes and his research that he went on looking, that he was not diverted. But time somehow shook itself and came out differently from before – and the space was filled with green, green mosses and her gentle bubbling knowledge. She spoke the language of science and turned it into a love song through her speaking and the mosses sang back the same tune in harmony.

Sometime after noon they came back to where they had started. He was hungry and got out his lunch box. She sat down beside him.

'Have you got something to eat?' he asked.

'No.'

'Do you want to share mine?'

'I'm non-vascular,' she said. 'I get what I need from the rain. That's why my wrinkles run up and down instead of across.' He looked at her face and saw that it was so. She went on, 'And of course it does mean that I revive very quickly even if I do get dried out. That's why I can go exploring, or for that matter,' she looked contented, almost smug, 'sit out in the sun with you.'

None of this seemed as strange to him as it should have seemed. He had reached a point of suspension, open to anything she told him.

'Are you...' but it did not feel right to ask her what she was. He changed the sentence, 'Are you all alone?'

'Yes, sadly,' she said in a matter of fact voice. 'I hoped for a long time that I would be monoicous. Nearly half of us are. But no, alas. I'm thoroughly female and as you can imagine that makes things difficult nowadays.' After a little pause she smiled at him, slightly shamefaced and said in a confessional sort of tone, 'As a matter of fact, that's what happened to my fingers. I was much younger then of course; I wouldn't try it now, but I did so want a daughter, I thought I might be clonal. You know, I'm not vascular, sensitive to pollution, often mis-identified or invisible, all those things; I hoped I might be totipotent as well. So I cut off my fingers and tried to regenerate the cells. But it didn't work. It was a bad mistake. I think we must have been though, somewhere in the lineage, because of our disjunctions and wide dispersal. That's one of the problems of evolution – losses and gains, losses and gains. Vascular was a smart idea, you have to admit, even at the price of all those vulgar coloured flowers.'

He realised suddenly there were no snowdrops; no green sprouts of bluebells, wild garlic or anemone; no primrose or foxgloves. 'Don't you like flowers?'

'Bloody imperialists,' she replied crossly, 'they invaded, imposed their own infrastructure and ruined our culture, stole our land. And anyway they're garish – I do honestly prefer the elegance, the subtle beauty of seta, capsules and peristomes.'

He did too, he realised, although he had never thought of it before.

They sat together, contented, in the wildwood, in the space outside of time.

But he lacked her long patience. He could not just sit all day, and eventually he roused himself, shook off the magic, stood up and took out his collecting kit: the little glass bottles with their plastic screw tops, a sharp knife, a waterproof pencil and a squared paper chart.

'What are you doing?' she asked him.

'I'm just going to collect some samples,' he said, 'so we can get them under the microscope.'

'You can't do that.'

'Yes, it's fine,' he said reassuringly, 'I've got a certificate. This is one of the richest sites I've ever seen. We'll get a team in here, later in the year, but I need some samples now – just to prove it, you know; no one will believe me otherwise.'

'I really cannot let you do that,' she said quietly, still sitting gently on the gentle ground.

But he just smiled kindly at her and moved away up the slope. He bent over a fine little feathered mat: a *sematophyllum* – *S. micans* perhaps; he knelt down, took his knife and scraped along its underside pulling free its anchoring rhizoids and removing a tiny tuft. He opened one of his bottles, popped in the small green piece and screwed up the top. So she killed him. She was sorry of course, but for witches it is always duty before pleasure.

Quite soon she knew, with great sadness, that she would have to move on. They would come looking for him and would find her, and rather obviously the crushed skull where she had hit him with the granite rock could not have been an accident.

Later still she realised that she could not just leave his body there. If they found that and did not find her, they might blame some other poor soul, some solitary inhabitant of wood or hill, some vagrant or loner. Someone like her, but not her. Justice is not really an issue that much concerns Moss Witches, but she did not want the hills tramped by heavy-footed policemen or ripped and squashed by quad bikes and 4X4s.

The evening came and with it the chill of March air. Venus hung low in the sky, following the sun down behind the hill, and the high white stars came out one by one, visible through the tree branches. She worked all through the darkness. First, she dehydrated the body by stuffing all his orifices with dry sphagnum, more biodegradable than J-cloth and more native than sponge, of which, like all Moss Witches, she kept a regular supply for domestic purposes. It sucked up his body fluids, through mouth and ears and anus. She thought too its antiseptic quality might protect her mosses from his contamination after she was gone.

While he was drying out, she went up the hill above the wood and found a ewe that had just given birth and milked it. She mixed the milk with yoghurt culture. She pounded carefully selected ground mosses in her pestle, breaking them down into parts as small as she could manage; she mixed the green ooze with the milk and culture.

When he was desiccated and floppy, she stripped his clothing off, rolled him onto his back among the thick mosses under the rocks and planted him, brushing the cell-rich mixture deep into the nooks and crannies of his body and pulling thicker, more energetic moss clumps over his now cool flesh. At first she was efficient and businesslike, but later she allowed her imagination to cavort. She painted *Aplodon wormskioldii* on his forehead and where his toes poked up through her main planting of *Polytrichum* because it grew on the dead bodies of deer and sheep and might flourish on his bones too. She festooned his genitals with *Plagiochila atlantica* because its little curling fronds were so like the curly mass there. She carried down a rock richly coated with the lichen *Xanthoria parietina* because it was the colour of his foxy hair. She looked at her little arrangement; it was clever, witty even, and secure, but she still felt there was something missing.

After a while she knew. She went round the massive granite boulder and up the slope beyond the oak trees and behind the hazel thicket to her artificial sandstone scarp. There, she hacked out one of the cushions of *Orthodontium gracile* on a piece of the reddish rock. Back where he lay she uncovered his face again, forced his mouth open and placed the sandstone in it, the little moss resting gently on his smiling lips. It was very pleasing to her, because he had been such a sweet man and knew the names of mosses.

Then she spoke clearly and firmly to all the mosses, the liverworts and the lichens she had planted. She told them to grow fast, to grow strong and to grow where she had told them. Bryophytes are not commonly obedient or compliant, they tend to follow their own rules, coming and going at their own random whim, but she knew this time they would do as she asked because they loved her. Within weeks his body would be part of the moss wood, a green irregular shape among so many others.

Then, sadly, singing all their names one last time, she turned northwards. She climbed high up the hillside and lay down and watched the dawn. When the morning breeze came with first light, she opened her mouth wide and exhaled; and her microscopic spore flowed out between her 64 little hydroscopic teeth and was caught by the wind, and carried up into the higher air currents that circulate the Earth.

And then... well nobody knows.

Perhaps she blows there still, carried on those upper airs, waiting for a new and quieter time when witches and mosses can flourish.

Perhaps she walked north and west and came at last to another small fragment of ancient woodland, a tight ravine leading down to the sea or a small island out beyond the uttermost west, and she lives there still.

Moss Witches, like mosses, do not compete, they retreat.

Perhaps there are no more Moss Witches; the times are cast against them. But if you go into ancient woodland and it glows jewel-green with moss and is damp and quiet and lovely, then be very careful.

Afterword:

Bryophytes

Dr. Jennifer Rowntree

I HAD A lot of chats with Sara about bryophytes and particularly mosses and suggested some books to read. I think she's been true to what we talked about, and has come up with many amusing and interesting things.

The way of finding Moss Witches that she invents, using the website, is brilliant. I'm sure it would work if there were such creatures. Bryophytes need water to complete their life cycle, as the sperm moves to the eggs across a film of water, but they can be found anywhere, even in very dry places. Many species can dry out completely, then rehydrate and start to grow again when water is available. They don't have an internal water transport system like most plants, but water moves over their outer surfaces and they absorb it directly through their cells.

That's why the witch puts the water on her skin instead of drinking it. The leaves of bryophytes are usually only one or two cells thick and because they absorb water directly, they can be quite sensitive to chemicals in the water, just as the Witch is. With many species, there are protrusions on the leaves that help guide the water around the surface, hence the vertical creases in the Witch's face.

The bryophytes' life cycle has two distinct stages, starting as a spore which grows into a leafy plant, the gametophyte. This then produces male and female sex organs. When an egg is fertilized it grows into a sporophyte, the second stage, which is essentially parasitic on the green plant and which produces the spores.

Some plants are dioicous, which means there are separate male and female plants. Monoicous plants have both sex organs on the same plant. The poor Witch hoped she might be monoicous, but sadly no, she's only female and cannot fertilize herself. The gametophyte has only a single strand of DNA, what we call haploid. The sporophyte has two strands of DNA like us which then divides to produce haploid spores. The witch cannot reproduce so she cut off her fingers to try to grow clonal children. A lot of Bryophytes are very successful at clonal reproduction. Some produce specific structures like little balls of cells or have leaves that easily break off and can grow into a whole new plant. Totipotent means that a whole plant can be grown from a single cell. Bryophytes have the ability to do this naturally.

Sara asked me to name one of my favourite bryophytes. I used to work at Kew Gardens as a conservation officer, managing a collection of threatened bryophytes from the UK. I worked quite a lot on one species, *Orthodontium gracile*, trying to reintroduce it. *Orthodontium lineare* is a non-native species, and a more successful competitor than *Orthodontium gracile*. Making a yogurt culture with cut-up leaves is one way to start a colony. I like that the Witch selected some *Aplodon wormskjoldii* to help hide the murder. It's a species that grows on rotting carcasses or dung, a good choice to cover a dead body.

At the moment I am not working with moss, but on understanding the importance of variation in natural systems. I currently work with pollinators, root microbes and parasitic plants trying to figure out how variation within and among species influences the way different species interact with each other. Understanding the role of biodiversity in natural systems, should help us to be able to determine how best to conserve them, particularly as climates change.

I thoroughly enjoyed Sara's story. It did a great job of imagining an intelligent, human-like creature who works like a bryophyte.

Dark Humour

WHEN THEY FINALLY got back to the cottage, the last of the light was vanishing although there was still a smear of almost peach-coloured sky along the rim of the hills to the west. The wind had dropped but the massed clouds, which had soaked them early in the afternoon, were being pushed away northwards and, above them, there was nothing but dark, navy blue.

'If you bath first,' she said, 'I'll light the fire. Then you can start supper while I return all my mud to its source. Don't use all the hot water.'

He gave the plan the briefest consideration. He slightly felt that he should offer her the bath first, but his own weariness as well as his superior culinary skills won out. He poured two glasses of whisky, slopped some water into hers, left it on the table and carried his own undiluted up the stairs.

When she heard the taps start running she took a long mouthful of the golden liquid and turned her attention to the fireplace. There was kindling and even matches, but she could see that at some point in the evening they would need more logs and now, while she was still dirty, seemed a better time to get them in than then, so she went out to find the woodshed. In the few minutes they had been inside the darkness had thickened and the blue sky turned to black; the air was much colder, there were a few first stars sparkling brightly and, when she sniffed the sharp air, she could smell frost. She grinned to herself at the thought of all those H_2O molecules huddling closer together as the temperature dropped, much as he and she were planning to do, reconsolidating their relationship after her three months in Geneva. The logs were neatly stacked under a tiled roof and a motion sensitive switch came on as she approached it; she gathered an armful, took them back in and efficiently set about lighting the fire. Afterwards she did not bother to get up, but stayed kneeling on the floor, watching the flames transfer themselves from firelighters to kindling and from kindling to the frayed edges of the logs. The damp from her trousers began to seep through into her thighs until she felt chilled and then her weariness hit.

It had been a good hard walk, leaving the car at Newbiggin and taking a bus up towards Alston. As always, she had left the logistics to him; he seemed to enjoy researching the complex minutiae of rural transport, making possible what looked to her un-manageable. They had taken the high path south along the Holdenhurth Band to Cow Green Reservoir, picked up the Pennine Way by the long cataract of the Cauldron Spout, came down to the High Force, then the Low Force and so back to the car. It was, she realised, a long while since they had walked so far together. She was allowed to be tired.

When he came down saying, 'Your bath's running,' she rose promptly and headed up the stairs. As she reached the turn he called,

'I thought I might do the skate wings in a sort of Thai broth. Is that good with you?'

'Sounds wonderful.'

'I won't make it too fiery.'

'I could use some heat. And I put a bottle of bubbly in the fridge.'

'I'll chuck in some potatoes then.'

'Very good. They're certainly earthy enough.'

'You're quick tonight.' They both laughed.

After her bath she put on leggings and an ancient, faded, red, ultra-long T-shirt: comfort first, and her whole body suddenly felt comfortable, glad to be here with him, glad to have been cold and wet and now be warm and dry. But as she went down the stairs, she saw that he was sitting at the table with his laptop turned on. She was about to remonstrate, when he looked up, smiled very sweetly and said, 'So, tonight she is putting out the stars.'

She felt a slight blush and was about to dismiss the compliment with a self-deprecatory joke when she caught something in his expression, and instead said, 'Ho hum. Not funny. Or not very. You are a crossword puzzle nerd. 3. 5. Red Shift. Clever clogs.'

'I said you were quick tonight. But I've been out looking at them, the stars – it does not bear thinking of, not seeing any, any more. I was watching them accelerate away from us, faster and faster, whatever the damn Dark Force is about. How will we be human, how will we stay humble if we can't see into deep space?'

'They coped splendidly before 1600. The Chinese, the Greeks, the Arabs.'

'There's stuff they could see that we won't.'

'We'll still see everything in our galaxy. The Milky Way, everything in the solar system, all the planets and the Moon. Surely that will be enough?'

'Not for me.' He looked so sad, suddenly. She thought, as she often did, that although she was probably cleverer and certainly better at her job than he was, he loved it more and that gave him an edge. She felt irritable with his sadness, his sentimentality, and knew herself well enough to know that sometimes she begrudged him the joy he could connect with. To banish the little tug of envy and the rush of tenderness that somehow went with it, she put on a stern expression and said, 'And why do you have that thing on? I thought we agreed.'

'Well,' he said, clearly unashamed, 'I could say I was looking up the recipe, but that would not be true. It's about the kitchen though; this kitchen is bizarrely over equipped

– there are too many bits and bobs, it is all a fidget and not elegant. It's too much.'

'So you can't have too many stars but you can have too many gadgets.'

'That's right. So I was thinking about clutter and I went back to your bloody particles. How can we be calling all this "fundamental"? I mean, come on: six different kinds of Quarks. Six! Seventeen different elementary particles! Never mind all the other crap. It's all an ugly, woolly mess. Stupid. And they'll be more soon, Dark Matter ones and so on. You know there will.'

'I jolly well hope so. It is, after all, what I'm supposed to be looking for. You can't expect me not to want them to be there – the more the merrier.' They'd been here before. He really did want a Theory of Everything, some sweepingly elegant simplicity. 'And anyway, they are there; and, if they are there, I can't just ignore them.'

'No one's asking you to. I'm not asking you to. I just don't like it. There's something missing. I... I don't believe in it.'

'But...'

'Yes, I know "but". In the Department it's OK. It makes sense, it works. But it's the angels on the head of the pin. Schoolmen, taxonomies. Here, out here, where it's cold and hard and real and the stars are dancing, I can't make it... I can't feel it's...' He moved his hands away from the keyboard and banged them on the table in frustration.

'Beautiful?'

'Don't bloody start.' He sounded angry but she knew he wasn't. 'Just don't start on stupid metaphysics. We don't even know what to do with gravity, never mind aesthetics.'

She came down the rest of the steps and stood with her hand on the newel post, waiting.

Eventually he said, 'Perhaps we need better names for them.'

'What?'

'Well they're silly, aren't they? Tau neutrino. Three – *three* – W & Z bosons. Hadrons. Kaons. Baryons. They're gobbledy-gook words, they don't mean anything.'

'"Baryon" does. It comes from the Greek for "heavy".'

She felt a sort of exasperation which she could only tackle by pouring them each another whisky, even though, as she did so, she could see how much he had had already, just while she was in the bath.

Her movement seemed to restore his benignity. He closed the screen of his laptop down, got up and went to the cooker. With his back to her, he said,

'I was reading, not just now, before, a while ago, I was reading about this woman, up in Scotland somewhere. Liz Holden, she's called, and she has a strange magical sort of job. She invents, discovers, whatever, good meaningful story-tale names for fungi. The mycologists – they've decided, at least they hope, people will care more about them if they have names; like flowers do. You know, forget-me-not and meadowsweet and lady's smock. Not just Latin technical terms. Stories. Perhaps that's what we need.' He made himself busy over a pan. 'All the old stars have names and stories to go with the names – gods and heroes and monsters and... sort of linking, connecting with other stuff, other real stuff... but now. Look at H11 regions. Those wonderful – and yes they are, they're beautiful, damn it – wonderful, complex, fascinating things. These swirling, heaving clouds of ionised dust birthing new blue stars, and do we call them Cybele or Hathor or Pachamama, or any of the great mother goddesses? No, we call them H11 regions; we call them things like NGC 406. How can anyone love something called NGC 406?'

'That's silly,' she said crossly. 'You're not meant to love them. You'll be wanting to call them Virgin Marys next. I hope you're not planning on some weird conversion number. A reversion to your family Catholicism perhaps.' She could hear the aggression in her voice and it faintly appalled her.

She took a breath. 'This is physics, not poetry; we don't want metaphors.'

'Why not? Metaphors carry meaning over, that is what the word means. We've lost it, you know. It's really exciting and expansive and bloody marvellous. But it's a mess – good theory ought to make things purer, simpler and yes, damn it, lovelier, more beautiful, but this stuff just proliferates and... and... we sort of have more and more intricacy without having anything to hold it together. And no images, no stories, either.'

'But...'

'No, wait. Remember when they thought they'd found those faster-than-the-speed-of-light neutrinos. Well it took about a week and we were all happily theorising it. I did it, you did it, everyone was doing it. At a completely abstract level we just explained it away, so we could have our cake and eat it. There were even public lectures on it. We simply let it get more complicated and more messy. Fancy proof of the new dimensions. And what was it? It was a bloody loose connection in an optical fibre. And that's not a metaphor, it's a parable.'

'Oh great.' She made a conscious, willed effort to stay pleasant and cool, to keep the sarcasm as hidden as possible. 'And what do you plan to do about it?'

'There's a question. Nothing I expect, but...' He turned back towards her and suddenly she could see he was grinning. 'Perhaps I should go back to magic. Become a wizard. Gandalf or something. Paracelsus. I could rather fancy the four elements; they are simple and pure enough.'

She tried to laugh too, 'Of course. Hence the potatoes. But it takes a long time to train as a wizard, if I remember rightly. And don't you have to be celibate?'

'That's a snag,' he said. 'But more generally it works nicely. I can be a post-Einstein wizard. Look: Earth, Fire, Air, Water. Gravity, Strong Force, Weak Force, Electromagnetic Force.'

'Come again.'

'Earth is gravity, holding everything down. Fire is the strong force, those quarks held together by a hot cauldron of exchanged gluons. Air is the weak force, somehow ethereal, like the neutrino it acts on. And water is the EM force, flowing and swooshing around the electrically charged particles. Same theory, different language. Maybe better language.'

Suddenly, happily, she laughed too, and recalled the sense of the air gathering its atoms together in the cold by the woodshed. 'Solids. Plasma. Liquids. Gas. I said you were a clever clogs.' And then after a pause, she added more slowly, 'Holdenhurth. The Cauldron Spout. High Force. Low Force. When we were coming down this afternoon, I knew it reminded me of something and I couldn't remember what.'

He laughed too, feeling generous because he knew she had generously made an effort to join him, 'You can't have Holdenhurth just because it rhymes with "earth". Metaphors – yes. Poetics – I think not.'

'No. Not. Hurth or hurst. In the south it usually means a copse or woodland, but up here it means an earth-bank or other elevated chunk of land – rock, sand or just earth. It's allowable.'

'Just.'

'Just is enough. Like the naughty neutrino games. You're right. Same theory, different language, better story.'

He transferred the skate wings deftly to two wide bowls; poured the poaching liquid over them and added some diced potatoes. She went over to the fridge, extracted the bottle of wine and removed the foil. She came and sat down at the table, twisting the wires free and making happy little murmurs of appreciation. The fish smelled wonderful.

Spooning down the spicy soup she said, quite playfully, 'Sometimes theory leads observation, like the discovery of Neptune; and sometimes the other way round, like Leavitt's Cepheid Variables, so I don't need an answer right now, but what is going to be the story about how the four elements mix in with each other, because experiment does not reveal it. I mean however much you mix water with earth you don't get giraffes.'

'I don't want to be contentious, but however much you stir around your elementary particles – and that cunning double-talk was an accident, not a clever-clogs thing – or even your basic atoms you don't get giraffes either. But actually you have missed the point. The Four Elements theory was highly theoretical, although they didn't probably call it that, because it wasn't actual water – the kind that was pouring down those waterfalls or swilling about, flavoured up, in your bowl. They were Platonists – it was pure or ideal water, or earth, or air, or fire. Theoretical elements, not the lowered sublunary kind we have down here. We are much more besmirched with materialism than Aristotle was. It wouldn't have occurred to them to put things in an accelerator and smash them back into their four separate parts. Idea and ideal went together for them.'

'Or deficient technology – how far in front of your technical capabilities can you imagine, or speculate?'

'We're all speculating now, well out in front of our technology or even our facts, our data. That's why you need stories, images, metaphors; to stimulate and integrate the imagination.'

Later, the Cava finished, he made her a mug of herbal tea and poured himself another whisky. She built up the fire and they sat on the couch, her legs tucked up under her as she leaned against his chest. The fire leapt and danced and they were peaceful for a while.

Then he said, 'I'm sorry. I'm feeling really down about it all tonight. It must be an excess of the Black Bile.'

'The *what*?'

The Black Bile. That's what I was looking up on the computer when you came down – and I never apologised for that either. It was bad of me. I'm sorry.'

'That's enough apologies,' she said. 'What's this black thing?'

'The four elements manifest themselves in the human body in what were called the four humours. Which oddly enough is where the word humour, as in wit and laughter, comes from. When they are balanced your health is good, when they get out of synch you get an appropriate illness and mood. Blood is air and makes you sanguine; Phlegm is water and makes you phlegmatic; Choler or Yellow Bile is fire and makes you irritable, choleric; Black Bile in Latin is *melan choler*; it is the earthy principle and guess what, too much of it makes you – melancholy, depressed.'

'Is there anything you don't know?'

'How to theorise gravity. Why I find you so beautiful. How many angels can dance on the head of a pin.'

'I believe the answer to the last one is infinity. How do we treat it – your superfluity of Black Bile?'

'Come, come, I'm a theoretical physicist; I can't know anything useful. I think you have to introduce a fire element – cupping and spicy food and that sort of thing.'

'Well you should be in recovery then after that skate.'

'So I should. But I'm not yet.'

There was a pause. Then she said, 'You've been a bit down since I got home, haven't you? Did you miss me?'

'That is such an unfair question. If I say "no" you'll feel hurt; and if I say "yes" you'll start thinking I resent your work. How about, "I was having low thoughts about work and therefore brooding too much on the meaning of life and I didn't have you to laugh at me."'

'I do not laugh at you. That is unfair too.'

'Yes it is. I've used up the apology ration, but honestly I meant, "I didn't have you to laugh at myself with."'

He fiddled with a strand of her hair. She waited.

'OK,' he said at last. 'I just don't think we are getting it right. And every time we hit a snag we just make up some new things. Superstrings, supergravity, a few new dimensions, another bunch of particles. There's no consensus, there's only fashions, and it all gets more and more... well you know what I mean... membrane-theories! Multiverses for heaven's sake. Well I'm with Lee Smolin: *There is only one universe. There are no others. Neither other universes nor copies of our universe – within or outside – exist.* I want there to be a Theory of Everything and I want it to be as pure and beautiful as Aristotle's elements – not this hideous, going-all-over-the-place-going-nowhere science fiction fantasy world stuff.'

'But,' she said, 'these things aren't fantasy; they postulated the Higgs Boson; it took a long time to get the technology up to speed – rather literally – and there it was. Just where it should have been. Theory-led, or if you prefer, speculation-led discovery works, it delivers.'

'Yes,' he said. 'Yes I know.'

After a pause she said, 'If you want stories, you ought to *like* the membrane universes. There they are, drifting about, and they bump into each other and generate a dear little baby universe; gives a brand new, if somewhat vulgar relevance to the Big Bang. Perhaps we can call them Casanova and Mata Hari or something if that would make you feel better.'

'Now who's being a clever clogs?' but he smiled. Then he stopped smiling and said slowly. 'Look, I do believe there has to be a Theory of Everything. You know I do. It's different for you. You're a terrier, you get in there and worry away at things, and you're so bloody smart that it's genuinely useful. I'm more like an old Blood Hound, doggedly on a trail, and the scent's gone cold. And the honest truth is, which is what has caused the Black Bile attack, I'm realising, I have to accept that I am not clever enough, even to imagine where to go to look for it. And that means that I'll have to spend all my life doing stuff I don't believe in; don't believe is going anywhere, and don't think is right. I mean correct, true.'

Under her cheek she felt him take a sharp breath, a sort

of quiver, and then he said, 'So I'm going to quit.'

There was a moment of almost perfect stillness and then a log shifted abruptly in the grate, throwing out a scattering of sparks.

'How would you feel if I did that? I mean stopped doing research. I could go and teach school; I'd like that.'

She uncurled her legs and sat up abruptly, looking at the fire rather than at him.

There was another, longer pause and then he said, very quietly, 'Or I could stay home and look after our babies.'

She stood up, took a step away from the sofa, faced him and said somehow coldly, 'Are you bloody drunk?'

She stood there for a moment or two, staring at him. He could see her eyes were filling with tears. Suddenly, she turned away, snatched up her jacket and went out of the door slamming it hard behind her.

It was sharply cold now, frosty and very clear. There was no moon but the sky was bright with the stars one never saw in the city – the whole pale sweep of the Milky Way and the big W of Cassiopeia high to the north, above the shadow ridge of the hills. She dashed the back of her hand across her eyes and then pulled her jacket on and walked slowly down the path to the gate. She stood there, shaken.

After about five minutes he came up behind her, put his arms round her, wrapping her into his own jacket, holding her against his chest.

'I'm sorry,' he said. 'You're right. It was a bloody stupid thing to say.'

'No,' she said quietly. 'No, it wasn't stupid, but it was shocking. I've never thought of it before. My mother always said that if I went on doing all that fancy physics, no man would ever want me to have his babies. I think I believed her. And I couldn't give it up you know.'

'I know.'

'So I just never thought about them. I didn't know you did.'

'Quite a lot actually; which is probably why I'm not such a good physicist as you. But I don't need them. I don't want to pressure you.'

They stood in silence, both looking up at the vast vacuity of space.

'There's Orion's Belt,' he said eventually, swivelling her round gently so she was facing in the right direction to see the clear line of three stars. 'He was a giant and a god of hunting, that's why you can only see him in winter, in the hunting season – and if you look behind him, right over there, you can see Scorpio chasing him. Orion foolishly boasted that no animal was strong enough to kill him – so the gods sent a little scorpion to sting him to death. It hasn't caught him yet though.'

'On a night like this it does seem nearly unbearable that they are all whizzing away from us, faster and faster. If I was starting again I'd try to do Dark Energy I think. So fascinating. But you probably don't want that. A fifth force.'

'As a matter of fact, Aristotle introduced a fifth element. It was called Aether. He didn't think the stars could be made of the same stuff as things on Earth – they had to be made of something more beautiful, more unchanging, even more absolutely pure and ideal. So my new theory, or rather my adoption of the old one, can keep up with yours. We can match Dark Energy to Aether. The Quintessence – the fifth element.'

'I think,' she said quietly, 'that you would make an excellent science teacher. You know lots of stuff and you tell great stories.' After a short silence, and with what felt to him like something adventurous or courageous, she added even more quietly, barely a whisper, 'and an excellent father.'

Later, inside, warm again, she said, 'What are you going to do with the Quintessence thing when it comes to bodies – Black Bile and Phlegm and all that?'

He ran his hand under her red T-shirt and said jokily, 'It has to be something pure and beautiful. Sex, perhaps.'

'Pure?'

'Very. Ideal.' Then very softly he added, 'Or love?'

Even later, in bed, she broke the long hush of shared delight and murmured, 'Hmmm. They say good sex is difficult, but it seems to me that it is a damned sight easier than particle physics.'

'Dark energy,' he says, and grins into the dark. 'More is unknown than known. Is sex a property of space itself, a fault line in the Standard Model theory of gravity, a new dynamic force, an ancient metaphor or a pure abstraction? This needs further experimentation. We need more data and better data before we can speculate.'

Afterword:

The Name Game

Dr. Rob Appleby

ONE OF THE most successful scientific assumptions ever made is the view that all things around us – trees, cars, other human beings, the sun and so on – are made of indivisible, fundamental, amazingly small lumps of substance called particles. This is a very old idea – indeed you could almost call it a 'hunch' – one which we've grown accustomed to in various guises. For example, the word 'atom' we learn at school is Greek for 'indivisible', but is a truly amazing idea. Take an apple and a knife and slice the apple in two, leaving two halves. Take a half, slice into two, and carry on. What this particle assumption says is that we cannot keep slicing the pieces of apple in two forever but eventually we'll reach a building block of the apple that cannot be sliced anymore. This is the fundamental part.

The modern worldview of particle physics takes this idea, stirs in some wonderful theories such as Einstein's relativity and the theory of quantum mechanics, and produces a model of the universe built of particles. What's amazing about this theory is that it has predictive power (we can calculate stuff before we measure it), it can be written (in a somewhat condensed form) on the front of a t-shirt and has been tested against nature to an unprecedented level of accuracy at places like the Large Hadron Collider. In essence, the fundamental particles (our building blocks) talk to each other through a set of fundamental forces, each transmitted by one or more force-carrying particles. These forces have

218

rather unemotive names, the electromagnetic force, the weak force, the strong force, and the gravitational force (although the latter is not yet in the same successful model as the others). The fundamental particles also carry names, such as the electron, quark and positron.

In 'Dark Humour', our two heroes talk about the four elements of earth, air, fire and water. Viewing the physical world as a composition of these basic matters dates from well before our highly developed, modern particle physics worldview but carries the same idea. Fundamental Building Blocks. Of course, the mechanism for building up more complicated objects from earth, air, fire and water is arguably less well developed ("I mean, however much you mix water with earth you don't get giraffes.") but this does not matter. The new worldview we have for how the universe around us is built is not new at all, but simply re-expressed in a modern, more exciting (and more precise) form as humankind develops its traditions and even myths. Along the way a certain language has formed to communicate our ideas and stories. For example, we try to describe the fiery cauldron of quarks and gluons inside a proton using the strong force and the language of Quantum Chromodynamics. But do the words matter? As our heroes point out "Earth is gravity, holding everything down. Fire is the strong force, those quarks held together by a hot cauldron of exchanged gluons. Air is the weak force, somehow ethereal, like the neutrino it acts on. And water is the EM force, flowing and swooshing around the electrically charged particles. Same theory, different language. Maybe better language."

The mycologists have decided that inventing emotive names for fungi might mean people would care more for them. "Not just Latin technical terms. Stories." So telling stories through names helps association and attachment and, in a sense, this is what we already have in particle physics. The

219

three quarks that combine to form the proton have their etymological origin in *Finnegans Wake* by James Joyce, where he wrote, 'Three quarks for Muster Mark.' So the word "quark" carries a narrative meaning. It tells you what it does. It tells its own story. The same can be said for the gluon, binding the quarks together inside the proton by mediating the strong force. Gluons. Glue. How much of the recent media interest in the discovery of the Higgs Boson, the greatly anticipated particle that completes our Standard Model of the universe, arises from the story of Peter Higgs himself, a very likable and inspiring human being? The Higgs Boson becomes real, as Peter Higgs is, telling a story. It can be taken too far... it was called the God Particle by one wit. However, not all of the names we give these particles and forces have a story to tell. One of the most important scientific discoveries of the past few decades was the discovery of the Z boson at CERN, which was a major success for the standard model of particle physics. It's difficult to imagine any kind of emotion or story attached to some beast called the 'Z boson', although its importance rivals that of our famous Higgs Boson. What if it was called the Glashow-Weinberg-Salam boson? Would it attract more column inches once their story was told? So these names we use are important in our story telling and in our scientific narrative. After all, "How can anyone love something called NGC 406?"

There are, of course, plenty of other examples of imaginative naming in physics. Many pages could be written (and have been written) about the naming of the strange quark, the kaon, the neutron and the neutrino. Indeed it may be possible to identify two different types of story behind the names of these fundamentals. There are those names that introduce us to the discovery story, the biography of the physicist behind it: the eureka myth, (like the Higgs Boson); and there are those names that take us down to the very bottom of things, to their fundamental properties, and attempt to describe how they might behave: the elemental myth.

The naming of the neutrino, by Italian physicist Enrico Fermi, as effectively a 'baby neutron' ('-ino' being the Italian diminutive), is perhaps a mixture of the two types – it tells us something of the scientist himself (his nationality) and something of the elemental properties of the particle (neutrally charged, like the neutron, only much smaller).

For an example of a purely 'elemental myth', let's return to our old friend the proton. We know it is built of quarks and glued together with gluons. The way it's glued together is encoded in a very successful quantum field theory known as Quantum Chromodynamics, developed in the 1960s. The 'chromo' part of this name means colour and colour is used as a metaphor for how the quarks are allowed to join together and form a proton. This works by giving the quarks a property called colour, either red, green or blue (they don't *really* have a colour, of course), together with their anti-colours. The trick is that any particle formed when the quarks join together must be colourless. This can happen with a red quark, a blue quark and a green quark, together forming a colourless proton. A particle like the proton with three quarks in a colourless state is called a hadron. In a similar way, particles called mesons can be formed with two quarks, one with (for example) red and the other being anti-red, again forming a colourless particle. So colour is representing something about nature. This can also explain why we don't see a quark flying around on its own. Nature does not like free, exposed colour and a free quark must very quickly form a colourless meson or hadron in a way permitted by our theory of colour, Quantum Chromodynamics. So this theory uses colour as a metaphor for the quantum behaviour of quarks. And the metaphor tells a story.

Indeed it's curious to see that in pursuing our 'hunch' for the existence of fundamental elements, we have called upon another, older example of fundamental elements – the primary colours – to express a new theory. Quantum Chromodynamics takes this older 'elemental myth' and maps it onto a modern problem in a way that gives new results. Similarly the heroes of this story are attempting to map the four humours of medieval philosophy onto the four fundamental forces of modern physics... to see what happens. Transferring stories, drawing out metaphors, mapping one tale onto another – this might actually be more than just dinner-table conversation.

We have always looked for the fundamentals around us. How many young boys and girls have taken apart a toy to see how it works? Many an aspiring physicist has taken apart a transistor radio to learn its secrets. We may even have a piece of wiring in our brain or in our DNA, driving us to search for the basic, fundamental building blocks. A genetic basis for the 'hunch'. Either way it has served us well. What we have accepted as the answer has changed as our understanding has developed, but the basic idea, the goal of the search remains the same. The four humours of earth, air, wind and fire were replaced eventually by the atomic picture of protons, neutrons and electrons, which was refined into four fundamental forces, and a Standard Model of seventeen fundamental particles. We even have the possibility of replacing our fundamental particles with superstrings vibrating in eleven dimensions! But the idea remains the same: there is an elemental story at the bottom of it all, with a finite table of particles, or a finite cast of characters, if you will. We tell the story of our universe through these characters. Their names may change over time, but they are all part of the same story. So the names matter.

Notes

1. Thomas, Doreen (1976) *Strike a Light, John Walker 1781-1859,* 2nd Ed, Middlesbrough, Cleveland County Council, p12.
2. *World's First Box of Matches*, North Mail, 6.4.1927.
3. O'Dea, W.T. (1964), *Making Fire*, London, Science Museum, p16.
4. Thomas, Doreen (1976) *Strike a Light, John Walker 1781-1859,* 2nd Ed, p41.
5. Bone, William (1927) 'The Centenary of the Friction Match,' *Nature*, p495.
6. Bone, William (1927), p495.
7. This story is based on Genesis 30: 25-43, which must be one of the earliest accounts of a deliberate and manipulative breeding scheme in the world. There are in fact some actual double helix staircases. There is a highly elaborate stone one at the Chateau de Chambord, which may have been designed by Leonardo da Vinci for Francis I, King of France in 1519; there is a perfect elegant bronze one in – of all places – the Vatican; there is also one in the huge shaft of St Patrick's Well at Orvieto, built in 1527, so that the mules going down for the water would not need to pass the ones coming up.
8. Norris, B. J. and Whan, V. A. (2008). 'A gene duplication affecting expression of the ovine ASIP gene is responsible for white and black sheep.' *Genome Research* 18 (8): pp1282-1293.

Consultants

Jim Al-Khalili OBE is Professor of Theoretical Physics at the University of Surrey where he also holds a chair in the Public Engagement in Science. His research over the past 25 years has established him as a leading expert on mathematical models of exotic atomic nuclei. He is also an author and broadcaster and has written six popular science books, between them translated into over twenty languages. His television shows include *The Riddle of Einstein's Brain* (Channel 4), *Atom* (BBC4), *The Big Bang* (BBC Horizon), *The Hunt for the Higgs* (BBC Horizon), *Science and Islam* (BBC4), *The Secret Life of Chaos* (BBC4) and the Bafta-nominated *Chemistry: A Volatile History* (BBC4). He also presents the weekly Radio 4 programme, *The Life Scientific*. He is a recipient of the Royal Society Michael Faraday medal and the Institute of Physics Kelvin Medal, both for science communication, and is the current president of the British Humanist Association.

Rob Appleby is a senior lecturer in the Particle Accelerator group and the High Energy Particle Physics Group of the University of Manchester, and an academic staff member at the Cockcroft Institute of Accelerator Science. He is also an associate of the beams division at CERN (APB), a fellow of the Institute of Physics and a member of the LHCb and COMET experiments. His research is into the physics of particle accelerators and fundamental particles, including the Large Hadron Collider.

Melissa Baxter is a stem cell research scientist at Manchester University. She is currently developing ways to turn stem cells into liver cells for drug testing and safer medicine. Her recent publications include the development of a new, efficient way to grow stem cells. During her PhD (2001 to 2005) she published research showing how adult stem cells age, and was the first to genetically correct diseased stem cells from bone marrow stroma.

Jamie Davies is Professor of Experimental Anatomy at the Centre for Integrative Physiology, at Edinburgh University. He is a fellow of the Society of Biology, the Royal Society of Medicine, and the Higher Education Academy, and a member of the Institute of Electrical and Electronic Engineers. His is also currently deputy Chairman of the National Centre for 3Rs. His main research interest is in the development of biological form in foetal life, and how knowledge of this can be applied medically.

Robin Dunbar is a British anthropologist and evolutionary psychologist and a specialist in primate behaviour. He is currently Professor of Evolutionary Psychology and head of the Social and Evolutionary Neuroscience Research Group in the Department of Experimental Psychology at the University of Oxford. From 2007-2012, he was Professor of Evolutionary Anthropology and the Director of the Institute of Cognitive and Evolutionary Anthropology at the University of Oxford and the Co-director of the British Academy Centenary Research Project. He is best known for formulating Dunbar's Number, roughly 150, a measurement of the 'cognitive limit to the number of individuals with whom any one person can maintain stable relationships'.

Charles Fernyhough studied developmental psychology at Cambridge University and is now a part-time lecturer in psychology at Durham University. He is the author of *Pieces* *of Light: The new science of memory* (Profile Books), and the novels *A Box of Birds* (Unbound), and *The Auctioneer*. His fiction has appeared in several anthologies, including *New Writing 11* and *New Writing 14*. He has been the recipient of several awards, from, among others, the Arts Council and the Society of Authors.

Robert Furness is Principal Ornithologist at MacArthur Green environmental consultancy, Professor of Seabird and Fishing Interactions at the University of Glasgow, a member of the Board of Scottish Natural Heritage, and a Fellow of the Royal Society of Edinburgh. Dozens of postgraduate students have worked on skua ecology under his supervision on remote islands in Shetland, Orkney and the Western Isles over the last 40 years, on topics esoteric, academic, and sometimes practical.

Linda Kirstein is a Lecturer in Earth Dynamics in the Institute of Earth and Planetary Science, Edinburgh University. She is also Earth Science Co-ordinator and Degree Program Convenor for Geology & Physical Geography at the university. She is a multi-disciplinary Earth Scientist specialising in the interaction of climate and tectonics on landscape evolution.

Gemma Lewis is the Collections Officer at Preston Park Museum and Grounds, which is run by Stockton Borough Council. Since 2005, she has worked in a number of museums in the North East, specialising in collections management and object interpretation.

Tim O'Brien is a Professor of Astrophysics and Associate Director of The University of Manchester's Jodrell Bank Observatory. His research concentrates on the study of exploding stars using telescopes around the world and in space, working across the spectrum from radio waves to X-rays.

CONSULTANTS

Neil Roberts is a research associate at the University of Manchester studying urofacial syndrome, a rare inherited bladder condition. His research aims to understand developmental systems and apply this knowledge to better understanding of disease states. He studied genetics at the University of Edinburgh and his PhD at The University of Manchester was an investigation of the genetic pathways controlling human pancreas development.

Jennifer Rowntree is a Research Fellow funded by the Natural Environment Research Council at The University of Manchester. Her work focuses on the genetics of species interactions and she is particularly interested in the ecological and evolutionary interactions of plants. Currently her research incorporates work on parasitic plants, pollinators and the microbes that interact with plant roots in the soil. Previously, she had a position as a Scientific Conservation Officer at The Royal Botanic Gardens, Kew where she worked on a project conserving the threatened bryophytes of the UK.

Tara Shears is a particle physicist and Professor of Physics at the University of Liverpool. She has spent her career investigating the behaviour of fundamental particles and the forces holding them together, and has worked at experiments at CERN, the European centre for particle physics, and at the Fermilab particle physics facility near Chicago, USA. Tara joined the LHCb experiment at CERN's Large Hadron Collider in 2004, where she currently works.

Ian Stewart is a Professor of Mathematics at the University of Warwick, and a widely known popular-science and science-fiction writer. He is the first recipient of the Christopher Zeeman Medal, awarded jointly by the LMS and the IMA for his work on promoting mathematics.

About the Author

Sara Maitland grew up in Galloway and studied at Oxford University. Her first novel, *Daughters of Jerusalem*, was published in 1978 and won the Somerset Maugham Award. Novels since have included *Three Times Table* (1990), *Home Truths* (1993) and *Brittle Joys* (1999), and one co-written with Michelene Wandor — *Arky Types* (1987). She is also the author of *The Book of Silence* (2010) and *Gossip from the Forest: A Search for the Hidden Roots of Our Fairytales* (2012). Her short story collections include *Telling Tales* (1983), *A Book of Spells* (1987) and *On Becoming a Fairy Godmother* (2003). Her short story 'Far North' was adapted for the screen by Asif Kapadia in 2007 and starred Sean Bean and Michelle Yeoh. Sara's science-inspired stories have also featured in several Comma Press anthologies including *The New Uncanny* (2008), *When It Changed* (2009), *Litmus* (2011), and *Bio-Punk* (2012).

ALSO AVAILABLE FROM COMMA....

Instruction Manual for Swallowing

Adam Marek

ISBN-13: 978 1905583041

Robotic insects, in-growing cutlery, flesh-serving waiters in a zombie cafe... Welcome to the surreal, misshapen universe of Adam Marek's first collection; a bestiary of hybrids from the techno-crazed future and mythical past; a users' guide to the seemingly obvious (and the world of illogic implicit within it). Whether fantastical or everyday in setting, Marek's stories lead us down to the engine room just beneath modern consciousness, a place of both atavism and familiarity, where the body is fluid, the spirit mechanised, and beasts often tell us more about our humanity than anything we can teach ourselves.

Praise for Adam Marek:

'Marek's fabulously meaty, funny writing makes the short story look really exciting again, pulling you, frame by frame, into a bright, strange future.'
– Maggie Gee

'There's a transgressive thrill to Adam Marek's debut collection of short stories that's not simply a result of the potency of the subject matter... delightful.'
- *The Guardian*

'Early Ian McEwan meets David Cronenberg... genuine, unsettling talent.'
- *The Independent*

'Marek is terrific at setting an off-kilter mood.'
- *The National Post*